D1564357

Folding Hearts

A Mitchell Family Series
BOOK 2

By: Jennifer Foor

This book is for all the guys out there who've taken on the responsibility of caring for a child that they didn't father. You're in a league of gentlemen. Thank you for proving that there is hope for kids after all.

To my beta readers. And their countless hours of time they give me. I am forever indebted to you.

Chapter 1
Tyler

Losing my girl to my cousin was bad enough, but sticking around while they tried to figure things out was probably the worst decision I could have made.

My uncle had just passed away and my cousin Colt wasn't taking it well. His girlfriend, my ex Van, had come all the way to Kentucky, courtesy of me, to support him in his time of need. Colt wasn't the type of guy to talk about his feelings. He would rather shut everyone out and drink himself numb. So, besides the fact that I came along with Van to navigate, now I was being her shoulder to cry on while she made the decision to stick by him or not.

If I could have changed the past, I would have. I lost her because I *couldn't keep my dick in my pants*. They were actually the exact words Van had used on the night I found out she was leaving me for Colt.

Last year I had been in an accident that left me in a coma for seven and a half months. During that time, Savanna had been abused by my ignorant friends and non-understanding parents. She stuck by my side, mostly because they made her feel like my accident was her fault. Unfortunately, my cousin Colt came to town, to help my parents get through a desperate summer of farming, and through the time they spent together, ended up falling in love with each other.

I probably deserved it, but my own cousin being the reason was pretty fucked up. I knew that she had been involved with someone while I was in the hospital, she had admitted that, but after her being so secretive, I started noticing things. They claimed that they tried to stay away from each other once I woke up, but obviously it didn't happen. I caught them the night after I asked her to marry me.

She only said yes because I put her on the spot. It was like a kick in the gut. When I say that I caught them, I really mean it literally. I left them alone at a bar and watched as they pawed all over each other on the dance floor. After a short amount of time, and some skin on skin touching, they took their little private party to my father's truck outside and fucked.

I don't know why I waited and let them finish. Maybe it was because I wanted a good reason to fucking kill Colt. He knew how long she had been mine. He saw her say yes to me the night before. I had just got out of the fucking hospital for Christ sakes. I just stood there leaning against a nearby dumpster as the windows of that truck began to fog up. I saw a hand pressing against the glass and watched as the truck rocked back and forth. I was even close enough that I could hear their panting. Even though I was watching it all unfold, I was in shock. Van wasn't the cheating kind, in fact neither of them were. I hoped that it was a bad dream? An effect of the pain medication I was taking, mixed with the alcohol? Maybe I deserve this for everyone I had slept with behind her back?

They were all of the questions that I was asking myself while I watched my heart breaking before my eyes. Sure, I had been a shitty boyfriend, but this was fucked up.

Five years of being together was over. The truth came out that night. Once she found out about my cheating in our relationship, I knew I didn't have a chance in getting her back. She had already made her choice. I wasn't sure about it that night, but she later confessed it to me, after I calmed down of course.

My cousin Colt was like a brother to me. We spent every summer together when we were kids. He couldn't help falling in love with Van. Anyone that didn't would be a fool. She was perfect in every way.

It hurt like Hell.

I may not have been faithful, but damn, I didn't expect my own cousin to take the only girl I ever cared about away from me.

I made the decision to forgive them, against my better judgment of course. I even went as far as to help Van get to Kentucky. She needed a friend and for some reason I wasn't ready to just let her go. Maybe I am weird like that, but I needed to be around them. I wasn't okay leaving things unsettled.

I spent most of the time that first week with Van. Colt was busy at the hospital and then later making funeral arrangements, so Van and I just hung out a lot. Miranda was with us most of the time, not that I minded. She was fun to be around and it also made Van more comfortable being around me. I had made several attempts at getting kisses and trying to talk her out of being with my cousin. I knew all along it wouldn't work, but damn I would miss those lips.

While Van and Colt struggled to work things out on what was in store for their future, I was left to hang out with a very pregnant Miranda more and more. She was Colt's cousin, but not mine. Their mother's were sisters, which meant we had no blood relation, although for years we had considered ourselves family. I visited a lot of times in the past when she was around. Her and Conner, her brother, had moved to the ranch when their father passed away years ago. I wasn't exactly sure what their mother did, but it had something to do with the cattle. The last time I had visited she was on a business trip looking to acquire some new steers.

When Van and I had originally arrived at Colt's ranch, I acted like I didn't know her to get a rise out of Van. She overreacted, even more than I could have imagined, and almost left without an explanation from Colt. For the few minutes it lasted, I had to laugh. Of course, I was the only person there that thought it was a damn bit funny at all.

A few days later, right before my uncle's funeral, Miranda went into labor. Van and I got her into the car and rushed to get her to a hospital in time. Regrettably, we didn't make it. Miranda delivered a little girl in the backseat of Van's car. I don't know how Van and I managed it, but we were able to get her through it. Miranda and her little baby girl were later taken to the hospital by ambulance, where it was determined that both were healthy.

Being there for that birth was the most scary, disgusting, and perfect thing I had ever witnessed. Parts were so fucking gross, I had to close my eyes, but when that little baby belted her first cries, something happened inside of me. It took everything I had not to burst into tears too. My heart started to race and I couldn't take my eyes off of her.

When the ambulance started to pull away with both Miranda and the baby, that she later named Isabella, I found myself running after them. I don't know what made me do it, in fact I think about it all the time. That little girl was so fragile and perfect, it was silly, but I felt like she needed someone there with her.

I stuck around the hospital that night, at least until the father decided to show his face, then I made a beeline to the outside of the room. His name was Tucker Chase and he was nothing to be proud of. Miranda introduced me as her cousin, which I was totally fine with. I wasn't there as some kind of love interest, or replacement boyfriend.

Her boyfriend appeared to be a real piece of shit. His arms were covered in tattoos, and not the kind that look remotely decent. They seemed to be hand done, maybe by himself or a drunk friend. He had one of his ears pierced all the way up his lobe with little studs throughout. He had a hoop between the cartilage of his nose that looked like the ones the cattle have and a tear tattooed under his left eye. He was a filthy looking punk. His clothes were dirty and he had made no effort to clean himself up to be around a newborn. When he got there, he paid more attention to his cell phone instead of his new baby girl.

It made me happy when Conner and my aunt finally showed up to give her the attention that she needed. They crowded in the room and I followed behind them, not really worrying about the creep. One thing I think I will never forget was how unresponsive he was to that baby. He held her for only a second and once the family came in, he made his exit promptly. Not one person from his family even showed up with him.

I hated the fucker. Miranda may not have been blood, but she was my family.

Due to the fact that we had to bury my uncle, I was able to stay in Kentucky for another two weeks. While Colt and Savanna swooned over each other more and more, I spent most of my time at the main house, which in turn enabled me to spend time with Izzy. Miranda hated that nickname and decided she was going to call her Bella for short, but that never changed my mind. I think I fell in love with Izzy immediately, but when I finally held her for the first time, I knew how special she really was to me.

Of course she was tiny. Her fragile little body could fit in one of my hands. I found myself holding her for long periods of time, even taking turns feeding her. I liked how I could put my finger against her hand and she would hold onto it. It was amazing she could respond like that.

My family kept making fun of me, even asking if I was using the baby to earn brownie points with Van. The funny thing was, when I was with Izzy, I never even thought of Van. Of course, at first, I did remember the times we talked about having kids. I was never really the settle down kind of guy, so it was all to appease her. However, this little girl, well I was pretty much in awe of her.

Being that I stayed in Kentucky for that extra time, I was able to make peace with Van and Colt. I loved them both and just came to the conclusion that I wanted them to be together. It seemed fucked up to explain, but they were the two people that I never wanted to lose. Their relationship was real and it was solid.

I didn't leave with my parents. Instead, I rode home with Van and Colt. They had to drive back to the Carolinas to get Van's belongings, which included her horse that *I* bought her. I had to laugh at how I was pretty certain she loved that damn horse more than she ever loved me. Anyway, Colt took one of the ranch trucks and I tagged along with them. They told me I talked entirely too much, but it beat the idea of them talking about each other or what they did when they were alone. To Hell with that shit!

Saying goodbye to them was hard, but they ended up leaving my parents with part of my uncle's life insurance money. It was enough to get my parents out of debt, pay my medical bills and still leave them with something saved. My father would be forever grateful, even though I knew he just wanted his big brother back.

After my uncle's unexpected death and the birth of Izzy, my family seemed to get closer. I spoke to Van on a day to day basis. Colt never seemed to mind. He would yell smart ass comments through the phone at me at least once a day, but I think he was just jealous that I never wanted to talk to him.

Chapter 2

Ty

The next few months went by pretty fast. Between my physical therapy for the metal pins that were permanently in my leg, and the legal issues impending from my car accident, things were hectic. I ended up getting seventy two hours of community service and a year of probation. It was a lot better than spending time in jail. Of course it took me another six months to get my license back. Because I was under the influence, I lost my license immediately. After my court date, I went through driving classes and even drug and alcohol counseling. The judge wanted to set an example for all of the college kids I associated with.

Even though I wasn't attending school, I still spent my weekends on campus at the frat house. It was weird not having to sneak around and the ladies were coming at me even more than before. Heather still had her hooks in me. That girl could give the best head in the whole state of North Carolina, not that it helped me with imagining it was Van giving it to me. When she found out Van and I were over, she assumed we would get serious, but the truth was I didn't need to commit to her to get a piece. The girl was already ready and willing.

I remember the day I got my license back. I called Colt and told him I was coming to visit. Surprisingly, he seemed excited about it, telling me that he had something important he wanted to talk to me about. I didn't want to think about a serious conversation with him, figuring he would be telling me that they were getting married or expecting a baby. I had made peace with them, but that was something that I couldn't even be prepared to hear.

Knowing that my visit had the possibility to be upsetting, I called my friends to find something to do. Shortly after leaving a few text messages, I got a call from one of my favorite blonde pieces of ass.

Heather arrived at the carriage house about an hour later. I never got up from the couch when she came in. Hell, I didn't even change my clothes. That was the thing about hooking up with her. There was no need to impress her. She just offered it. It was degrading, but hey, it was her own fault, not mine.

I smelled her perfume even before I glanced away from my Xbox game to greet her. She was wearing some short sleeve zip up jacket and a skirt, like a tennis player would wear. "What the fuck are you wearing? I ain't in any shape to play tennis." I joked.

She bit her lip and climb over me to straddle my body. Immediately, my hands reached around to her ass. "This is my easy access outfit baby." While explaining, she started unzipping the jacket, revealing her naked breasts. As she threw the jacket to the side of the couch, she lifted up her skirt and smiled with her vixen eyes. "See. Easy access."

No panties.

This girl gave the word booty call its name. I groaned and pulled her over my pants where my dick sat, so she could feel my rapid arousal. Her soft ass cheeks moved with the motion my hands were guiding. Heather grabbed the button to my shorts and loosened them enough to reach her hand down my pants. "I want it in my mouth." She offered without even a sign of uncertainty.

For two years she was the one person who was willing to fuck at the drop of a hat, with no strings attached, well on my part. My intentions were always clear. It was just sex for me, but as the time went by, I noticed her striving for a real relationship. When she pushed me about it, I would stop calling her for a few weeks. After she calmed down and realized this was all I was offering, she shut up and enjoyed the ride.

I watched Heather begin to slide down onto the floor. I couldn't help but lick my lips as I watched her yank down my pants, just enough to be able to pull out my cock with her hand. She looked up at me while taking her tongue and sliding it up the main vein at the base of my erection. I could feel the force as it pressed firmly and stroked it once again. Her eyes never left mine as she took the base of my shaft into her mouth and started bobbing her pretty little head up and down it. I considered grabbing my Xbox paddle and playing my paused game, but didn't want to take the chance of her stopping, or biting me.

Like every time, I closed my eyes and imagined it was Van with her lips wrapped around me. I think since I enjoyed getting head so much, Van purposely hated it. I would beg and beg for it until she became so pissed off and eventually gave in, or in some instances, just went home.

I tried to shake off my thoughts of Van, to be able to concentrate more on Heather and her lips around my dick, but it was easier said than done. Van haunted my mind every time I got aroused. I couldn't control it, believe me when I say that I tried.

After at least ten minutes, Heather climbed up on top of me. "My mouth hurts, baby. How about we just fuck?"

I shrugged and grabbed her by her hair, putting my lips close enough to brush against hers as I spoke. "Let's see how bad you want me." I slid two fingers down in between her legs.

After I had grabbed a condom and slipped it on, I looked over to Heather. I had no respect for her and she knew it. If I hadn't been so depressed and desperate, I would have just sent her home. I wasn't trying to be heartless, but this was as good as it got for me. I was miserable, with no light at the end of the tunnel.

She was already panting for me when I swung her around to lean over the coffee table. I scooted myself off of the couch and positioned my body to be right behind her. My hand pushed down on her back and I slid deep inside of her. Heather was great about not complaining. She knew what this was, even if she couldn't admit it to herself.

I pushed up the ruffles to her skirt so I could watch while I smacked her tight little ass. The harder I thrust, the louder she screamed out for more. Visions of Van filled my closed eyes and I felt myself growing on the verge to finish. Once I had blown my load and collapsed back on the couch, she got up and looked at me. I couldn't say anything to her that she wanted to hear. She needed to move on and find somebody that cared about her. She would have been a great girlfriend, but I could never respect her.

"Thanks for stopping by." I said before hitting play on my game.

She slid down next to me on the couch. "Can I stay for a while?"

Reluctantly, I hit pause again and looked toward her. She was already zipping up her shirt. "Heather, we talked about this."

"I drove all the way out here. I just wanted to stay for more than a half hour Ty. You keep getting worse instead of better. I just thought that after all of this time you would feel something for me." She said sadly.

I rolled my eyes and brushed the hair out of her eyes. "Look, I can't help it I still love her. You knew this was all we could be Heather. I know it isn't what you want to hear. Why can't you just move on to someone who can give you what you want.?"

"Because I love you Ty. We are so good together. Why can't you just see that? Nobody can satisfy you like I can." She started to cry.

I shook my head. The truth was that neither of them really satisfied me. That was my problem. I just never saw it that way back then. It was like the pussy was the devil and it kept calling me. I never could say no. It was a big problem that I didn't know if I could ever change, or even wanted to. I always pictured Van, every time I had cheated on her, but when I was with her, it just didn't make me feel fulfilled. I was always looking for that one person that could leave me completely speechless.

I liked to fuck, but it ended as quickly as it started.

Every time.

"Why do you keep doing this?"

She looked right at me with those sad eyes. "You know

why."

I ran my hand over the back of her arm. My brow creased and I suddenly realized I had no reason to sugar coat things with this chick. Maybe if I was mean enough she would be able to just let go. "You beat the shit out of my girlfriend. You are one of the reasons that she fell in love with my cousin. She left me for him. Do you know how much that fucking hurt? How much it still hurts? I can never feel anything for you Heather." She gasped and more tears seeped out of her eyes. "We fuck. That is all it is. To be honest with you, I still have to picture Van to get off....."

She stood up and threw the remote at my face. I put my hands up and blocked the impact. "What the fuck...I am just being honest!"

"Screw you Ty. Lose my fucking number you prick! I hate you!" She stormed out, slamming the door behind her.

I let out a laugh. Five minutes ago she loved me. Within a week she would be calling again. Her desperation was a real turn off. When I heard her car pulling away, I hit play and went back to my game. I wasn't going to let her ruin my night.

Chapter 3
Miranda

"Your daughter is nine months old now, Tucker. I was just wonderin' when you were going to step up." I was enraged. He hadn't even talked to me in two days. I had sent texts several times with no reply. I had even gone so low as to text his friends. The idea of them making fun of me pissed me off more.

"Don't start this shit with me again Miranda. You know I have a bunch goin' on right now. I don't even know why you keep buggin' me about it. Your family is loaded. You know why I haven't been callin'. I need money. Why don't you just ask your aunt for some. If you helped me get out of some of this trouble than we could be together more."

I looked down at my phone and considered throwing it across the room. "Tucker, I can't ask my family for somethin' like that. I don't want their money. I just want you. We don't need it. Things will work out."

"Look Miranda, I don't have time to argue about this right now. We are gettin' the Chevy ready for the race this weekend. I need to figure out how I am goin' to make some fast cash. I gotta go."

"Wait! When will we see you? You need to come visit with your daughter. She needs diapers," I said desperately trying to get him to come over.

"You know I don't have any money for that shit right now. Just ask your mother for her credit card." He said rudely.

"What happened to your job?" He was working at a body shop outside of town.

"I quit. Ain't nobody goin' to tell me what I can and can't do."

I felt so angry. We had a child to think about. I was helping part time at the farm, but it wasn't enough to start a life with. Why couldn't he want to start our future together? "Now what are you goin' to do? You can't keep livin' like you are right now."

"Don't worry about me. You just keep livin' on that ranch with your rich family. I will figure somethin' else out babes."

"She's nine months old, Tucker. I am startin' to feel like we are never goin' to be a family. She needs her daddy ya know."

I could hear him sighing through the phone. "She don't know any different. She's just a baby. Listen, I gotta head over to Charlie's. He's havin' people over later, so I will just call you tomorrow."

"I want to go with you," I stated.

"It's just a bunch of guys. Just stay home and hang out with your daughter. I will call you tomorrow."

My daughter? She was also his daughter....

"Fine, I love you."

"Yeah, me too...bye."

I hit end on the phone and set it on the table. There wasn't a second to consider he had just blown me off, because I heard Bella crying and made my way to her room instead. When I saw her in her crib, just laying there, waiting for me to pick her up, all I could do was cry.

I had been so stupid to think that he would drop what he was doing to come hang out with me and our baby. In the past nine months he had spent the night less than ten times. I picked up my beautiful daughter and started comforting her to still her cries. "It's okay, baby. Momma's got you now. I will never choose anything over you. I promise."

She settled quickly and began her daily cooing and raspberry blowing, while it took me a little more time to calm myself down. I hated being a wreck around her.

After I changed her diaper, we headed into the family room to play. Ever since my uncle passed away suddenly, the house just seemed empty. Even with Van moving into Colt's place and them having dinner at least three nights a week here, it just wasn't the same. My aunt was an empty shell of a person. She tried to keep herself busy during the day, but nights were the hardest for her. Many times, when I got up in the middle of the night with Isabella, I found her in my uncle's study. She would just sit there in his chair and cry.

My mother had a house on the ranch too, but she and Conner were fine by themselves. I insisted that Bella and I stay here in the main house. We basically had an entire wing to ourselves since only my aunt and her housekeeper Lucy still lived here in this big mansion. Her daughter had just left to go to college, so it was just us girls left here. Because there was little cleaning to do in the house, Lucy spent her days in front of the television watching soap operas. During intense parts she would sometimes yell at the television, or come into the kitchen talking all about these characters as if they were real people. "Can you believe he cheated on her? I knew he was the father. She isn't really dead ya know."

I had heard it all.

Today was no different. I heard her arguing with the television again. Friday's were the worst for her, because they always left with some major cliffhanger. She came walking into the kitchen shaking her head. "I just can't believe he did that," she said as she approached Bella. "How is my favorite baby today?"

"Say...I am just fine, Auntie Lucy," I said in a baby voice. Bella smiled with a mouth full of pureed bananas.

"Have you heard from her father lately?" She started wiping off Bella's face.

My family hated Tucker. My mother begged me to dump him, but he was the father of my child. I loved him and he loved me too. He just had his priorities all wrong. One day things would change and we would be a family.

"We talked this morning."

"You don't sound very happy about it missy," she said sarcastically.

I gave her a quick fake smile. "I just wish he would grow

up. I want us to be together." I wiped off Bella's mouth and turned around to face Lucy. "Hey, do you think you could babysit tonight for me? I want to surprise Tucker."

"Sure. Not that I want you hangin' with that riff raff, but I would love to spend quality time with this little cutie." She said as she approached Bella and talked in a sweet voice.

"Thanks, Lucy. I don't know whether my mother would say yes considerin' she wishes he would drop off the face of the earth. I just wish I could make him see what he's missin'."

She patted my shoulder. "Sweetie, I think some men just never grow up. Your mom just wants more for you and Bella. That man is no good for you. Bella needs a daddy who wants to be around her, not one that can't make the time to."

I gave her a smile and started cleaning up the mess on the high chair. I had never planned to get pregnant and lose out on the college life. I didn't want to spend my whole life on this ranch. I wanted more for me and my daughter. I just couldn't do it alone.

I never expected to get pregnant with Bella when I did. I met Tucker at a party. He broke up a fight between two guys that were fighting over a girl. Everyone was pretty drunk and I was the sober person to clean up his bloodied nose. We hung out after that, taking shots and groping all over each other. That night he looked at me like nobody else ever had, and after a few hours, we ended up in the back of his pickup truck.

It was hard for me to date with my brother and Colt always threatening everyone that was interested. Those two were like the country songs about fathers waiting at home with a shotgun loaded up, ready to tear a guy a new ass.

Tucker wasn't afraid of anyone, but I didn't show him off at first anyway. Instead, I snuck out to meet him. I found out I was pregnant about a month later. I knew it was Tucker's baby because I hadn't been with anyone else in months. We had been having such a good time that I thought he was really into me. When I told him, he freaked out and begged me to get an abortion. After I refused, he didn't speak to me for three months. When he did start coming back around again, he was distant.

He made wise cracks about my weight and the stretch marks that I had across my stomach. He refused to have sex with me during the rest of my pregnancy, even after my doctor confirmed it was perfectly healthy to do so.

I heard from one of my friends that Conner saw Tucker out one night racing and gave him hell. He must have really laid into him, because after that he came around a lot more.

My family still begged me to just dump him. Every day they had some new reason that it needed to happen. I couldn't help but hope that one day he would see how important family was to me. I lost my dad when I was a little girl. We did everything together. It was so hard for me to believe that I would never see him again, or sit on his lap again. I remember coming home from school and waiting for him to get home at night. When I heard his car pulling into the gravel driveway I would run to the front door and open it up. He would pick me up over his shoulder and plop me down on the couch and tickle me. He did that every night.

When he died I refused to sit on that couch. The memories were too painful for me. Soon after, my mom moved us to the ranch. My aunt and uncle put a nice double wide on the property so that we wouldn't have to worry about money. We had been here ever since.

Tucker knew what losing my father did to me, so I couldn't fathom how he couldn't understand why I needed him to be here for me and Bella.

I realized I had completely dazed out. "I just want Bella to have her daddy. It means so much to me."

"Bella will be loved no matter what," Lucy said as she stood up and started washing a dish. "Before I forget to tell you, Tyler is coming to stay for a week. He will be staying in one of the guest rooms here."

I knew he didn't want to stay with Colt and Van. Those two

couldn't keep their hands off of one another. "Okay. I am sure Bella will like the attention."

"It still amazes me how he acts around her," Lucy admitted.

"Yeah, it weirded me out at first. It isn't even like we were really close before. I guess it all changed after he helped deliver her."

"You be careful with that boy. I hear how he is with women," She warned.

I laughed. "Seriously Lucy, we are just friends, almost cousins even. I have never considered him anything but family. I am sure he feels the same. He even has me telling Bella to call him Uncle Ty. I hardly think there is anything more to our friendship in his eyes."

She didn't need to know that Ty would listen to me cry over Tucker sometimes late at night. We video chatted a few times a week and it was almost always so that he could talk to Bella and act like a moron to get a smile out of her, but several times we stayed connected and talked for hours. He gave good advice, probably because he was such a womanizer himself. I heard what he did to Van and I also knew he still loved her.

"When is he gettin' here?" I asked.

"This afternoon I think."

"I guess I will see him before I go out then," I said as I carried Bella out of the room. I needed to pick out something hot to wear. I had tried everything else. Maybe seducing her daddy would get him to see what else he was missing. I was willing to try anything at this point.

Chapter 4
Tyler

19

I packed up my Jeep and headed to Kentucky. Part of the reason was to hang out with Colt and Van, but the other was to see Izzy. She was getting so big. All of the pictures I had from text messages and internet video chatting did nothing compared to how she was in person. She was turning nine months old and her cheeks were so chubby. I swear the child smiled constantly. She had two matching dimples on either side of her cheeks that made you just want to kiss them. That little girl was the only thing to take my mind off of my totally fucked up life. Maybe using a baby to bury my problem was selfish, but things were difficult.

I'd lost everything. I just needed something to look forward to.

Van and Colt had expected me for dinner at the cabin, but I had stopped at the main house first. I wasn't sure if she would recognize my voice, but when I walked into that house and said hello, in my best baby talk voice, she got the biggest smile. After it got dark, I realized I had been there for hours. Miranda kept me company, and called me a weirdo for playing with Izzy for so long.

When Miranda said she had to get ready for a night out, I volunteered to hang out with Izzy. We sat watching a video with a bunch of brightly dressed adults dancing and singing. I moved her hands around to act like she was dancing. She giggled and made squeaking sounds the faster we danced. Her little teeth were the cutest thing about her smile.

Miranda came out of the bathroom smelling like heaven. She wore a tight tank top that pushed up her already large breasts and low rise skinny jeans. She did a spin in front of me. "How do I look? I still feel like I am so fat."

We had become pretty good friends in the past few months. I think sometimes I freaked her out always asking about Izzy and even giving her my own nickname, but she still called every now and again to catch up or vent about her douche bag boyfriend.

I had to admit, this was the first time I had really looked at her as a woman and not a family member. I couldn't take my eyes off of her, especially her tits. Her curves were perfect and I imagined how fucking awesome it would feel to bend her over something.

I needed to shake that feeling.

It didn't help that she was blonde, which was so sexy to me. Van was the only brunette I had ever been attracted to. Today Miranda had curled the bottom of her hair. It flowed down her back. She could have been the sexiest Dallas Cowboy Cheerleader. I pictured her in that little outfit they wear and got a big smile on my face.

I tried to hide my expression, so that she couldn't tell I was mind-fucking her. The idea of doing that to her just seemed wrong, but I couldn't stop. Having a baby had caused the girl to have never ending curves. "Uh, you look fine."

That was all I could say.

She turned around again and ran her hand over her ass. "I was hoping I looked better than just fine. These jeans are new. Are you sure they don't make my ass look fat? They are so tight, but I need to be sexy. Tonight is important."

I kept my smile to a minimum. Did every woman ask that question? "Are you going for a sweet relaxing good time, or more of a 'I want to get laid' look?"

She turned around and rolled her eyes at me. "Seriously Ty, I wanted your opinion. You have been with a lot of people, you know what guys like. Do I look sexy enough? How are the boobs?"

A lot of people?

The idea of her being with that little dickhead made my skin crawl. She obviously wanted to fuck him tonight. I wasn't going to help her do it. "We are related. I am not answering that."

She turned around to face me, leaned over and put her hands on my knees, teasing me with those breasts.

Close your eyes. Do not lick your lips.

"We are not really related. Look at me and be honest.

21

So…….I need to know if I look hot? Do you think he will want me?"

If he doesn't than he's a fool.

She was too close. I could smell whatever she had put on her body and it smelled delicious. I wanted to lick her skin. Her tits were pressed together in her shirt and I had to put my hands into fists to keep from reaching up and trying to touch them. I couldn't do this, for so many reasons. She was something I could never want and never have. I stopped staring at her tits and looked straight into those beautiful green eyes.

Oh God that was just as bad. "We are family. I can't answer that."

She stood up and put her hands on her hips. "Picture me as someone else then. If I had a bag over my head and you didn't know it was me would you want to hit it?"

I laughed out loud.

God, her use of words were killing me. "Miranda you look really hot. I am sure you will have a fantastic night." I smiled and tried not to look at her rocking body anymore. It was wrong to look at her the way I was. She was just so beautiful. No wonder Van felt threatened, even when she was pregnant. Now we were such good friends. In fact, I knew too much about her to look at her like I was.

"Tonight has to work," she said as she looked down at her chest and adjusted them once more, in front of me.

"What do you mean?" I was curious.

"He won't take our future seriously. All Tucker wants to do is run around with his friends and get into trouble. I need him to be here for Bella and I."

"What exactly did he do to get into trouble?" It was more like what hadn't he done.

She looked at her fingernails and avoided eye contact. "He stole metal from scrap yards and then took it back in for cash the next day. He would do it at different places and eventually they caught on to his scheme."

"Sounds like it isn't a big deal."

"Do you have any idea how much copper is worth? Some of the yards give almost three dollars a pound for clean copper. Some days he was makin' over a grand. I think that is how they caught him. They recognized the copper. Large amounts of it are easy to spot."

"Sounds stupid."

She gave me a dirty look. "Everyone makes mistakes Ty."

"You are right. Sorry. I just can't see having a baby at home and risking it all for a few bucks. Has he ever just looked at her and saw how perfect she is?" I could see it and she wasn't even my kid.

I overstepped my place, but it was obvious I was crazy about that kid. I had held her mother's hand in the back of that car and let her head rest on my lap as she pushed. I had brushed away her tears when she cried in pain and been the one to tell her she would be okay. Izzy's birth was so special to me.

Obviously I made her mad. She shook her head and wouldn't answer.

"Good luck," I said looking down and noticing that Izzy was crawling away. I jumped down and followed her acting like a dog. She crawled faster and made excited coos as she tried to get away.

"I guess I will see you in the morning?" She asked.

"Sounds good." I grabbed Izzy and held her up to face her mother. "Tell Mommy you love her," I said against her cheek.

Miranda leaned in and took a kiss from her daughter. Her face was so close to mine that I breathed in her sweet scent again. "You smell nice." I said as she walked away.

I couldn't help watching her leave. That there was the finest ass I had ever seen. Tucker was a fucking fool. I'd lost the love of my life and I would never get her back, I knew it, but damn he had a family. How could he ignore that?

She really did look totally hot and she didn't need a paper

bag over her head for me to see it. I shook off the urge to chase after her and instead spent the rest of the evening with my favorite little girl.

Sometime later Lucy came in to check on us, but I had already changed Izzy and given her a bottle. The old woman gave me a raised eyebrow and took a second look at the sleeping baby on my chest. She walked away shaking her head claiming she would be back down to check on us later. I got myself comfortable and made sure both of my arms were securely wrapped around her before closing my eyes for a short nap myself.

Chapter 5
Miranda

It was already dark when I left to head to Charlie's house. He lived in a small trailer in the middle of nowhere. It had become the local party house on weekends because the cops would never get called. I was so nervous about seeing Tucker. I had missed him so much.

After spending almost an hour getting ready and seeing the look on Ty's face when I leaned over, I knew I looked hot enough to prove my point tonight. My friends always said 'if you got it flaunt it', well that is what I planned to do tonight.

When I pulled up into the driveway, I noticed the slew of cars already parked in it. After checking myself in the rearview mirror one last time I climbed out of the car. I knew for a fact I would be totally overdressed, but that was the point.

The commotion of the party was coming from the backyard, so I headed in that direction. I couldn't help but notice half of the voices were female. Tucker had told me it was just the guys tonight. My cheeks instantly flushed with anger. This wasn't the first time he had lied to me about being around other women. As I made the turn around the back of the trailer I started looking for Tucker. I heard whistles and realized they could see my figure, but didn't notice who I was yet. I kept walking toward the crowd. Charlie and Nick, Tucker's two best friends stood up and headed in my direction.

"Miranda? What are you doin' here?" Nick asked, almost preventing me from looking past them.

"What do you think I am doin' here? I want to have a good time. Where is my man?"

Charlie was giving me a once over and licking his lips. I waved my hand in front of his face. "Hello? Up here."

"Sorry, you just...well you look hot Miranda. I guess I haven't seen you in a while. You sure do look different," Charlie

25

stuttered out.

"Thanks, but I am here to see Tucker. Where is he? I saw his car out front."

I pushed past them and they followed trying to say something, but I ignored them. He clearly wasn't outside so I headed for the trailer.

"Miranda. WAIT!" Charlie yelled behind me. He ran up in front of me. "He isn't inside."

Just as I started to believe him, the back door flew open. Tucker was laughing with his beer in one hand and a redhead's ass in his other.

"What the hell?" I yelled as I ran toward them. "Tucker?"

His hand quickly moved away from the little ginger. "Miranda, I can explain."

I started walking away and knew he was following. "I don't see how you are going to talk me out of what I think I just saw Tucker. Is this why you didn't invite me?"

He grabbed both of my arms. "She means nothin' to me babe. We were just messin' around. I was tellin' her about you."

I pulled away from his grasp. "Do you really expect me to believe that lame ass excuse? Did you sleep with her?"

"Hell no!"

I folded my hands across my chest. "Really? Why don't I go find her and ask myself then."

Adrenaline filled my veins and I knew it was much better than him seeing me cry. I wanted answers and I wanted them now.

"She likes me, but I never returned the feelin's. Let's go somewhere and be alone. We can talk this through."

"No! I am a mother of a beautiful little girl and I will be damned if I let her daddy walk all over me."

I turned and started walking away. There was no way that I was going to let him see me crying.

"Miranda wait! I will go with you," he offered by grabbing

my arm.

I yanked myself out of his strong grip. "Get the fuck off of me! I can't even look at your lyin' ass right now. Do not follow me. Go back to that little whore and have a great night, you son of a bitch."

He backed away and stood there watching as I skidded down the driveway. I couldn't catch my breath for at least ten minutes. My car sat at the end of the road until I could stop crying enough to be able to see out of my tear filled eyes.

How could he just pretend that we didn't exist? How could he ignore his responsibilities the way he was? How was I going to do all of this without him?

All of those questions made me cry even more. Every time I saw headlights in the rearview mirror, I thought it would be Tucker coming to apologize, but he never did.

When an hour had passed, I had become so angry that I decided to go back and give him a real piece of my mind. Part of me wanted to call my brother, but I knew he would beat the living shit out of Tucker and end up in jail over it. I wasn't willing to risk my brother getting into trouble.

I pulled in across from Charlie's trailer and climbed out of my car without being seen. Just like last time, I could hear the laughter coming from the backyard. I walked around the opposite side of the house and peeked around it slowly so I wouldn't be spotted.

My heart dropped when I spotted the same redhead, sitting on Tucker's lap, with her tongue down his throat. I closed my eyes and put my hand over my mouth to keep from crying out. Unable to accept what I had just witnessed, I looked again. This time the redhead was wrapping her legs around his waist and his hands were on her ass. She leaned back and his face went against her neck. Before I could make a move, he stood up with her still attached to his hips, and carried her toward the house.

I slid over to hide again and I tried to control my breathing and shaking. The door opened and shut and I could hear laughing coming from inside. Since I had been in the trailer many times, I knew exactly where each room was located.

I walked right in the door, without anyone even noticing I was back. There was nobody else in the house, which made it easy to follow the moaning to one of the bedrooms. The door was closed, but I took my boot and kicked the sucker in.

"Miranda? What the fuck?"

Before I even knew what I was doing, I pounced on that little bitch. I grabbed her by her hair and punched her in the face three times before I felt Tucker ripping me off of her. She lay there in her skimpy little bra backing away from me, while I fought to get free.

"Get off of me you lyin' sack of shit!" I kicked and I screamed, but he wouldn't let go.

"Calm the hell down Miranda," Tucker demanded.

"Screw you. How could you? How could you do this to me?" I cried.

He pulled me into his chest and I started punching him with both hands. "You need to leave so I can talk to her right now," he said to the other girl. I tried to fight my way free to attack her again, but he made sure to hold me tight.

"Get off of me, Tucker."

"Sit down and shut up Miranda. You weren't supposed to be here tonight, so don't you dare get all pissy with me. I was just tryin' to have a good time." He was drunk. I could smell the liquor on his breath and hear it in his voice.

"So you are admitting that you cheated?" *Please don't cry. Please don't cry.*

"We just aren't going to work out Miranda. We don't want the same things," he confessed while standing over me.

"How could you say that? We have a baby. How could you not love her?" His words crushed me.

"Honestly, I asked you to get an abortion. You knew I

didn't want a kid." He shook his head and let out a laugh. "I am glad you caught me tonight, because I am just sick of hearing you bitch at me every day. There ain't no bitch in this world that is going to tie me down."

I stood up, causing him to back away. He knew what he said and what those words did to me. I clenched my fists. "You can't mean this. You can't regret her."

"Dammit girl. Are your ears clogged? Just get your shit and get out of here."

I don't know what came over me, but anger filled my lungs. I pointed my fingers in his face and backed him up against the wall. "You will never see my daughter again. If you come near me or my family I will fucking kill you myself."

"Don't you threaten me. I will take that little girl away and you will never see her again."

Oh Hell no!

I grabbed my phone and hit the red emergency button while hitting the speaker button.

"Nine-one-one what is your emergency?"

"Yes, I know where you can find Tuc..." My phone went flying across the room and the battery popped out.

"Get out of here now, before I do somethin' I swore I would never do to a woman." He threatened.

"What? You goin' to hit me? Go ahead and give me another reason to turn your ass in. I dare you!"

His eyes were big and they bore into me, but he said nothing.

"That's what I thought you lyin', no good cheater. Stay away from me, or you will be sorry."

Charlie and Nick ran past me as I was walking out the front door. My phone was in pieces in my hand, but I managed to pull out my keys and drag them from the front of his black shiny car all the way to the trunk. A small smile covered my face, even as the tears poured out.

I had been such a fool. I fell too fast. So much for true love and being a family. My little girl would never know her daddy and it was all my fault.

I was reluctant to go home at all, but I had nowhere else to go. My aunt and mother had gone to some spa for the weekend, so I was alone in the house with Lucy and now Ty. After looking at the clock I noticed it was pretty late. Everyone would be asleep and I could just sneak in without having to explain how my life was a total mess.

I drove slow up the driveway and tiptoed into the house. I noticed the television was still on. Even as I tried to sneak past, I couldn't help but notice what I saw. My hand went over my mouth as I saw Ty lying there with Bella asleep on his chest.

Why couldn't Tucker want this? How could someone with no relation love my child this much and not her own father. I sank to the floor in front of the sleeping pair and started bawling my eyes out. I tried to be quiet, but between the sobs and the sniffles, I must have woke Ty up.

His hands first went to Bella to make sure she was safely on his chest, then he turned to look at me.

Chapter 6
Ty

I didn't realize I had fallen asleep until I heard Miranda crying. She was sitting on the floor next to the couch. "Hey", I whispered.

It was hard to sit up with a sleeping baby on my chest. The moment I moved she woke up. She started to cry, but I grabbed her pacifier and calmed her enough to sit up. Miranda shook her head and went to get Izzy a bottle. I followed her into the kitchen and handed her Izzy when she finally had the bottle ready. While she walked her daughter to the nursery, I waited in the kitchen.

I grabbed us two glasses and found some whiskey. After adding some coke to each glass, Miranda came walking in. "I hope this is strong," she said before taking a giant gulp. Her face was red and she still had tears falling from her eyes.

"Do you want to talk about it?" I asked.

"Not with you Ty," she said rudely.

I set my glass down and reached my arm out to her, but she backed away. "Seriously, just don't. I can't deal with another guy like him tonight."

Like Him? "Look, I don't know what happened, but I am nothing like Tucker."

She shook her head and gave me a dirty look. "Oh really? You don't fuck girls for fun, no matter who you hurt? You don't sit there thinkin' with your dick instead of worryin' about your future?"

I swallowed the lump that was now in my throat preventing me to speak. "I was a fool," I said into my drink.

"That's what I thought." She shook her head and leaned against the counter. Her sobs got louder. "Why couldn't he want us? She doesn't deserve this. None of this is her fault."

I knew that she was referring to Izzy and it pissed me off immediately. "What happened?"

"He said he never wanted her. Can you believe that? Who says something like that?" Her cries became worse and she covered her face with her hands. "I just can't believe this. Everything is messed up. How am I going to raise her alone?"

I walked behind her and rubbed her shoulders, in the most non-sexual way possible. "You are not alone Miranda. This family would never let you be. We all love that little girl. Don't ever think that."

She didn't pull away from me. "Tell me why Ty?"

"What do you mean?"

"Why do you have to cheat? Why can't you be happy with one person? Is this just something all guys do?"

I wanted to tell her it was, but she and I both knew one person who would never do it. Damn Colt had to be the proof she needed. She just wanted to hear me confess to being an asshole, like somehow it would make her situation feel better. "No, not all guys do it. I can't tell you why. I guess it's different for everyone."

"So why did you do it?"

I was standing behind her, leaning against the fridge. She wouldn't turn around to face me and that was okay with me considering her question. "For the longest time I wondered about that, but after months of being without Van I came to realize it was never about her. I loved her, but she was never the right girl for me. Hell, in one weekend she gave Colt more than she ever gave me. I guess part of me did it for the attention. Van was always so sweet and innocent. Every time we did something she would freak out like we were going to get into trouble. As we got older she was better, but she never really was comfortable. Now that I know some of the things she has done with our cousin, I know it wasn't me holding her back. I just wasn't the right person for her either." I shook my head realizing how much I had said.

She turned around and handed me the empty glass. "Can I have some more?"

I refilled both of our glasses and turned back around to

face her. "She wasn't even pretty."

"Who?" I asked.

"The redhead he was hookin' up with tonight. Does that make me ugly too? Maybe he has low standards."

I reached over and put my hands on both of her shoulders. "Miranda, you are sexy as shit. He's a fucking idiot for taking you for granted."

She pulled back and rolled her eyes, while putting the glass to her mouth. "That's real funny coming out of your mouth. How many girls have you slept with now? Thirty? Fifty? One hundred?"

Did she really think that? "You aren't even close."

"Oh my God, it's more?"

"No! What the fuck? Do you really think that highly of me? Damn." I shook my head and finished off my second drink.

"Sorry, I just assumed it was a bunch of people."

"I was faithful to Van the first couple of years. She was everything, but girls kept tempting me, offering to do things that she would never do. One night I caved and after I got away with it, I continued to do it. I cheated with the same two girls in high school, then in college it was a couple more. Oh and one time I visited Colt and hooked up with some random chick here." *Holy shit, I had never told someone that.*

I expected Miranda to be mean, but instead she started laughing. "What's so funny?"

She shook her head and continued to laugh. "It doesn't matter."

"You can't do that then not tell me why. Spill."

"No, you will think I am a whore. I ain't sayin' nothin'."

"Fine. Just so you know, I never told anyone that. Not even Van." I put my glass in the sink and drank from the whiskey bottle. Van was going to find out the truth and hate me more now. I knew how close she was with Miranda.

"Don't do that." She said grabbing the bottle away from me.

"Hey, give it back." I tried to grab the bottle but somehow got my arm caught up around her waist. When our faces almost touched, we froze.

She was so close. I could still smell her sweet perfume. Her eyes were a mess and all of the makeup had run down her cheeks. "I should probably call it a night," She said as she handed me back the bottle and walked out of the kitchen.

I had no idea why she wouldn't tell me what was so funny. I wanted to know. Without thinking, I followed behind her, hoping she would explain. She must not have heard me coming, because she was already starting to pull off her tank top when I walked into her room. When the door creaked she spun around and I just stood there.

Her hands naturally covered up the lace of her bra. "Ty? Get out of here? What the Hell?"

I turned around as quickly as possible. "Sorry, I came up to talk to you. I don't see what the big deal is. I have seen my share of breasts." None of them looked at good as that though.

"You can turn around now pervert."

I spun around to see she had changed into a long t-shirt. I sighed in relief. "I wasn't being a pervert. I was trying to be a friend."

"You really should just go into your own room now Ty. Right now I hate every man on the planet. I wouldn't be good company." She confessed.

"Miranda I don't think you understand my intentions. I was there for Izzy's birth."

"Bella." She interrupted.

"Izzy is my name for her. Just let me finish." I smiled at her disappointment. "I watched her being born. Something that day made me fall in love with that little girl. I can't explain it, but I feel like I always want to keep her safe. If Tucker did something to her mother, then I want to know about it. I know you think you need him in your life, but that bastard doesn't deserve either of you."

"Who are you and what have you done with my asshole cousin?" She joked.

Sometimes I hated that she thought of me as her family. This day had been one of those times. "Stop making fun of me. Can't I be nice? I was never mean to Van. Even she will tell you that."

"Sorry. It's keeping me from losin' it again. He said he never wanted her and that I should have got an abortion."

Before she could say anymore I lost it. "HE SAID WHAT?" I yelled. "Tell me where I can find his little ass. I will fucking kill him."

"Ty, please just leave it alone. I told him to stay away from us."

I ran my hands through my hair. "If I see him, I will hurt him."

"I don't want the family to know Ty. Please keep this between us. They can't know."

"Are you afraid of him?"

She shrugged. "I am not afraid of him right now, but if you or my brother go after him, there is no tellin' what he will do. I can't worry about that. I need to keep my focus on Bella. Please promise me."

I shook my head. "Fine. If I hear about him hurting you, it's on."

"Thank you for carin'. Sometimes I feel like I can't talk to anyone about him. I know you hate him too, but at least you made me feel better. Safe even."

I walked out of her room and gave her a high wave as I turned away. One day I would find that fucker and kick the shit out of him. It would be on my bucket list.

Chapter 7
Miranda

Even after I told Ty I was fine, I still cried myself to sleep. I kept replaying the night in my head. I saw Tucker's lips and tongue kissing that girl over and over. I wanted to throw up. He told me he loved me. He said we would be a family. How could he take it all back? How could he not love Bella?

That was the part that upset me the most. She was the most perfect little baby. How could someone not love her? For goodness sakes, Ty was infatuated with her. He video chatted with a infant because he was so crazy about her. Sometimes he would tell me to put the computer next to the crib while I got a shower or had to get changed. They would play peek-a-boo. He would keep her occupied through the screen of a laptop and her own father wanted nothing to do with her. When Tucker was with her, he would play on his phone while she cried or crawled at his feet.

I should have known he was no good, but I wanted to believe he would change. I had been so stupid, so infatuated with the idea of us being a family.

The next morning I woke to sounds coming from Bella's bedroom. After the shocking revelations the night before and the lack of sleep, it didn't register that it could be Ty. I entered the doorway and froze as I saw him bent over the changing table, singing to Bella, while changing her diaper.

You are my sunshine, my only sunshine...you make me happy, when skies are gray.....

I folded my arms across my chest and smiled from cheek to cheek. It was the cutest thing I had ever seen. "Again, I have to ask...who are you and what have you done with my cousin?"

He picked up Bella and turned to face me. His grin was huge. Bella grabbed a chunk of his shabby hair and got his attention. "Ouch, gentle Iz!"

I couldn't help but giggle at the two of them. I was so thankful that she was too young to see what I was going through and Ty being here was a godsend. Had I come home last night and been alone, it would have been horrible.

"I like your hair in the morning. The eighties look really appeals to you." Ty joked.

"Give me my, child smart ass," I said while reaching out for her. I hadn't even considered that I looked terrible.

I have no idea why she did it, but instead of reaching out for me like she always did, she put her head down on his chest. "Ah, you see. She wants to be with her uncle Ty."

I looked at Ty shocked. "There is no way she wants you over me. You haven't even seen her that much."

He rocked her around in his close grip. "I was the second person she ever laid eyes on. She won't forget me. She loves me."

I groaned and rolled my eyes. "I can't believe you changed her diaper."

"She was wet. I didn't want her to get a rash on her little hinny," He said in a baby voice.

Feeling defeated, I told Ty I would meet him downstairs after I got changed. When I made it into my room and caught a glance of myself in the mirror, I wanted to scream. I had black mascara smudges in lines down my face. My hair was a giant matted mess and my eyes were blood shot from crying.

I grabbed some clothes and ran into the bathroom to grab a quick shower. It amazed me that I could shower and get ready in seven minutes flat, since having a child. When the beads of water started trickling down my body it felt so refreshing. I leaned back against the shower and tried not to think about anything going on in my life.

I didn't know whether to be more mad at myself or Tucker. I had been such a freaking fool to not consider that everyone in my family had been right about him from the beginning. I should have done things so differently. I let my love for him blind the truth about the kind of person he really was.

After an extra ten minutes, I climbed out of the shower feeling determined that things were going to change for Bella and I. She was my life now and I would do everything I could so that she would have a good life as well.

I threw on a pair of yoga pants and a sweat jacket and headed downstairs. Ty was leaning against the kitchen counter while Lucy was sitting in front of the high chair feeding Bella. "You guys didn't have to do that. Go on about your day. We can manage from here."

We heard the front door shut and all of us turned to see my brother walking into the room. "The douche bag just pulled in. I told him he couldn't come inside, but he's insistin' on seein' you Miranda."

"I have nothin' to say to him."

Before I could give Ty a warning look, he threw me a wink. I appreciated that he wasn't going to tell Conner. My brother hated Tucker and his temper would get the best of him.

Conner grabbed an orange off of the counter and started walking out of the kitchen. "I'd be happy to tell him that."

I followed him to the front door and noticed that Ty had caught up to him. "Conner, wait up. I want to hear what this dumb ass has to say."

Great now I had the two of them to worry about.

They walked out the front door and headed in the direction of the driveway. I spotted Tucker's car and him leaning against it. My heart started pounding when I saw what was in his hand.

A baseball bat.

I went running out of the house trying to reach my brother and Ty before Tucker had any opportunity to hurt them. "Guys wait!"

They turned around to see me running toward them, but doing that caused Tucker to have the upper hand. He started walking toward them pointing his bat. "Your little bitch sister keyed my car last night. I want her to fuckin' pay for what she done to it."

Ty stood in front of me, sheltering me from being able to see Tucker.

"Don't you dare threaten my sister you common freak!" Conner shouted.

"Fuck you, Conner. I ain't scared of you. Walk a little closer and I will prove it." Tucker threatened.

"STOP IT!" I screamed. "Just go wait inside while I talk to him."

Conner and Ty just stood there staring at me like I had three heads.

"Just go. I don't need you both gettin' into my business any more than you already are. I can handle this myself."

"I ain't leavin' you out here alone with this scum bag," Conner said, not budging from his stance.

I looked over to Ty. "Please help me here."

"I'm not okay with this asshole being around you with that bat," He admitted.

I grabbed them both by the arm and pulled them in the direction of the front door. "Seriously you two, get a grip please. I can handle him. Go wait inside before things get ugly." I said in a whisper.

They carried on about it, but finally went inside. I could feel them staring from inside of the house as I walked back in the direction of Tucker and his car.

I stood about a foot away from him and tried to really study his body language. He was pissed. "I know you keyed my car you bitch."

"I am not sayin' whether I did it, but you probably did deserve it." I stared him right in the eye.

He scrunched up his face and walked toward me. "Let me tell you somethin'. There ain't no way I am leavin' here without getting paid for the damage you did to my car. Go inside and get your damn aunt's checkbook."

"I am not givin' you shit! Do you know how much it costs to raise a baby?"

"GIVE ME THE MONEY DAMMIT!" His eyes got big and I actually felt scared.

"Back away from me before my brother comes out here and beats the shit out of you," I threatened.

I took a step back trying to keep a good distance from him. His hand clenched the bat and he kept hitting it against his boot, to remind me that he had it.

"I ain't scared of your brother, or that punk ass cousin of yours."

"So you just came here for the money? What about apologizin' for what you did? I will never forgive you, Tucker."

He looked down to the ground and started laughing. "You catchin' me was the best thing that could have happened. She and I are together now." He waited a moment to let his hurtful words sink in. "You should have never had that kid Miranda. I told you it wasn't goin' to work, but you just couldn't get it through that thick head of yours. Look, I don't have time for this. Just go get me my money so we can just be done."

I was fuming. He called my daughter *that kid.* "You will not get a penny from my family. Get the hell off of my property before I call the police and tell them where to find you," I threatened.

"You want to play it like that? Okay. You will pay for this you little whore." He started to climb into his car and I backed away.

While hanging his head out of the window he spit at my feet. "You were never more than an easy fuck. Tell your family that what comes next is all your fault. See you soon bitch."

I watched him drive past me and then heard a loud crashing. He had taken the bat and smashed the passenger mirror on Ty's parked Jeep. I heard the guys come running out toward me.

"What the hell? He busted out my mirror dude," Ty said to Conner.

"You need to call the police Miranda. Get a restrainin' order before he does worse. We can't afford to have him messin' with this ranch. You should have never been with a guy like that in the first place. We warned you this would happen. How could you be so irresponsible?" My brother's words were like daggers. I should have known better.

"Where is Bella?" I asked in a panic.

"She's with Lucy. Are you okay? Did he threaten you?" Ty asked while grabbing my arm.

I just pulled away from him and shook my head while I ran into the house without answering. Tucker's words hurt me. How could I have been so blind? They were together now?

By the time that my brother and Ty came back into the house, I had already heard enough Spanish from Lucy to sing the LaBamba forty times. She only did that when she got really mad, so I knew she'd had enough of my boyfriend drama. What everyone didn't realize was that behind the anger, I was devastated. I opened my heart to this guy whether he was a bad person or not, I still loved him, or I thought I did.

Van and Colt came walking in the door about ten minutes later. I could hear the loud voices coming from the foyer as Ty and Conner explained everything that had just happened. Because Tucker threatened the ranch, Colt was going all hog shit over it. I took Bella and carried her up to my room. I just wanted to be alone with my baby. She was all that I needed in my life. I couldn't regret her for a second.

Chapter 8

Ty

I had a hard time sleeping with Miranda crying down the hall. I don't think she even realized how loud she was being. A part of me felt so bad for her. My friends used to joke about girls with kids, claiming they were a no-no. In light of my new found affection for Izzy, there was no way I would ever feel the same about that statement. Miranda was smoking hot and she was a great mother. It wasn't her fault that her pansy ass boyfriend couldn't act right.

I loved that little girl so much, in fact when I heard her cooing this morning, I couldn't help but go into her room and play. I hadn't expected that Miranda would come in looking like death, but at least she knew that Izzy had a clean diaper and a smile on her face.

I thought about how my friends would chew me a new ass for being such a sap about that little girl, but I didn't give a shit. Every time I looked into that little girls eyes I knew that she was special.

After the douche bag came and busted up my mirror, Conner demanded that Miranda tell him what was really going on. Since Colt and Van had showed up, I suggested that we go into the other room and give them some alone time. Colt wanted to hear about the drama, but Miranda seemed to genuinely be upset about the whole ordeal.

Once we got into the family room, Van pulled me to the side and gave me her accusing eye.

"Don't I get a hug?" I said grabbing her and pulling her into my chest. Colt rolled his eyes.

"We thought you were getting in yesterday. I tried to call you all night." She said.

"I did get here last night. I uh, well I got caught up with Izzy and after Miranda went out we fell asleep on the couch together.

When I woke up I saw all the missed calls."

"Wait. Who did you sleep with?" Colt asked accusingly.

"Izzy. Miranda went out to see that dickhead," I explained.

"You babysat?" Van asked with a smile on her face.

"Lucy was here too, although I told her to leave us alone and that I was fine. Obviously I was." There was no need to say I wasn't capable of taking care of her. She was easy to watch.

"What has happened to you?" Van joked.

I shrugged my shoulders. "What can I say? The kid likes me."

"I don't think that is what Savanna means. I think she's sayin' that you are not the type of guy to play with kids and be so caring. It's kind of disturbin'," Colt admitted.

"Screw you guys. It doesn't matter what any of you think. I love that kid and she loves her uncle Ty too."

Colt changed the subject immediately once he sensed my anger. "What's up with Tucker now? Man I am tellin' ya, that guy is trouble. He has been caught stealin' and I think the police came lookin' for him last week. He has Miranda brainwashed. That girl needs to stay away from him."

"He seems like a real douche," I added.

Colt gave me a funny look then let out a cackle.

"What?" I asked.

"I just think that is funny comin' from you." He held up his hand. "No offense."

He really just called me a douche!

"None taken. Look, I know I am not the best boyfriend, but my family has always been important," I argued. "That little bitch is nothing like me. Tell him Van."

She sat beside me on the edge of the couch and patted my back. "Calm down. We know you aren't like him. I think Colt is just worried you might want to ...I don't know...hook up with Miranda."

I looked from Colt to Van and shook my head. "Is that

43

what you both think? You think I came here to screw around with Miranda? Are you fucking kidding me right now? We are just friends."

I put my head down and shook my head again. I didn't want to talk to either of them about this anymore. I hadn't come here to sleep with Miranda. I wanted to see Van and Colt and of course Izzy. "Miranda and I are just friends. We are practically family. Nothing is ever going to happen between the two of us. I can promise you that." *Not like I had never thought about it before, but it couldn't happen anyway. Damn I was thinking about it again.*

I started to get up and walk out of the room, but Van grabbed my shirt and pulled me backwards. "Wait! We have to talk to you about some things."

Could this conversation get any worse?

"Ty, look, I am sorry if I made you mad. Miranda is my cousin and I just get sick of her goin' down the same path time and time again. She needs to stop goin' for guys that are nothin' but trouble. I didn't mean anything by it. I just think she shouldn't get involved with anyone right now." Colt's words weren't making things better, but I decided to keep my cool for Van.

"Whatever, dude. What do you have to talk to me about? When is the date?" I was already guessing it was a proposal since Van had her hand stuck in her hoodie since she had been around me.

Out came her hand, revealing a giant rock on her second finger. I swallowed the painful lump that managed to creep into my throat. I gave a fake smile and avoided eye contact as I hugged Van and shook Colt's hand. "Congrats guys. So when are you taking the plunge?"

"Next June. Right after graduation. We want Izzy to be the flower girl," Van noted.

"And I want you to be my best man," Colt added.

I was flabbergasted. "That isn't a good idea guys. I

appreciate the thought, really I do, but I just can't be in your wedding." I looked over to Van who seemed genuinely upset. "I'm so sorry. I just can't do it."

This time she didn't grab my shirt as I walked out of the room. I passed by Conner walking toward where I had just come from, but kept walking to go out back. I just wanted to be alone. They had a lot of nerve asking me something like that. Everyone knew I wasn't over Van leaving me. I couldn't watch her promise to love my cousin forever. I may have been okay with not trying to interfere, but I couldn't promote it. It was like they were dangling their happiness in front of me.

Fuck that.

I found Miranda out by the pool. There was no way for me to know she would have been there, and I was just as shocked to see her there as she was to see me. I wasn't crying, but I certainly wasn't displaying a happy face.

"Hey," she said while crying.

I looked behind me to make sure that we were alone. "You look just as happy as I am."

"Guess you heard the big news."

"You should have told me last night. Maybe I could have prepared myself more."

"Sorry. I had a lot goin' on last night. I guess I just figured you knew, but from the look on your face, I can tell that you didn't."

I ran my hands through my hair and looked behind me, just making sure nobody was following. "Yeah, they kind of told me that they had news when I got here. I figured it would be that, but nothing can prepare you for handling it."

"You really do still love her?"

I sat down next to Miranda. "She's the only girl that I have ever told that to. If I hadn't been such an idiot, I would have never lost her in the first place. She would be wearing my grandmother's ring and planning our wedding instead of theirs. It doesn't matter. I cheated and the rest is history. Maybe I don't know what love is."

We were both quiet for a few seconds. Miranda was looking down at the water in the pool. "Conner is callin' the police and reporting Tucker for vandalism. He wants me to get a restrainin' order." She shook her head and covered her face. "I just can't believe that just yesterday I thought we had a chance for a future together."

"I know how much it must hurt, but you have to know that he isn't any good for you. I heard the way he talked to you, and it ain't right."

She started crying again in her hands. I wanted to reach over to comfort her, but the last thing she wanted was someone like me touching her, someone that she compared to the douche bag. To Miranda, I was the same type of guy as Tucker. I hated it, but I had made my choice to live my life the way I had been. No one could be blamed for my actions except me.

I stayed there next to her as she continued to cry. What she was going through sucked big time. She had a baby that needed a father, unfortunately he wanted nothing to do with either of them. It really pissed me off. He had no idea how lucky he was. I was alone and wished I had someone that wanted to love me back. It was a shame.

I was considering what I could say next, when Conner and Colt came rushing out of the door. "Randa, we already called the cops. They are headin' over to take our statements. You best tell them the truth if you know what's good for ya. They need to catch him and put an end to all of this nonsense," Conner said rudely.

"Whatever, Conner," Miranda said rudely. "It isn't like they are goin' to catch him. He's just goin' to get more pissed off about it. You are adding fuel to the fire."

"I don't give a shit what you think about it Miranda. I want this guy away from my niece and I would expect you to want the same for your daughter. He's bad news and that is never goin' to change." Conner stated.

"Why are you even tellin' me then. You have made your mind up. Just leave me alone. You obviously can't understand what I am goin' through," Miranda said before walking back into the house.

"She knows he's a loser. She just needs some time," I suggested.

Conner looked from me to Colt. "What's this new interest with my sister Ty? Don't get it in that head of yours that you can get into her pants next. It ain't happenin'," He threatened.

Colt shook his head as I didn't back down from Conner's threat. "Not that it's any of your business, but we are just friends. I never said anything about being with your sister."

"You think that we haven't noticed how you have been acting around her and Bella?" Conner said accusingly.

"The only thing I am guilty of is loving that little girl. I was there when she was born and I feel close to her. As far as your sister's pants...well they are safe around me, because I am not interested!" I pushed past my family and walked into the house. Once inside, I looked around for anyone, but I was alone.

I was already making myself a sandwich when Colt and Conner came walking back into the house. I tried to ignore them the best that I could, but Conner came to lean against the opposite side of the kitchen island. "Look, I am sorry that I got in your shit about my sister. You need to understand that neither of you have the best track record. For a while that girl was givin' herself out to anyone. I know she's an adult, but she needs someone lookin' out for her. I am not sayin' you are a bad guy. We have always been on good terms and I've considered you family, but my sister is off limits. She doesn't need to be in any kind of relationship. So, it wasn't personal."

"I know. I can assure you for the third time that I did not come here to get into your sisters pants. She and I are just friends. I talk to her about V......well about things that upset me, and she talks to me about the same things. Just friends!"

Colt rattled his hands on the countertop like it was a makeshift drum. "When y'all are done, I need to talk to Ty alone."

I stuck out my hand to Conner, who started to shake it then gave me a friendly nudge. "You up for goin' out tonight? My girlfriend has this friend goin' out and I told her I may have someone to come with us too."

Wasn't he just threatening me about pants?

"Yeah, I guess that would be cool." I turned to Colt. "You guys coming out too?"

"Savanna wants to," He replied.

"Let me guess, you'd rather stay home alone?"

"Not like your thinkin'. It just isn't my scene anymore."

"Nine months ago you were all up in that shit. I recall the night pretty clearly."

"Speaking of that, we need to talk."

I rolled my eyes and walked back outside with Colt. "Whatever you have to say isn't goin' to change my mind. I can't stand up there and watch her promise to love you forever."

"I thought we were past this. You know how much it would mean to Savanna. She cares about you."

I shook my head and ran my hands through my hair, trying to grasp the words that needed to be said. "It still hurts. I know that she and I are over and honestly I don't know if I even want to be with her again, but the fact that she's with you is what drives me crazy. If it was some stranger, I think I could have let go by now. You were my idol and now you are marrying who I always thought was my dream girl. It's like a kick in the balls."

Colt got one of his famous half smiles. "I can't force you to change your mind, but I hope by next summer you will have. I love her and I want her to be happy. She wants you there with us. Just think about it." He put his hand on my shoulder. "When I was younger and got engaged you were the one person I wanted standin' next to me. I know the past year has been hell, but I haven't changed my mind. You are like my brother and my best friend. I hope you reconsider."

Why was it that he and Savanna could make me feel bad for them?

"I will man. I promise I will."

Chapter 9
Miranda

I wish everyone would just leave me alone. Couldn't they see how much they were adding to my frustrations? I needed time to get over the shock of the previous night and what happened this morning, before dealing with even more drama.

My brother was getting on my last nerve. He needed to understand that my heart was breaking for myself and my daughter. I could tell that he was lookin' out for me, but he needed to back off and let me breathe first.

While the baby took her nap, I sat in my room as Van lectured me on what I need to do next to keep me and Bella safe. She didn't have a kid. She had no idea what it was like being responsible for a child. She meant well, and I could tell she believed she was doing the right thing, but it wasn't helping me at all.

The father of my child had said the most painful words that a mother wants to hear. He didn't want our child. He didn't even love her.

The stinging of my eyes felt like it was going to be permanent with my new found drama. When I couldn't take it anymore, I asked Van to give me some time alone. I appreciated her, just not right now.

While burying my head into my pillow, I heard the fancy doorbell ringing. Voices followed the sound of the door opening and I knew it was only a matter of time before they called me to come down. This was a bad idea with a capital B. This would push Tucker over the edge. They thought the vandalism was major. I had no idea what would come next.

Two hours later the officers made their way out. My brother looked far too pleased at what he had done. I felt the knot in my stomach tightening. The repercussions of his actions were not going to be what he thought. Conner always had to be in control. This was going to end badly.

The officers said that since they were familiar with Tucker and his family, they would pay his mother a visit later in the day. He didn't talk to her much, but she would make sure he knew what my family had done to him. It was a good thing that my mother and aunt were due home sometime in the evening, otherwise I wouldn't have even considered going out tonight with the whole gang.

I hadn't seen Ty since we were outside together, but I was actually happy about that. While he and Conner were having words, I was upstairs standing at the bathroom window being nosey. It wasn't like I wanted there to be something between me and Ty. He was telling the truth about our friendship, but for some reason it hurt my feelings. I didn't understand why, but it just did.

He was such a big help with Bella and everyone could tell that he loved her. In light of my newest daddy issues, it made me happy that someone cared about my daughter. I always had my family and that meant the world.

Knowing that my family wanted to go out to one of our local establishments meant that I needed to get my ass in gear and find something to wear. Since this was the first official night in months that I was single, I wanted to take advantage of the situation. I picked out a tiny little black dress. The bottom was a short skirt that puffed out a bit, but the top was just two separate pieces of black fabric that covered each of my breasts and tied around my neck.

I had these great red high heels that I had never worn before that popped with the dress, so I knew I had to wear them with it. I pulled my hair up and had small curly pieces falling out of the up-do. I did the makeup around my eyes to look smoky, making the green color in them pop, and added just a bit of powder and lip gloss. For an added touch I put on some of the lotion that my aunt had gotten me on my birthday. Last night I had gotten dressed up to seduce my then boyfriend, tonight I just wanted to forget he ever existed. I needed to feel eyes on me and know that I didn't have to answer to anyone. I deserved to have a little fun or at least feel better, even if it was temporary.

There was a bunch of commotion when I finally walked downstairs. It seemed that everyone must have been waiting on me and Ty to be ready. I hadn't even noticed that he was getting ready upstairs, my only focus had been on myself. Van was holding Bella and pointed toward me when they saw me walking downstairs. My little girl got the biggest smile on her face when she saw me. A part of me just wanted to stay home and cuddle with her all night.

Everyone's eyes were on me as I grabbed my daughter and showered her with kisses. The front door opened and my mother and aunt came rushing in the door causing their own interruptions. They immediately snatched up my daughter and began telling us about everything they had bought for her while they were away.

I was used to them spoiling her. It was just what the two of them loved to do.

When I noticed Conner moving in on them, I grabbed him by the arm and shook my head. "Not tonight, please."

He shook his head, but didn't say a word.

We were all standing around chatting when I heard footsteps coming down the stairs. Ty was in dark jeans that had holes randomly placed on them. His hair was disheveled all over his head and down around his ears. His shirt was tight against his hard chest and it was a dark red like my shoes that popped against his olive skin. The V shape in the neck showed off some of the definition to his chest. I tried not to be obvious about checking him out, but as he caught my eye, I caught the scent of his cologne. He smelled better than any scent ever to exist on a man. I felt like one of the girls in those Axe commercials. I wanted to pounce on him right there in front of everyone. With no regard to anyone else, he looked at me and got a huge grin on his face.

Our eyes froze into each other for only a few seconds before Van cleared her throat. "You two ready to go?"

Without turning around again to see his face, and give away any obvious signs that I was swooning over him, even when I shouldn't be, I kept my eyes fixed on my daughter as I kissed her goodbye. I caught up to everyone outside. Conner had to pick up his girlfriend, so Ty and I rode with Colt and Van. Colt gave me a dirty look as I climbed into the backseat behind him. Van let Ty sit in the front seat because he was so much taller. The Mustang didn't have that much leg room in the back.

The ride to the bar was uneventful. Ty and Colt talked about some baseball game when they were kids, while Van and I played on our phones in the back. I went into all my social networking apps and changed my status to say single. While Van seemed occupied by her own phone, I pulled up Ty's profile on mine. His profile picture was a group of his friend's doin' keg stands. I had to laugh when I pictured him holding my daughter being so responsible. After goin' through a few more photos I found a bunch of he and Van. It made me sad. I heard him saying that there was nothing between us except for friendship, but this just confirmed that he was not ready to move on.

Still, when we climbed out of that car to go into the bar, I felt his eyes on me again. I wasn't denying that I worked hard to make myself look irresistible, but the fact that Ty wouldn't stop looking made me all tingly. The night was looking up, well that was until my brother and his girlfriend pulled up. Sitting in the back was Courtney Timmons, former Ms. Kentucky.

They got out of the car and immediately approached us. By the look on Conner's face, I could tell this was a setup. She came here to be hooked up with Ty. I should have known that my brother would cover all his bases to prevent anything from ever happening between us. This was low, even for him. How could he bring the prettiest girl in all of Kentucky to paw all over Ty?

Right away I could tell he was interested in her. They shook hands and both got ridiculous smiles across their faces. I wasn't sure whether I wanted to scream or cry first. I tried to shake it off and concentrate on all the other available guys around us, but my eyes kept going back to the one I couldn't have. His strong arms led Courtney out onto the dance floor. I had never wanted Ty. Sure, he was one of the most gorgeous guys I had ever seen, but I never really looked at him as available.

"You okay?" Van asked, breaking my train of thought.

"Yeah, fine. Just didn't know she was going to be here." I pointed toward Courtney and Ty.

She led me over toward the bar. "Conner thought it would take Ty's mind off of my engagement. She seems to be doing a good job."

"Yeah, whatever!" I said sarcastically.

Van looked over at me with a concerned look on her face. "You can't like him Miranda. You know that right?"

"Are you sayin' that because you still want him for yourself?"

"Of course not!" She said immediately. "I just don't think it's a good idea for the two of you to get involved, especially so soon after what happened. Plus, he's family."

"We are just friends anyway. He made that clear earlier today with my brother."

She started laughing and made a quick glance over my shoulder. "You should stay that way. He's better at being a friend than a boyfriend anyway."

Van didn't warn me that Ty and Courtney were coming up to the bar. I felt a hand on my shoulder and turned around to his smiling face. The more I looked at him, the more I felt like a teenager with an impossible crush. "Hey."

Get a grip.

"Hey, you look like you are havin' fun. Good thing Courtney came along."

He shrugged and looked over at her talking to Van. "She's alright."

"You do know she's the former Ms. Kentucky?"

"She told me, like ten times already. It's getting old." He said close to my ear in an almost whisper.

I pulled away from him and looked at his face, but before I could say anything else he smiled at me and looked down at my body. I started to shiver as his eyes started at my face, but slowly moved down every inch of my figure. When his eyes met mine again, I felt like they were on fire, burning into me. Before either of us could say anything, he was handed two beers by Courtney and being hauled back out to the dance floor away from me.

He turned to look back at me as he walked away, giving me a half smile.

Van filled the empty gap between us and giggled as Colt came up behind her. I spotted my brother and his slutty girlfriend grinding all over each other in a corner of the bar, while Colt and Van made company next to Ty and Courtney. I found a stool located at the bar and sat down on it, spinning around every now and again to watch everyone else having a good time except for me.

My brother was such an asshole for bringing me out, but making sure that I couldn't hang out with Ty. Maybe nobody else noticed his schemes, but I wasn't going to pretend Ty's hookup was a coincidence. He was rubbing Ty's love for anything with a vagina in my face. He wanted me to see that he was the type of guy I didn't need in my life.

A few mixed drinks later, a slow song came on. I didn't even want to turn around and watch Ty grinding all over that blonde tease, so I just kept flirting with the bartender. When I felt someone spinning me around I started to scream. Ty's face lit up in front of me. "How about a dance?" He asked while offering his hand.

I didn't waste a second as I grabbed his hand and let him

guide me onto the dance floor. "Where is your date?"

"She ain't my date and she went to the bathroom. I hated seeing you over there all by yourself. I thought we were going to hang out more tonight," he admitted.

I could feel the redness rushing to my cheeks and tried to look down so that he couldn't notice. His hands were wrapped around my waist, and he kept them there instead of letting them linger around my ass. I would have been fine if they wandered around, but he seemed content the way they were. "I thought we were goin' to hang out too. I think my brother thinks there is somethin' goin' on between us. I told him that he was crazy and we were just friends." *You smell so good that I want to take you outside and let you do whatever you want to me.*

"Yeah, I told him we were just friends too. He's just looking out for you. He knows my track record and doesn't want you getting hurt. He's your brother and it's his job to protect you. It doesn't help matters when you look so fucking hot in that dress."

Ahh, he did notice.

"Well I just wish he would mind his own damn business. If I want to hook up with someone than I can damn well do it. He can't control my life ya know." *Maybe I shouldn't have said that.*

The man smelled so good. I felt like I could just lick every inch of his skin. His hands remained firm on my waist, but it made me hot just thinking about what else they were capable of doing to me.

Ty slowly pulled his face back enough to be able to look at me. "It's not like you have someone in mind to hook up with right?" He asked with a smile across his face.

I opened my mouth to speak and felt someone tapping on my back. "Mind if I cut in?" Courtney asked.

Yes I mind. Damn, I was in the middle of something. "No he's all yours," I said as I let go of Ty's shoulders and backed away from them. Before I turned to walk back to the bar, I caught Ty glaring at me. When he caught my gaze, he smiled back at me.

Was something really happening between us?

I glanced over at my brother and his girlfriend and then back to Colt and Van. They were all too busy with themselves to even notice Ty and me dancing. I headed in the direction of the ladies room to freshen up, but felt someone tugging on my arm. I really thought it was Ty, just trying to get me alone for second, but the face in front of me wasn't him. Tucker gritted his teeth and spoke into my hair. "Walk outside with me and do not make a fuckin' scene if you know what's good for you."

Chapter 10

Tyler

I never expected my visit to Kentucky to result in me having fantasies of being with someone I had always just considered my family, but every damn time I got around Miranda now, I felt like it was undeniable. She was gorgeous and witty, and not to mention an excellent mother. Who cared about her past relationships, or her taste in men? It was obvious that she had bad luck with guys and I could understand how her sex appeal would get her into trouble.

The girl could walk into a room and turn heads. She didn't have to wear skimpy dresses or doll her face up in makeup. She had it naturally. I know because I had seen the way she looked when she woke up. Her hair may have been a mad mess, but she was adorable anyway.

I knew what Conner was doing when he picked up Courtney, and part of me wanted to thank him for the gesture, the other part, well not so much. If I were at home and met this girl under different circumstances perhaps I would have liked to take her home and show her a good time, but ever since I walked down those steps and saw Miranda, she was all I could think about.

I don't think she had any clue what she was doing to me. While Courtney continued to throw herself all over me on the dance floor, I couldn't stop peeking over her shoulder to catch just a glimpse of Miranda. The way that dress came down so low and showed off her breasts made me crazy. It also made her ass pop and I wanted to reach my hands under it and touch her soft skin. She could have been a swimsuit model. The girl was perfection.

My leg was really starting to throb, so I excused myself from the next dance to take a seat at the bar. I headed in the direction of where Miranda had been sitting, not noticing yet that she was nowhere to be seen. I took a few more looks around the crowded bar as I sat down and ordered a drink. Courtney plopped down in the stool next to me and slid her hand up the thigh of my jeans. I still couldn't believe I was considering turning down such an easy lay.

"You're even hotter than I pictured," she purred.

I considered allowing her to keep thinking that she had a chance with me, and maybe even being nice just in case my next visit here didn't go as well and I needed an easy out-of-town booty call. She was definitely going to be pissed if I told her I wasn't interested and part of me was saying what a fool I was being for denying myself a piece, but I couldn't stop thinking about Miranda. Hell, I didn't even know if I even had a chance with her at this point. Not only had we both talked about just being friends, but also we had never made a move on each other. I just had this feeling that I couldn't shake. I needed to find out why I couldn't stop thinking about her.

Reluctantly, I grabbed Courtney's hand and pried it off of my leg. "Look, you are really hot and I appreciate you hanging out with me tonight, but I just can't hook up with anyone right now."

I thought that my words were nice enough to get her to back off. "I know all about your relationship with Savanna. I wish you would reconsider, because I am sure that after one night with me, I will make you forget all about her."

Don't picture her naked...

"Yeah, it's just not going to happen. I am sure it would be a great time, but I just can't tonight."

"It's too bad. You don't know what you are missing. I have a lot of special talents that you don't know about."

"I bet you do." I shot her a smile and continued to look around the bar. "Have you seen Miranda? I haven't seen her since our dance ended and she doesn't have a car here to leave."

Courtney crossed her legs and gave me a dirty look. "I can't believe you are actually blowing me off to look for your whore of a cousin."

I tried to remain calm to the best of my ability, but I knew I was doing a piss poor job. "What the hell did you just call her?"

"I called her a whore, a slut, a ho, because that is what she is. Everyone in town knows how easy that girl is. Then she went and got knocked up by that drifter criminal. How much lower can you get? Look, I am sorry, but your cousin is far from perfect. She probably left with some stranger, knowing her."

I wanted to smack the bitch. I knew to never lay a hand on a female, but this chick was asking for it. Even if I only considered Miranda my family, I couldn't believe she would have the nerve to say such horrible things about her. "The person you are calling a whore is someone that I care about. She isn't just family to me, she's one of my closest friends. How can you sit there and hit on me, after only knowing me a couple of hours, but accuse her of being easy? If you ever had a chance in hell at being with me, you just lost it all together, you spoiled little cunt. If you'll excuse me, I need to find Miranda because I know she isn't doing anything like you suggested."

Yeah, I said that word. The word I never should say to a woman. She deserved it! Screw her and her little Goddamn title. She can take that little crown and shove it up her tight ass!

As I walked away, I caught the appalled look on Courtney's face. I wanted to walk back and jump in front of her yelling 'HA', but I kept on walking. Conner must have spotted our confrontation, because he walked toward me, while his girlfriend ran toward Courtney. "What happened?"

"Look, that bitch was talking trash about your sister. Maybe I was out of line, but I told her where to go."

"She don't like my sister cause Randa slept with her boyfriend a while back. My sister doesn't have the best track record with guys. Most girls can't stand her around here."

"Your sister is my friend and I didn't appreciate that bitch saying those things about her. She's a good girl who made bad choices. She's a great mother and an honest friend. She didn't deserve that."

"Thanks for takin' up for her. So where is she? She didn't hear y'all talkin' did she?"

"I haven't seen her for at least two songs. I thought maybe she went to the bathroom, but nobody has come from that direction in a while."

Conner finally seemed genuinely concerned for his sister. He began probing the entire bar again for any sight of her. "I will go check the bathroom. Do me a favor and go check out by the car. Sometimes phone service in here sucks. She might just be checkin' on the baby."

I gave Conner a nod and walked in the direction of the exit. After walking toward the back of the bar I could hear someone talking. When I saw Tucker, I ducked down behind a car to see exactly what he was doing. From the angle I was standing, I couldn't see who he was talking to. My first instinct was to just jump him before he caught wind of me being behind him, but I didn't have anyone there to back me up and he was obviously with someone. One wrong kick to my leg and I would be back in physical therapy again.

I could hear him gritting his teeth, but couldn't figure out exactly what he was saying, or who he was saying it to.

Slowly, I crawled one more car closer, trying to get a better look. Immediately, I spotted Miranda. He had her by the throat and was licking her cheek. I still couldn't make out his words, but it didn't matter because I ran right toward him, throwing myself full force at his pathetic ass. He went down quickly and Miranda backed away from us. With two swift punches to his jaw, I had forced his face to hit the concrete.

I could hear Miranda crying as I watched Tucker try to get back onto his feet, the whole time spitting out blood from his mouth. "Stay down if you know what's good for you!" I threatened.

"Fuck you. The bitch deserved it."

Since I had no idea what he meant, I looked over toward where Miranda was standing. She was hunched over a car and holding her face with her hand. "Hey, you okay?" I asked.

She just nodded and never took her hands down. I turned my attention back to Tucker who was now sitting down, leaning against his car. "What did you do to her?"

He didn't answer. I kicked him. "What the hell did you do to her?"

"I taught the bitch a lesson about runnin' her mouth. What's it to you anyway?" He asked.

Conner came up behind me before I could answer. When I heard him approaching I turned to look at him heading in the direction of where his sister stood. He leaned over her and pulled her hands away. Her face and hands were covered in blood. She was crying. I heard Colt's voice behind me, giving the address to the bar. Assuming that he was speaking to the police, I looked back to Tucker. Before I could react, he took out my legs and sent me flying down to the ground.

As I moved myself away from his legs, I saw Conner jumping on top of him. They started rolling around on the concrete parking lot. Within seconds, Conner had Tucker pinned down to the ground. "Stay down you little punk ass bitch!"

"Fuck you!"

I couldn't contain my anger. I took my foot and forced it hard into Tucker's side. The sudden pain must have ripped through him. He crunched himself up into a ball holding where my foot had been. "That is for laying a hand on a female." I kicked him in the face. "That one was for busting out my mirror."

"This changes nothin'!" He yelled from on the ground. "She's still nothin' but a common whore. You think your family can keep all of her dirty laundry hidden? Everyone knows it."

I gave him one final kick in the side before I heard the sirens coming our way.

I have no idea how long it really took, but the police arrived and Colt forced me to walk away. While Tucker was being subdued and put into handcuffs, I rushed to Miranda's side. She was already surrounded by Conner's girlfriend and Van. Colt suggested I steer clear of the cops due to the fact that I already was on probation in another state. Even though it was nothing compared to a violent type of crime, it still wouldn't help with my future if I continued to get into trouble with the law.

They had to force me away from Miranda's side. Colt handed me his keys and suggested I wait it out in the back of the car. All I could do was think of Miranda. I needed to see that she was okay. The last thing I saw was her face covered in blood. She needed to go to the hospital.

After at least thirty minutes, I noticed the police cars driving away. Colt headed in my direction, followed by Van holding a very distraught Miranda. Colt leaned over and got the seat pushed down so that Miranda could climb into the back. Just like when she was giving labor, I pulled her head on top of my lap. I stroked her hair away from her face. She was still crying out and it wasn't just from being upset. I could sense from the way her body was tensed up that she was in a bunch of pain.

"Are we taking her to the hospital?" I asked as we pulled out of the parking lot.

"Yes, we will be there in fifteen minutes. Van, can you call my aunt and tell her to meet us there?" Colt handed her his phone as he continue to drive.

"What the hell happened back there? Did anyone see that asshole come into the bar?" Colt asked.

"Not that I know of. She was dancing with me ten minutes before. That bitch Courtney cut in and the next thing I know Conner and I were looking all over for her," I explained.

"I told Conner that his threats were goin' to cause more problems. Damn him for not listenin'."

Colt was pissed and I could tell from the way his foot hit

the accelerator on the Stang. "Let's get her taken care of and we can figure out what to do next." I suggested.

Van turned around and shot me a look. "There is no 'we'. You are going to go home Ty. You can't be here for any of this. You are on probation already. We don't need you being involved in any of this anyway. We can handle it ourselves."

"You can't ask me to leave, not now."

Colt looked in the rearview at me. "She's right Ty. You need to pack up your shit and head home. We can take care of things here. You don't need any more trouble on your plate."

I kept shaking my head. "Hell no! I am not leaving!"

We pulled up to the hospital and got Miranda inside. Luckily there was no wait and they took her right back. Conner came rushing in behind us and went into the back with her, while me, Van and Colt waited in the designated waiting area.

Miranda's mother came running in a while later. She had Izzy with her and approached us as soon as she spotted us sitting there. "What happened?"

"It was Tucker. He got her alone and jumped her," Colt explained.

"Oh my God! I need to go see her. Can you take the baby for me?" She cried.

I stood up and grabbed Izzy out of her reluctant arms. I think it still shocked the family that I had a connection to her the way I did. "It's okay. Go ahead. We have her taken care of."

She handed us the diaper bag and made her way toward the triage nurse to be let into the back where her daughter was being cared for. Two hours later, they came back out. Miranda's face was cleaned up, but it looked so bad. The bridge of her nose was busted open and had butterfly stitches. Her left cheek was swollen and already turning purple. Dried blood was caked over her scalp. Her busted lips were both swelled to double in size. Miranda had a sling on her right arm and walked like she was in pain elsewhere.

We all rushed to her side, but she never spoke. Her mother took Izzy out of Van's arms and the three of them made their way to her car instead of Colt's. I understood, but I couldn't help but want to make sure she was okay.

The ride home was quiet, with the exception of Colt and Van telling me I needed to pack up my shit and leave first thing in the morning. They didn't want the police to know that I had been involved. The plan was to say that I came home a day earlier and had nothing to do with being at the small dive bar.

I argued with them, but left as they suggested. I was so pissed that I made it home in record time. I was glad that I could kiss Izzy goodbye, but Lucy said that Miranda stayed the night with her mother and I didn't want to wake them to say goodbye.

Chapter 11
Miranda

I should have screamed or at least let someone in that bar know that I felt threatened by Tucker's presence. I should have known that he was going to hurt me.

For three days my mother stayed by my side and nursed my wounds. Tucker had slapped me before, but it was nothing compared to the beating that he gave me. I had two cracked ribs, a broken nose, and contusions all over my face and a dislocated shoulder.

I couldn't hold my daughter and if I thought the pain of losing her father was bad before, well, knowin' what he was capable of, made me feel so sad for her. I had a family that would make sure she never wanted for anything, but I knew firsthand what it was like to grow up without a father. Not having that in my life caused me to rebel against my mother more than I wanted to admit.

After three days, I left my mother's small house and headed to the main house. My mom and aunt argued with me about it, but I needed my space. My shoulder wasn't better, but I had Lucy to help me with Bella and could manage the rest by myself.

The truth was that I was tired of being judged. They refused to admit they were doing it, but I could see it in their eyes. They blamed me for this happening.

Nobody ever considered that all of this might be hard on me. I mean, first I catch my no good boyfriend cheating, then he says he wants nothing to do with our daughter, and finally he beats the shit out of me in a public parking lot. How could I not be a bit messed up over all of this?

To make matters worse, I hadn't been able to talk to Ty since it happened. Sure, he had been calling and texting me like crazy, but after everything I didn't know what to say to him. I had been ready to throw myself at him that night with no regard as to what would happen afterwards. We were friends and he had made it clear that was all we were. Whatever happened between us was just us thinking without our minds. Neither of us wanted to get involved with each other.

I had seduced my share of guys and none of those times had ended with a healthy friendship. Ty and I needed to take a break from each other, in order to forget that either of us ever considered taking things further.

Tucker was convicted of assault and sentenced to one year in jail. He was ordered to attend drug and alcohol classes while incarcerated. As much as I appreciated that he was behind bars, it still didn't make me feel any better about my life or current situation. I had nothing to show for as far as a future for me and my daughter.

A month went by before I was able to pick up the phone for one of Ty's calls and then I felt so embarrassed for waiting so long that I couldn't figure out what to even say. He asked a million questions about Bella and even if he could video chat with her. I felt bad for keeping him from her. He hadn't done anything to deserve being shut out. I was acting like an immature child. He clearly cared so much about my daughter. I was an asshole.

I spent the next four months trying to get my life back on track. Since Lucy's kids were both moved out, she actually enjoyed watching Bella while I took cosmetology classes. I was lucky enough to have a mother that offered to pay for any kind of further schooling I was interested in, but I had to admit that school just wasn't something I was ever really good at.

With me being so busy, I hardly had time to even think about my friendship with Ty or lack thereof. I couldn't say it was for lack of trying on his part. He called or texted at least three times a week. Apparently he had gotten a job at a local shop working on cars. He said the money was pretty good and he didn't mind working a nine to five job during the week. What that really meant was that it helped him not be so lonely. He rarely talked about Van, but I knew he missed having her around. They still talked often, but with her and Colt's wedding coming up, I could imagine the conversations weren't to his liking.

Speaking of the wedding, it was getting closer. Van had decided on an outdoor theme here at the ranch. Colt and Conner had been working to restore an old red barn where the service was to be held. The thing hadn't been usable in at least ten years and was filled with random farming equipment. I got that Colt wanted everything to be perfect for the big day, but he could have built a brand new barn in less time.

Things finally seemed almost normal. Our family was back to the way they were before. Mundane days led to relaxing nights curled up on a couch watching sitcoms, and that was exactly what I was doing when I got the call.

I was sitting next to Lucy watching a popular singing competition when my cell phone rang with a blocked number. I had no idea who it could have been, but I answered it anyway. My friends played jokes and cranked called people when we were younger so I just assumed it was going to be a fun kind of call, in fact I answered it with a sarcastic tone and waited for whoever to hand me some punch line.

The voice on the other end sent the fear of God into me.

"You think you can just go about your life like you didn't ruin mine? You better watch your back you little bitch. I am getting out early and when I am through with you, they won't be able to identify either of the bodies. I am goin' to cut you slow so you can watch yourself bleed out."

I threw the phone on the floor and just stared at it for a moment. Bella was asleep in the porta-crib just feet away, so I knew she was safe. I picked up the phone and started screaming into it. "Don't you dare threaten me or my family you.......hello? Hello?"

Lucy had already stood up and grabbed the phone out of

my hand. The call had probably ended before I got a word in.

"Who was it?" She asked.

I couldn't answer her. I was still in shock from hearing Tucker's threat.

She started grabbing the house phone and dialing some numbers while she talked in Spanish. I tried to grab the phone to stop her, but just one look at my innocent child and I knew that this was more serious than I could handle myself.

It only took my family about ten minutes to be standing in the living room with all of their hands on their hips, demanding a detailed explanation.

I put my hands in my face and shook my head. "Tucker threatened Bella and I. He says that he's getting out early and.....," I started getting choked up. "And he will make sure that you can't identify our bodies when he's done with us."

I had my face still buried in my hands, but I could hear the gasps fill the room.

"This shit has got to stop. We need to call the police," Conner said angrily.

"We can't prove this call ever happened and even if we did, he could still get someone else to come after them. Even with this little prick behind bars, he's still threatening my family. If you ask me I think we need to get them as far away from here as we can." My mother was shaking and holding Bella tightly. I could tell she was honestly scared for our safety.

"Mom, I don't think he's serious. He's just sayin' what would hurt me the worst."

"Get your head out of your ass Randa. This guy was trouble from the beginning. You need to start thinking about your safety first. When does he get out?" Conner asked.

"I have no idea. I didn't even know he was gettin' out early at all." I argued.

"The first thing we need to do is call whoever is in charge of Tucker's case. When we have more details we can figure out what to do next," my aunt chimed in.

"What happens if they don't believe me? It isn't like anyone else heard what he said to me."

"Miranda, you need to think about you and Bella. Have you forgotten what he did to you?" My mother seemed petrified to think about what Tucker had done to me in that parking lot. Remembering how I looked when I left the hospital that night made it easy to see her side. Being a mother myself, well, I couldn't imagine seeing my own child go through what I was.

"No Mom. I remember every detail of what happened. All I am sayin' is that we don't know whether this is just some kind of joke. We may be panickin' and he isn't getting out of jail early. We just don't know."

"Well I will not be taking the chance with my only daughter and grandchild," my mother said assuringly.

My aunt was already on the phone with someone. I had no clue who she could be calling around nine p.m., but she was talking up a storm, explaining the whole situation.

Colt and Van were deep into a conversation with my brother and my mother and Lucy were trying to settle Bella. I felt like I was in the middle of some worm hole, listening to all of them decide what was going to happen. If it weren't for my aunt making a few phone calls, I would have just assumed this was all a hoax, but finally her calls paid off.

She pulled my mother into the kitchen and we could hear them talking, but not clear enough to figure out what they were saying. I think we were all thrown a loop when they called everyone except me and Lucy in there with them.

"Guess we aren't at liberty to hear what they are deciding?" I said sarcastically.

"You know that whatever they are saying, it's for your own good. You have to make the right decisions here missy. That Tucker is a dangerous man. You need to get as far away from him as you can." She started to tear up as the words came out of her mouth.

I grabbed her and hugged her tightly. "I love you Lucy. I will do whatever it takes to keep her safe."

Everyone came walkin' out of the kitchen. Their faces told me everything I didn't want to know.

"Over-crowding! He's getting out early on account of overcrowding. Do you believe this shit? He committed an act of violence and he's being let out six months early." My brother was not too happy.

"Honey, sit down!" My mother said as she sat down on the couch and waited for me to join her.

"He beat the shit out of her. Does anyone else have a problem with this? I don't care if he has had good behavior or some dumb shit that qualified him for an early release. This is horse shit," Conner slammed.

The room was filled with sudden animosity and I knew whatever they were about to tell me couldn't be good.

"When does he get out?" I asked.

"As early as three days from now." My mother answered. "They said that you would receive a letter."

"You really think I am in danger?"

"We have all made arrangements for you and Bella to go away for a while, at least until we can tell you aren't in any imminent danger," My aunt explained.

Tears filled my eyes. "Where am I supposed to go? How long? Is anyone goin' to go with me?"

"We have a place for you to go. It's out of state and you will have help there. I have made arrangements for you to stay with family in North Carolina. They have plenty of room and you and Bella will be safe there. It isn't forever honey, just until we know for sure that you are safe." She looked over to her son Colt and gave him a quick nod. He and Van left the room without saying a word to me.

"When do I have to leave?" I asked.

71

"Tomorrow. We will help you pack up enough of your things before you make the trip," My mother explained.

I started to really cry and my mother wrapped her arms around me. "I have never left home before. I don't want to go. I don't even know the people where I am goin'. This isn't fair."

"You aren't staying with strangers. You are going to stay with Tyler and his parents. They have a small farm and a carriage house that you and Bella will be comfortable in for the time being. Honey, this is temporary."

The only word I heard out of her mouth was Tyler. I was shaking so bad, but I definitely heard her right. "You are sendin' me to stay with Ty?"

How could they want me to go stay with the one person they made a point to try to keep me away from?

"Yes. I know it isn't what you want, but just go there and lay low, at least until we can figure out if there is anything to worry about," My mother suggested.

My brother looked out the window. I could see him clenching his jaw. He didn't like this idea one bit. "This is only temporary Randa. We just need to make sure this son of a bitch is not goin' to be a problem for you. Give it a couple of weeks and then you can come home."

For the next hour my family tried to convince me that leaving was my best and safest option. It wasn't like I was fighting them; I just wanted to be able to make my own decisions. When it was all said and done, the decision was final. Tomorrow morning I would wake up and pack as much as I needed and be on my way to a different state. By the time the discussions were done it was too late to call and talk to Ty about how his parents really felt about me coming to stay with them. I was sure that the last thing they wanted was for a baby to be in the way of their everyday life.

The next morning was hectic. My family got me up at the crack of dawn. They insisted that I drive Van's new car instead of taking my own, on account of Tucker not being able to tell whether I was still in town or not. My aunt handed me a envelope full of cash and a new cell phone before I pulled out with a road map and a long trip ahead of me.

I felt like I was going into a witness protection program. My family was famous for overreacting, but in this case, I wasn't really sure what Tucker was capable of. I couldn't take any chances when it came to Bella.

It was hard to watch everyone kissing Bella goodbye, and it honestly felt like it was a forever instead of just a few weeks. At any rate, it sucked something fierce.

When I had finally pulled out of the ranch, it was already one thirty, so with all of the stops it was nearing dark before I pulled onto the farm road. Bella was great the first two hours and then she got on this crying fit that forced me to pull over five separate times. It didn't help that it was pouring down raining for most of the ride.

I wanted to call Ty and let him know how close I was to getting there, but my new phone had no numbers programmed in it. I figured that he would be standing there waiting for us to arrive, but that isn't exactly how it went down.

Chapter 12

Tyler

It had been months since Miranda and I had seen each other. Ever since I was forced to leave the ranch, we hadn't been as close. It was probably for the better to keep some space between us. When I was there visiting, I started thinking that maybe I wanted more from her than I should.

Apparently, Miranda must have caught on to my sexual innuendos because she backed off from our friendship and hadn't really been the same since. I tried to talk to her and still do occasional video chats with Izzy, but something changed between us.

The longer I was apart from Van, the more I started to understand that I had considered her more of a possession then an actual partner in our relationship.

Most of my friends were starting to get into serious relationships while I was still single, and quite frankly pretty miserable. My booty calls became less frequent and eventually had almost become non-existent. It wasn't like they weren't still coming in. Hell, even Heather called every once in a while. I don't know why she couldn't just give up, I mean, I hadn't been with her since before my visit to Kentucky.

I missed Izzy more than I wanted to admit. I couldn't explain the connection I felt to that little girl, but it was always there, almost making me want to be a better person. It was like the strain on mine and Miranda's relationship had caused me to re-evaluate the things that I wanted in my life. Well, that, and the fact that everyone seemed to have someone to share their life with, while I went home to an empty house every night.

Life had been hard for me in the past year. I got so bored being at home that I went out and found myself a full time job working on cars. It wasn't what I pictured my future to be, but it gave me a steady income. It wasn't like I had many bills. I was living at the carriage house rent free. My parents would, in due time, leave me the farm anyway, so they weren't very pushy about me moving or having to pay rent. Since my uncle's life insurance had paid off their house, they were doing good financially.

Being that I worked five days a week, I was tired by the time I got off at night. It had been pouring down raining all damn day and my mood was being affected by the gloomy weather. My phone had been blowing up so much with calls and text messages that my boss had asked me to leave it in the car after lunch. I figured someone was almost certainly having a big party and I didn't really feel like going anyway. By avoiding the calls, I didn't have to piss anyone off for not showing.

After stopping by the liquor store and grabbing a case of beer, I headed home. There was no telling which one of my friends would end up crashing later on, so on weekends I kept the fridge stocked with beer and waited for people to show up.

My mother hated it, but she couldn't argue with the fact that I wasn't drinking and driving. When I finally got inside, all I wanted to do was get a hot shower. Smelling like gasoline and motor oil got old after a while. I popped open a beer and went into the bathroom. I let the water pound down on my back until it started to get cold. That is when I hopped out and heard someone knocking at my door.

I figured it was just one of the guys, so I wrapped a towel around my waist and headed for the door. A drenched Heather stood in the doorway, taking in my almost naked appearance. I rolled my eyes. "What are you doing here?"

"You going to let me in or make me stay in the rain?"

I didn't answer, but instead opened the door wider so that she could walk in. She took off her jacket and of course was in some red little skimpy number.

"Seriously, Heather, I am not in the mood for you tonight."

"I miss you Ty. I was hoping that I would be able to change

your mind."

Heather was a pretty girl and the old me would have loved her dropping by unannounced, offering free pussy or a damn good blow job, but the bitch had done too much for me to have any respect for her. I tossed her the jacket. "You should probably just leave. Sorry you wasted your gas driving out here."

She sat the jacket down beside her and walked toward the door. "I had guessed that you would react this way, so I came with reinforcements to get you out of this funk you are in."

I had no idea what the hell she meant, but with one wave out the door another blonde came walking in. "Shew, it's so cold out there tonight."

"Who the fuck is this?" I gestured to the girl.

"This is my roommate Lauren. She has been dying to meet you," Heather introduced us and stood behind her friend. Slowly she removed the girl's jacket to reveal a very tight, very leathery corset and panties.

Heather's hands reached for her friend's waist and she slowly took her fingertips and slid them over her friend's breasts. "Isn't she hot?"

Holy hell!

"Is this for real?" I asked, trying really hard to not look at Heather feeling up her blonde roommate.

"That depends on what you want," Heather teased.

"You aren't playing fair." I needed to think of something non-sexual, like chairs or picture frames.

"You have two choices Ty. You can drop the towel and join us, or tell us to leave, in which we will go home and enjoy ourselves without you."

Oh shit! Don't picture them touching.......Stop thinking with my cock...Stop thinking with my cock!

Without saying a word, I stood up and headed to the fridge to grab a new beer. I knew what decision I had to make, but my body was putting up a fighting struggle with my mind.

I didn't have to answer to anyone. It was just one night of fun. One night to forget about everything I had lost and all that I didn't have.

Just a one-time thing.

Fuck it!

I headed toward the girls and grabbed the towel to release it from my waist, when suddenly; knocking came at my door again.

The girls looked confused as I walked away from them and opened the door without even looking to see who was on the other side. I didn't even think to turn around until I heard a crying sound entering my place.

Miranda stood there, with Izzy in her arms, staring at the two half naked chicks in my living room.

"Miranda? What are you doing here?" I was without words. I looked around toward Heather and Lauren and they both just stood there with their hands on one another.

"I.....your mother was supposed to tell you we were coming," She stuttered, never taking her eyes off the girls.

Izzy started crying again and I reached my arms out to her. At first, the little one reached back for me, but Miranda pulled her into her chest. "I think we will just take our things to your parent's place." She turned and started heading out of the door.

I grabbed her by the arm. "Please wait. This isn't what you think."

"Yes it is! Who is she Ty? Do you have some kid by this little tramp?" Heather's words were the last and final straw for me. Nobody had the right to talk to Miranda like that.

I held on to Miranda's arm, while I took my other hand and pointed outside. "Get the fuck out of my house!"

"I ain't leaving until you tell me who this is? Do you have a kid? Does your precious Van know?"

What the fuck? Couldn't she get a hint?

"I am serious, Heather. Leave now!"

"Screw you, Ty. You don't know what you're missing. Call me when this bitch leaves," Heather yelled as she started walking out into the rain.

About time!

I slammed the door just as they hit the threshold then turned my attention to Miranda. "Please let me explain."

She shook her head. "I am so sorry Ty. I didn't mean to interrupt your night. They made me come here."

"Who did? What's going on? Why are you here?" She hadn't even been close to me. She had no reason to visit me, really.

"It's Tucker. He's gettin' out of jail early. He called and threatened me and Bella." She started to cry and held her daughter tighter. "The things he said implied that he wanted to hurt us. Kill us."

I clenched my fists just thinking about that dick head threatening them. "What the hell did he say?"

"He says they wouldn't be able to identify our bodies when he got through with us." The more she started to cry the more Izzy cried.

"Jesus Christ! Give her to me so you can get that jacket off," I offered.

She was still crying. "You aren't even dressed. I am not handing you my daughter while you are in a towel."

I looked down and remembered she was right. "Give me a second!" I said as I headed into the bedroom to grab some shorts and a shirt.

When I came back out she was taking Izzy's sweater off. She was still screaming though. "Okay, are your things in the trunk or the backseat?"

"Both. Just grab the stuff in the backseat for tonight," She suggested.

I ran out in the pouring down rain and grabbed the bags out of the back. When I came in, Miranda was on the phone. I sat down the bags and held my arms out for Izzy. She reached right back for me and I grabbed her into my arms, giving her a great big kiss.

"Hey pretty girl. I missed you so much." She put her hand over my mouth and squeezed my lips while laughing for causing me pain with those tiny little nails of hers. "Ouch! You are hurting Uncle Ty," I joked.

She giggled more.

Miranda hung up and sighed loudly. She ran her hands over her face.

"Are you okay?" I asked.

"Not really. I just drove the longest ride ever with a screaming baby. My ex threatened my life and I walked in on you having a threesome. My night can't get any better." She said sarcastically.

"There was no threesome."

"Spare me the lies Ty. I pretty much just caught you red handed. Besides, you are a grown man. You can sleep with as many women as you like."

I loved the twang in her southern accent. I could listen to her talk for hours.

"Believe what you want. I am not going to argue about it. I was telling you the truth and that is all I can offer." I swung Izzy between my legs and pulled her back up to my lap. "How are you doing other than what you told me?"

"I thought I was doing good, but now I don't even know. I mean one second I am getting my cosmetology license and the next I am running from a convict. How am I supposed to be?" She asked rudely.

"I wasn't asking to piss you off. I was asking because I wanted you to know you could talk to me," I admitted.

"I'm sorry! God! I keep pissin' off everyone I care about. I just don't know what's going to happen. They packed me up and sent me on my way. Bella cried the whole way here practically. I don't understand what's wrong with me tonight. I think I am just tired."

"Why don't you take your things in the bedroom and take a nice hot shower. The water should have heated back up by now. Izzy and I will make us all something to eat," I offered.

"Bella!"

"Izzy!"

She rolled her eyes and gave up the fight. "She has been fussy all day. There is no way you can handle her while you cook."

"I will manage. Just go relax for a while. We got this under control!"

Miranda shook her head and walked in the direction of the bedroom. When she reached the small little hallway she realized how tiny the place was. "One bedroom? You mother said there was plenty of room for us out here."

"She probably meant for me to stay in their house while you are here. It's no biggie. Just put your stuff anywhere." I suggested.

She disappeared into the bathroom and I heard the water turning on. I grabbed Izzy and sat her on the counter beside me. "Are you hungry princess?"

She pointed toward the bathroom "Ma ma."

"Yeah, Mommy is getting a shower. Did you give her a hard time today?" I said in a baby voice. "Uncle Ty missed you so much."

I didn't keep much food in the fridge, but luckily my mother had made stuffed shells and brought them out last night. She must have known about Miranda coming because when I opened the fridge, not only were the shells in there, but it was surprisingly full of food. I hadn't paid any attention when I put the beers inside of it. "Looks like someone was prepared for you to visit me."

The messages on my phone were apparently from my mother. It figured that the one day I didn't check them, they were important.

Izzy and I put the food in the microwave and grabbed some paper plates, well I held her and pretended like she was helping. She started chewing on the edge of her plate, leaving a drool covered chunk on one part of it. "Don't eat your plate silly girl."

She had gotten so big. Her blonde hair was longer with ringlet curls and her eyes were the same as her mother's, a bright green. Her little mouth was full of teeth and from the way she continued to chew on her plate, I imagined more were coming through.

Miranda came out of the bathroom just as the microwave sounded. She ran past us and went outside. When she came back in seconds later, she was holding a seat that hooked to the table. "Mommy remembered your chair," She said as she attached it.

Izzy started to crawl across the table to get to her seat. Once she was inside, Miranda started cutting up small chucks of pasta for her to grab with her tiny fingers. When she had a good pile in front of her, Miranda sat down and stared at me.

"What?" I asked.

"Did you make this?"

"Hell no! My mother did yesterday. I worked late so she brought it over for me to have tonight."

"You didn't even know I was comin' did you?"

I shook my head. "Work had been slammed. I never even checked my messages. I wish I had because I never would have let those bitches be standing in my living room the way they were. I am so sorry about that."

"It's none of my business. I shouldn't have judged you."

I looked up at Miranda, who I'd avoided eye contact with this whole time. She was beautiful, especially with wet hair streaming down her chest. Her little tank top revealed that she was chilly as her tiny nipples protruded. I bit down on my lip and looked to her face again. She rolled her eyes and acted like she hadn't just caught me checking her out. "I didn't invite them over. I swear."

She shook her head and let out the smallest air filled sigh. "I don't care about it Ty."

"Whatever. I really missed you guys. I have been working non-stop. I am really sorry I missed Izzy's birthday party. I have her gift. Can I give it to her now?"

She took a huge bite of food and rolled her eyes. "Sure."

I grabbed Izzy and carried her to the bedroom. In the corner was a huge item wrapped in the worst wrapping job ever. Izzy tugged at me to let her down. I watched her walk all by herself over to the package. I walked over and started pulling away the paper, showing her what to do. Izzy thought it was funny and started hitting the paper then finally ripping it with me.

It had taken me forever to make, but her hand carved rocking horse was the perfect size for her. I used my old one as a model when I built it. My mother helped me assemble the yarn hair and paint the eyes. Izzy started slapping on the seat. I lifted her on it and slid it out on the carpet until we were facing her mother.

"Oh my gosh. That is so cute!"

"I made it for her."

"You what?" She put her hand over her mouth and stared at the wooden horse. "It's the best gift ever. Thank you so much Ty." She looked down at Izzy who was already trying to get the thing to keep moving. "Do you like your horse honey?"

Izzy gave a mean look and her face turned red. "Go!" She said.

I looked at Miranda. "Has she ever said that before?"

"Not that I heard. Every day she says more and more."

I was so happy to see that little girl on the horse I'd made her. It didn't matter how depressing my life was, because the moment I saw her my mood changed. I loved that kid. She had me wrapped around her little finger. "I know this is off topic, but how long are you staying?"

"Tryin' to get rid of us already?"

"No! You can stay as long as you want. You are safe here. I won't let anything happen to either of you. I promise." I meant it too. There was no way in hell I would let anyone hurt them.

Chapter 13

Miranda

I guess I should have gone to the farmhouse before heading straight to the carriage house. I thought my mother had explained that the place was sitting there waiting for us to arrive. I had no idea it was where Ty had been residing. I think we were both just as shocked to see each other when I opened that door. I mean, how could I have ever imagined that he would be havin' some kind of freaky threesome with two girls?

I didn't know whether to turn back around and get in my car to drive home, or just sit in it and wait until he was finished doing whatever he had planned for the night. I didn't want to be some party crasher, but I had a little girl that was completely miserable, crying in my arms. As embarrassed as I felt, I couldn't leave.

Ty insisted that it wasn't what it looked like, but what else could it have been? He was standing there with two almost naked girls. I didn't even know what to say to him, and he appeared to be just as speechless. After what seemed like twenty seconds, he turned to the girls and told them to leave. I didn't appreciate the look I got from either of them as they exited.

Apparently, he had been busy at work and not gotten his messages from his mother stating that Bella and I would be staying with them. I felt bad for barging in, but we had nowhere else to go. After being there for ten minutes, Ty dismissed the earlier events and threw himself into entertaining Bella.

When I saw that horse that he had made himself, I felt like crying. He had put so much work into that thing. The details were insane and I was sure it had taken a long time for him to do.

Bella fell in love with it, and cried when he picked her back up and sat her in front of her food. She kept pointing down at the wooden rocking horse as she cried with a mouthful of food. I think between the long ride and her being hungry, she was just in a really foul mood.

When I realized that she was wasting more food than she was eating, I cleaned her off and let her play with her new toy. Ty cleared my plate, but quickly made a beeline for the floor where Bella sat. He slid the horse around the carpet while she held on and giggled. It was so funny seeing the two of them together. Colt and my brother were the only two men that she saw on a day to day basis, and Bella always seemed shy around other men, well except for Ty. Obviously it didn't matter how long of a time period the two of them spent apart, she always went to him with welcome arms.

Watching the two of them play made me feel happy. Our ride here was horrible and she had gotten herself so worked up. I half expected her to have fallen asleep by now, but she was having too good of a time to do something like that. Ty was so amazed by the way she was walking around by herself. He walked around the room grabbing everything within her reach after she grabbed the cord to his Xbox and sent it flying across the room. I wanted to laugh, but his face looked like his best friend had been killed. I thought he would be angry, but he smiled as he moved it up to where she couldn't reach and went back to playing with her again.

Finally, she started yawning an awful lot. I knew she was ready for bed because she was grabbing for her ninny and laying her head down in random places. Ty thought it was cute and took a dozen pictures of her doing it with my new phone.

When he finally sat down on the couch, she climbed on to his lap and fell fast asleep. "I have no idea how she remembers you and takes to you every time you are around."

He played with one of her long curls. "I was the first guy she ever met. She probably just can't forget my handsome face," He teased.

I let out a little laugh. "I don't think she thought you were handsome, in fact I am pretty sure she has no idea what that even means."

"Are you mad that she loves me so much, like are you jealous?" He took his leg and kicked me so that I would look at his snarky grin.

"No, I am not jealous that she loves you. Obviously she does."

"I think she really likes the horse."

"I still can't believe you made that for her. It's so perfect. If you would have come to her birthday party, nobody else's presents would have been appreciated. She loves it!"

"Thanks. I spent a bunch of nights working on it. I couldn't wait to give it to her. I am sorry I didn't make it. I had just started my new job and I couldn't take the time off."

"I hope that was the reason." I put my head down and couldn't look at him. I had left things badly with Ty and I had a feeling that he was avoiding me the past few months as a reaction to how I had been.

"I have to be honest. I didn't understand why you stopped talking to me so much. I mean, we were really good friends and then you just stopped talking to me. I know lately things have been better between us, but what happened? Did I do something to make you mad?"

I shook my head, but refused to answer him. I had just arrived at his family's farm. I wasn't ready to tell him the real reason I backed off of our friendship.

Bella was fast asleep against Ty's chest. He noticed me looking and smiled when he saw she was asleep. "Looks like I still have the magic touch."

"I guess so," I said as I grabbed her gently and carried her into the bedroom. Ty followed behind me and at first I assumed that it was going to turn into something, but he started picking up the room and removing things within her reach.

"There are some extra pillows in the closet if you want to put them around the bed. I don't want her to roll off," he whispered.

I grabbed the pillows and positioned them around my daughter. "If she wakes up she will just climb out of bed and find me. She has been sleeping with me a lot lately."

We walked out into the living room and I slowed my pace when I realized that for the first time in a long time, Ty and I were completely alone together. He must have got the same feeling, because he quickly walked into the kitchen and started cleaning the counter off.

I sat down at the breakfast bar and played with my fingers, trying not to make eye contact. It wasn't like Ty was still wearing just a towel, but the t-shirt he did have on hugged his arms and every time he moved his muscles would flex.

"Did you get a new tattoo on your arm?" I asked as I noticed one peeking out from his sleeve.

"Yeah, it's just a tribal design with my last name in it. I didn't want anything like Colt has. That one on his back is giant."

"I have a couple. My newest one is Bella's name."

Don't ask where it is...

"I want to see it."

Of course he would. I should have just not said anything. I climbed off of the stool and took a deep breath as I lifted up my shirt to reveal my hip and abdomen. In fancy letters surrounded by hearts was the name Bella.

I don't know why I was being so shy. This guy had seen parts of me that I didn't even want to know, but for some reason showing him seemed so much more of an intimate thing.

"That looks awesome! I like where you put it too."

"Thanks Ty. So are you sure it's okay if we stay here for a while? I mean they say just a few weeks and I can probably head home."

"Stay as long as you want. Tomorrow I will move some of my things back into my parents and be out of your hair." He looked away from me when he said it.

"Bella likes it when you are around." I admitted.

"God, I really miss her." He leaned against the countertop. "I miss you both."

I wondered if he was being honest. *Didn't he say the same things to Van?*

I smiled but didn't answer.

"Miranda, I need to talk to you about what happened. I need to talk to you about that night."

I couldn't talk about it. I never should have gone out to that parking lot with Tucker. I should have never assumed that he wouldn't hurt me. I put myself in danger and I was tired of everyone telling me about it. I was here now because of that loser. There was no need for constant reminders. "Let's not rehash the past Ty. Let's just never talk about it again. It was a mistake. I know that now.

Ty scrunched up his face and seemed upset by my words. I didn't understand why he would want to talk about it anymore. Because of that night, he was forced to come home and our friendship had really taken a toll over it.

"So, do you have any plans for this weekend?" he asked, changing the subject.

"No, this all just happened. I didn't have time to plan for anything. Honestly, I don't even know what there is to do in this town."

"Well, aside from parties, and late night bonfires, there ain't much, but for a kid, there are a few things. Down the road is a petting zoo. If the weather lets up we could take her tomorrow."

"You don't have to keep us company Ty. I don't want to interfere in your life here."

"I was offering to take you and the little girl I am crazy about out. You aren't interfering. In fact, I don't really do much anymore. I work a lot and I am tired when I get home at night. My friends are all settling down and getting serious and the few that aren't party too much for even me."

I watched him walk into the living room and sit on the couch. He patted the seat next to him for me to sit. Luckily he patted it far enough away that I sat a whole cushion away from him. "I think that Bella would love to see the animals. Thanks for everything. It's been a hard couple of days."

"Don't thank me. I know you think you are imposing, but I couldn't be happier that you are here. I really did miss you. Hell, I can't believe they suggested you come here. Conner really seemed to be wedging himself between us last time I visited. I mean, I told him we were just friends and he had nothing to worry about."

I don't know why I ever thought there had been something between us. He was always a good friend to me. What he did with other girls was his business. He cared about my daughter more than he needed to and I could only be grateful to him for that.

Chapter 14

Ty

I still couldn't believe they were here, in my house, spending the night. Izzy had gotten so big. She loved her birthday present and I couldn't have been happier about that. My mother would really get a kick out of that little girl when she saw them in the morning. The last time she had seen her was when she was first born, but I had shown her pictures every time I got new ones. It was funny that her pictures were the only ones in my wallet. In fact, the last time I used my credit card someone commented that I had a cute kid. I didn't have the heart to tell them that she wasn't mine, so I just agreed with what they said. It was so cool to see her walking around on her own, getting into things and laughing while she did it.

Miranda looked exhausted. I knew what kind of stress Tucker had put on her in the past, but threatening her was the most evil thing a guy could do to the mother of his child. Saying things like that about his own child was just unacceptable. I would like to hunt him down and beat the shit out of him for doing that.

Miranda stared at the television, almost as if she were in a daze. "Hey, you still with me?"

She turned and gave a quick smile. "Sorry. It's just been a long day. I think I am still in shock over all of this. How could I have been so stupid Ty? How could I ever think that he could be anything but the devil?"

Her confusion over her poor choices had stressed her more than she wanted to admit. I wasn't really sure how she would react, but I held out my arms for her to slide into my chest. "I won't bite you know."

She reluctantly slid her body over so that she was pressed up against my chest. I folded my arm around her shoulder and across her arm, pulling her into me closer. Very gently I pressed my lips into the top of her head. She remained silent in my arms and I was fine with that. I just wanted her to know that she was safe.

I had started watching a new hot rod show on television. Miranda leaned her body on mine and let me just hold her like that. She looked up at me. "I am really sorry that I have been so distant with you. I should have never shut you out like I did. You are a good friend Ty. We are lucky to have you in our lives."

She said the word friend again, which I was fine with, if that was all she really wanted. Unfortunately, just being with her for the past few hours stirred up some buried feelings that I was trying to deny having for her. She was so attractive and the fact that she was vulnerable and needy made it easy to want to be there for her. We needed to talk about what had happened between us that night, but she kept telling me to drop it. I felt like we were on the same page, but she continued to shut me down. I wasn't really sure what to do about it.

"You are both important to me. I don't know who else I could have talked to about losing Van. It meant so much to me to have you giving me advice. I don't really talk to anyone else the way that we talk," I admitted.

"Yeah, well with Bella, it's hard for me to have any kind of social life. Besides Van and my brother's occasional girlfriends, I really don't have many friends. Van is great, but she's so involved with her wedding plans right now. She really doesn't have time for my drama, especially since they all told me to stay away from him so many times."

She repositioned herself a little more away from me so we were face to face. It should have made things easier, but her gorgeous eyes looked intently into mine, causing me to look down at her lips. I knew it was a mistake. I never should have even thought about doing it, but I leaned over and pressed my lips against hers.

I kept my eyes open, worried about her slapping me in the face, but she closed her eyes right away. I avoided using my tongue, or following through with a deeper kiss. I just let my lips linger against hers. As I pulled away, I watched her open her eyes slowly.

"What was that for?" She asked.

I have wanted to do that for so long.

"I ...well...I don't know. Are you mad?" Since she hadn't pushed me away or done worse, I figured what I had done was at least okay.

She shook her head. "No. I just didn't expect that."

Me either!

"I should probably head over to my parents." Things had just become awkward.

I stood up before she could say anything. The kiss was over, but tension had filled the room. I could have just fucked everything up. I needed to get out of there. I didn't regret what I had just done, but I didn't want to face negative consequences, either. She had finally smoothed everything over with me and I had possibly screwed it all up.

She let me walk to the door before she stood up and put her hands into her back pockets. "So, will we see you in the morning?"

"If that's what you want?" I leaned against the door frame.

She nodded her head up and down. "Yeah, I think Bella will be looking for you at the crack of dawn."

"Should I set my alarm?" I wondered.

"Of course not! Just come over when you wake up."

She wouldn't make eye contact. "Are you sure you aren't mad at me?"

She walked closer to me and leaned against the edge of the couch. "Not at all. It was just a kiss Ty. It was sweet. We are friends. It's okay."

There was the friend word again....

"I don't think anyone has ever called me sweet before," I admitted.

She looked down at the floor and let out a tiny snicker. "You act different around me. I mean, people say you are one way, but I don't see that side of you Ty. You have always been so sweet to me and especially Bella."

"Izzy," I interrupted.

"Bella!" She laughed. "I think you should show everyone this side of you. You obviously have a big heart."

I shook my head and disagreed. "Nah, I think that having my heart broken has changed the person that I want to be. The sex and the girls was something that I did to pass the time. They never meant anything to me, it was all for fun. I don't know whether it was the accident, or the fact that I finally lost Van, but whatever it was made me rethink the decisions I was making. I am not saying that I am abstinent or never going out again, but I just don't do it a lot."

"All the partying is what got me Bella. I will never regret her, but I wish I hadn't run around like I did. For shits sake, her daddy is a convict."

We both laughed.

We stood there just staring at each other for a couple seconds. I grabbed the door and was thankful when I opened it and realized that the rain had slowed to a drizzle.

"Guess I will see you in the morning."

"Okay."

I gave Miranda one more smile before heading out away from the carriage house. It was surprising to find my mother still awake when I walked into the house. She was sewing some huge ass blanket.

"Hey Mom."

"I tried to call you and tell you she was coming." She shook her head like she was pissed at me.

I sighed. "I know you did. I didn't bother checking my messages. It's all good though. I got a surprise visit from my favorite girl. She's getting so big Mom. Wait until you see her tomorrow."

She sat her blanket down and looked up at me. I knew the look well. I sat down without being asked to.

"That girl is here because she's running from trouble. It would be in your best interest to keep her at a distance."

I chuckled. "Seriously? I think I can make my own decisions when it comes to Miranda. She has been nothing but a friend to me when I was at my worst. If she needs a friend then I am going to be there."

"You know that I ain't talking about a friend Tyler. She has trouble written all over her."

I pointed my finger at my mother. "You stayed up to give me this half ass lecture didn't you?"

"Perhaps."

"There is nothing that I won't do for that little girl. I know you don't understand it, but it's the truth. Please be nice to Miranda while she's here Mom. I know how you like to feel in control of my life, but damn it, I am a grown man now. I make my own money and wipe my own ass. You can't continue to meddle like you do."

She raised her eyebrow. "I am afraid to tell you that I will always have an interest in your life son. I don't want to see you get hurt like you did before, or worse."

I expressed amusement in her last comment. "What's that supposed to mean?"

"Maybe she will try to trap you. Girls like that are always looking for someone to help raise their kids. I can't blame her for having eyes for you."

I rolled my eyes and shook my head again. "She doesn't have eyes for me. Jesus Christ!"

"Don't use that talk around me."

"Whatever! I am going to bed before I say something else to get you into a tizzy. Goodnight Mom."

My mother didn't say goodnight as I walked away from

her. I got that she was suspicious of someone that she didn't know, but Miranda was not looking to trap me, in fact she had never even made a move on me. I was the idiot trying to kiss her tonight. I had to remember that my overbearing mother had been looking out for me again. She needed to stop her meddling, but I saw the good in what she thought would be considered looking out for me.

After Van and Colt had left, things were tough for me. I spent most of my time alone, sulking in defeat. Karma is really a bitch and it dealt me with the biggest payback possible. I knew all along that Van was too good for me. While she sat at home planning our future, I was out banging chicks. I was selfish and worried about getting my dick wet. When I finally opened my eyes to look into that mirror they call 'truth', well I didn't like what was staring back at me at all.

I was left with nothing to show for.

No college degree.

No future in football.

No driver's license.

No girl.

After weeks of sulking, it was my mother who had drug me out of my depressed stupor. Well, it was her and Miranda. Of course she would rather take all of the credit and not give any to the single mother staying in our carriage house.

It appeared that my mother had nothing to worry about anyway. Even if I was interested in Miranda, she had made it clear that we were just friends more than once. It was ironic considering that the more I felt like I wanted there to be something between us, the more she kept shutting me down. I wasn't used to so much rejection. Maybe all of my cheating had left me with the inability to ever be trusted again. Maybe I needed to move to another country where nobody knew me.

For the next two hours I laid in my bed and pondered on every conversation that Miranda and I had ever had. It left me even more confused.

Chapter 15

Miranda

It was just a friendly kiss. He missed our friendship and was overwhelmed with our surprise visit.

I kept telling that to myself while I lay next to my daughter, trying to fall asleep. I couldn't get over the fact that Ty seemed so different. He hadn't thrown himself on me, or given me any reason that he wanted me sexually. He just offered a shoulder and an ear. I needed to stop making something out of nothing.

If the timing was different I could see myself being with Ty. Of course that would require him to return an interest in me, but he was great. Van said that he was a good friend. Although, on more than one occasion she said that he wasn't a good boyfriend. I couldn't just think about myself anymore. My daughter had to be my first priority. I couldn't use sex as a tool to get a guy, especially a guy like him. He loved my daughter so much and that was a big deal. I wasn't going to let some secret feelings ruin their relationship.

I woke up to my daughter rambling. I sat up and noticed that she wasn't even in the room. It took me a second to take in my new surroundings before I jumped up and rushed out into the living room. She could have walked into the bathroom and been playing in the toilet, or worse.

I froze when I spotted Bella, sitting in her chair, eating her dry cereal, while Ty sat across from her. "How did you get in here? Did I lock the door wrong?"

"No. I used my key. I figured that you would be awake, so I just came in. Izzy must have heard the door open, because she came running out of the bedroom carrying a bra and a diaper." Ty had this half smile going, especially when he said the word 'bra'.

I put my hand over my very embarrassed face.

"I changed the diaper, but the bra didn't fit her at all." He reached his hand out and handed me my pink bra.

I tucked it behind my back. "Smart ass!" I walked over and tossed my bra back into the bedroom. Bella must have been awake for a little while, because my whole bag was ripped apart on the bedroom floor.

When I got back out into the kitchen, Ty was still cackling over my underwear. I rolled my eyes and noticed that he had a cup in his hand. "Is that coffee?"

"Yep. There is a whole pot in the house, as well as some waffles. I came over here to tell you. I can't believe that you were still sleeping. Izzy could have walked out and rode off on the horse."

"Your morning humor is not exactly entertaining. Thank you for taking care of her. I will have to start closing the bedroom door and make sure nothing is within her reach. She gets into everything now."

The tiny little cereal that was just on Bella's tray was all gone. Ty shook the can to get her attention. "You want more?" She held out her hand for him to give her more. He opened the can and handed her a couple before picking her up. "Do you have another jacket I can put on her?"

I went back in the bedroom and grabbed her some clean clothes. Ty put her clothes on while I went and brushed my teeth. After getting her presentable we headed to the main farmhouse.

I looked around but noticed immediately that there was nobody else in the house, that I could tell. "Where is everyone?"

"Mom ran into town to do some church thing and my dad is around the farm somewhere. Coffee is fresh in the pot and how many waffles do you want?" He asked.

I sat down on a stool across the counter from him. After running my hands over my face a few times, I looked back up at him. "How in the hell are you so wide awake right now?"

He shrugged and turned to the coffee machine, where he poured me a big cup. He grabbed the milk and sugar and slid them over to me. "Here. This will help you wake up. My mother makes it thick. I am just warning you."

I shook my head and started pouring the sugar bowl into my cup while Ty pulled out a box of frozen waffles. He started laughing when I giggled. "I was wondering how you were going to make waffles. Now I see that you only need a toaster."

"I can cook. Stop complaining and tell me how many you want. Izzy is going to make you breakfast." Ty handed Izzy a waffle and she put it to her mouth. It was frozen and the cold must have felt good because she kept chewing on it. He put one waffle in the toaster then showed her how to put hers in. She started banging her waffle on the top of the toaster. "Don't beat it up. We want Mommy to be able to eat it." He teased.

"So I get to eat the slobber waffle?"

He laughed and sat Izzy on the counter while still holding her. "I will eat the slobber waffle if you can't handle it."

"That is disgusting. If you knew the things she tried to put in her mouth, you wouldn't be sayin' that." That child put everything in her mouth. God only knows what she had eaten that I didn't know about.

Just like he had said, Ty took out the waffles and took a giant bite out of the one Bella had chewed on. "It tastes great to me!"

"That is so gross."

He made more until we both had two each and we started to eat. Bella sat on his lap and he fed her small bites of his food. I think she was just sucking off the syrup for the most part.

"Did you call home and tell them everything is fine here?" He asked.

"Yes. I did it last night. I left a message. Things weren't exactly happy when I left. I didn't want to go anywhere, but they pushed the decision on me." I explained.

"Well I am glad you came here. Working so much sucks because I can't come visit. Izzy is getting so big so fast. I can't believe how good she's walking and saying words."

"It amazes me how much you love her. I wish her father would have felt that way about her." I started to tear up. Not because I missed Tucker, or even wanted him to change now, but because there were men out there that weren't even blood related that would do anything for her. How pathetic was that?

"She definitely has my heart. Ever since she was born I have felt that way. I hope it doesn't bother you. I mean, I never would have chosen to be there that day, but now that it has happened, I couldn't imagine not being there." He reached for his back pocket and pushed his wallet across the table. "Look inside of it."

When I opened that wallet, I never imagined that it would be filled with pictures of my child. There were at least six pictures, all of Bella. No hot models or pictures of him and Van like I would have thought. "How long have you been carryin' these around?"

"Well, when she was born I wanted to have a picture when I told the story, then I just kept collecting them. Is it creepy?" He got a worried look on his face.

I looked at my daughter sitting on his lap and thought about how, if things were different, I would love to be with someone like him. I was aware of his past, but for some reason it just didn't matter to me. He loved my daughter and made it clear we were just friends, so I had to settle for that. "She's lucky to have an uncle like you. Thank you, for everything Ty. I really mean that."

He smiled and looked down at Bella. "Who is ready to go pet some stinky animals?" He said in a baby voice. "Say 'I am Mommy'." He raised Bella's hand causing her to giggle.

We cleaned up our mess and headed out for a day at the petting zoo. Ty insisted on driving since he knew where he was going. Since my one jacket had been damp from the rain the night before, he lent me one of his college hoodies. It was too big, but very warm in the crisp spring air.

I was surprised at how close the place was. Ty later admitted that he knew the people his whole life. When we first got there he gave some old man a wave before getting Bella out of her car seat. I think that it wouldn't have mattered if I even went. He carried her around and made a big deal about every animal they came up to. Bella was reluctant to touch most of them, but after Ty showed her it was okay she started to open up. By the third animal she was squealing and getting all excited every time she got to touch one of them.

After about an hour of touching every stinky animal she could get her hands on, Ty led us over to a few picnic tables. He told me to wait there for him to return. He came running back from the car moments later with a cooler in his hand.

"Where did you get that?" I asked.

"I put it in the car this morning before going into the carriage house. I packed all kinds of shit too, so you better be hungry."

I shook my head and let Bella play in the grass while he got everything out. It wasn't anything fancy, but he had managed to pack the cooler full. "When did you have time to buy juice boxes?"

"Actually, they are mine. I still pack them in my lunch every day."

I snickered. "How old are you?"

He stood up straight and put his hands on his hips. "I will have you know that those juice boxes supply me with half of my daily required vitamin C for the day."

I rolled my eyes. "Only you would say somethin' like that."

"Don't you ever wonder where this perfectly sculpted body comes from? It's from eating Wheaties and drinking my juice boxes. I also like spinach out of the can, just like Popeye the sailorman."

"Well I got my big breasts from eatin' lots of chicken," I joked.

With his index finger, he pointed toward my chest. "Yeah, I can tell."

I blushed and looked over at Bella. I hated that he noticed things about me, but only ever considered me a friend. When he said things like that I felt my body starting to tingle. Sometimes I just wanted to feel his touch, whether it was wrong or not.

We ate our food and enjoyed the sunshine for a while longer. I could tell that Bella was starting to get tired because she had become cranky and nothing settled her. After spending a good twenty minutes with a very friendly llama, that licked everything in sight, and also seemed to know how to actually spit, we took a slobber filled faced child back to Ty's for a nap.

Luckily, she fell asleep before the car left the driveway. Ty couldn't stop talking about how excited Bella was when she got to touch the animals. I think he was the one who was more excited. Since Bella was sound asleep when we pulled back up at his parent's farm, Ty suggested we watch some television and relax. I don't think he realized how much a child can tire someone out.

"That was draining!" He said as he plopped down on the couch after laying Bella down.

"Yeah, you have to get used to it. Thanks for taking us. She really seemed to have fun."

He snickered. "Yeah, until she got spit on by a damn llama."

We both began to laugh.

Ty stood up and pulled off his hoodie. As he was doing it, his t-shirt pulled up over his abs and back. God, his stomach was so firm. I turned away quickly when he turned to look at me. I got the impression that he knew I was checking him out when he shot me a half smile.

Instead of him calling me out on my wandering eyes, he started flipping through the channels. I let out a big sigh thinking I had gotten away with it.

That's what I thought.

"So aren't you hot in that sweatshirt?" He asked, without taking his eyes from the television.

I cringed just knowing that he *had* caught me. "No. I am just fine." I lied.

After nearly an hour, I was sweating my ass off. Ty kept randomly making conversation while I tried to prevent the beads of sweat from dripping down my forehead. I don't know why I was so determined to act stubborn, but I didn't want him to have the upper hand. Ty had been known to be a womanizer. I had seen firsthand how women approached him. He knew he could pretty much get whoever he wanted. Hell, I wanted him too, even if I couldn't have him. Opening that can would be just added disaster to my already chaotic life.

When Bella woke up, she came walking out of the bedroom with no pants on. "Bella, what happened to your pants honey?" I grabbed her and went looking for her pack of diapers. "Uncle Ty doesn't want to see your hinny."

I no sooner got Bella changed when my new cell phone started ringing. "Ty, can you get that?"

I heard him talking on the phone as I approached, but he handed it to me immediately and started shaking his head. I didn't understand but I grabbed it and sat down. Ty held his hands out for Bella and started swinging her around.

Hello?

Miranda, it's me. Conner

Hey. What's up?

Look, I am not goin' to beat around the bush. We got a few disturbin' calls last night. They are all from a blocked number, even the texts.

Well, was it Tucker?

We don't know. The voice was raspy and deep, like they were holdin' somethin' to disguise their voice.

You said you got texts too?

Yeah. They said 'it's only a matter of time'. Another said that 'you will pay'.

What does Mom say?

She's glad that you are stayin' with Ty. I think it's a bad idea, but for the time bein', I guess it's alright. He best keeps his damn hands to himself.

Please don't start with that Conner. I did what you all said. Ty is keeping us safe, isn't that what you want?

Of course it is. I just don't want him tryin' to get into your pants. Don't you let him either. That ain't why we sent you there.

I started gritting my teeth. *Thank you for keepin' me posted about the phone calls. Goodnight Conner. Tell Mom I love her.*

I hung up the phone before he could piss me off anymore

"He thinks I am going to deflower you." Ty joked.

I rolled my eyes. "Ha ha! I think it's too late for me to be deflowered."

"You know what I mean. I answered that damn phone and he started asking what I was doing near you. Was I not supposed to be around you?" He asked.

"Don't listen to him. He thinks he can control my life. He threatens everyone I am close to," I admitted.

"Are you saying we are close?" he asked as he pushed the hair away from my face.

I tried to pretend like his touch didn't affect me. "He says that my old phone had been getting threatenin' phone calls."

"Nothing will happen to you while you are here with me Miranda. I promise you that."

He pulled me into his chest and just held me there for a few seconds. "Thank you. This is my first real time away from home. It makes it harder having Bella. She's a good little girl, but I never wanted this for her."

He put his hands on either side of my face. "I know I already said this, but I am really glad you came here. I missed Izzy.....," he looked directly into my eyes, "and I missed you."

I licked my lips and glared at his.
We started moving closer.
My heart was beating out of my chest.
Yes...yes......
Then someone knocked on the door.

Chapter 16

Tyler

Leave it to my mother to drop by the carriage house at the worst time possible.

I was inches away from feeling those soft lips again, when she came beating on the door. Then to make matters worse, she just came bursting in. "Sorry to just barge in. I wanted to give Ty his cell phone. It has been ringing in his room all day."

My mother looked around the living room. "Is the baby sleeping?"

Miranda had scooted at least two feet away from me, but I could tell that both she and my mother sensed the tension in the room.

"I took them to Jeb's farm to pet all the animals. It wore her out."

"So how are you doing Miranda? Do you have everything you need out here?" My mother asked.

Yes, thank you for lettin' us come here. I know the circumstances aren't ideal. I apologize for the inconvenience," Miranda explained.

"It's no trouble. It's a real shame that boy is threatening you and your baby like that."

Miranda gave my mother a quick smile. "I thought he would change once she was born. I swear I truly believed that once he saw her for the first time, he would want to be a family."

"He's a damn fool." My mother shook her head and turned her direction toward the bedroom door.

Izzy came peeking around the corner. She was looking straight at my mother but being shy because she didn't know her. Miranda had her back facing the bedroom, so she wasn't seeing the hide and seek that was going on. "There's my favorite girl," I announced in an excited tone. Izzy got a big smile on her face and came walking out into the living room toward me. I held my arms up and offered to pick her up. Just like every time, she jumped right up. "Don't be shy. This is my mommy."

"Mama." Izzy said as she pointed toward Miranda.

"Yes that is your mama," I agreed and laughed.

My mother approached us and held her arms out for Izzy. Instead of reaching back, she turned her face and buried it into my shoulder. "No!"

We all started laughing even though my mother seemed genuinely hurt that the baby hadn't made friends with her yet.

"She's shy at first. Just give her a little while and she will open up." Miranda explained.

I tickled Izzy's neck with my whiskers and got her to finally look up. "There she is!" I looked over at my mother. "Grab that container of cereal and hand her some, Mom. She can't resist them."

Miranda handed her the cereal container and she took a few pieces in her hand. In hindsight she looked like she was trying to lure out an angry or scared puppy, but instead it was just a cute little girl.

I got a very excited look on my face. "Izzy, look what she has for you."

Izzy peeked behind her and saw her favorite cereal in my mother's hand. She had sat down on the couch and I sat down next to her. "Don't you want one?" My mother asked kindly.

"Mine." Izzy announced as she grabbed all three out of my mother's palm.

After shoving them all in her mouth, she climbed down and started gibbering about something. It was clearly baby talk and none of it made sense, but to appease the child, my mother pretended to know every word she was saying. "Is that so? Tell me more." She leaned over and played with one of Izzy's curls. "You have such pretty hair. I can see why Uncle Ty is so crazy about you. You are the cutest little thing."

Izzy looked up and pointed at me. "Ty."

My heart skipped a beat. It had been clear as day. I looked over to Miranda, who now had her hand over her mouth. "She said my name. She pointed to me and said my name."

"That is incredible. She has never said that before. I mean, she has been sayin' random words more and more, but I don't remember her ever hearin' that. It was perfectly clear Ty." Miranda said, still shocked I was sure.

I couldn't stop smiling and when I turned to look over at my mother, she had this sparkle in her eyes that I hadn't seen in forever. She ended up staying and hanging out with us for at least a half hour. When she finally headed out, she invited us to dinner and told us she wouldn't take no for an answer.

When I walked her outside, she pulled me into a hug. "Please forgive me for being so protective of you. I don't know if there is anything going on with you and Miranda, and you are right, it's none of my business, but I want you to know that I see how easy it was for you to fall in love with that baby. She's perfect."

I smiled and looked at my mom. "She is. I know they came here because they were running away, but I am so glad to be able to spend time with her, with both of them."

My mother nodded and started walking toward her house. "See you in an hour."

I was shocked at how she had turned around, but I knew that the little girl had also made me have feelings that I didn't know existed. All of the partying and sex could never give me the happy feelings that I felt when I spent time with Izzy. Her little smile sent a charge straight to my heart. I understood how grizzly old grumpy men could become puppy dogs when they saw their grandchildren, or how people in the armed forces could shed those tears of joy when they saw their babies for the first time through a computer screen. Suddenly, the life I was living seemed so empty. Sure, I had family and friends here, but when I came home at night I was alone.

Last year I thought that I had my future all pegged out, but after the accident, the coma and losing everything else, it was clear that I was left with nothing to look forward to. I had been a shitty boyfriend to Van. I had treated her like a possession while I went out and screwed around on her. I never thought about getting caught or what would happen if I did. I always just assumed she would be there.

The thing was, when I actually did lose her, I realized just how unhappy we both were. We were living in the fantasy of it all. Van and I didn't have much in common. She was her own person and I had never taken the time to get to know her. I was more worried about myself.

I had fucked up, but the worst part of it all was that she found that happiness in my cousin. I had to see her when I visited my family. I had to hear about their upcoming nuptials and how I should be a man about standing up beside Colt, being his best man. Did anyone realize how much that hurt me? Not just because it was Van, it was because after losing her, I realized it may have been what I wanted all along. I didn't know how to be in a faithful relationship, with someone that was my best friend. I was completely jealous of their life.

Having Miranda and Izzy come to stay had forced me to rehash all of the feelings again, reminding me of how lonely I would be when they left. I had an instant ache in the pit of my stomach just thinking about it.

I needed to stop being a selfish prick, get over what happened last year and move on. For the second time, I had almost kissed Miranda and I was certain this time that she wanted to kiss me to. We had been friends for a while and talked about everything, in fact she knew all about my feelings, because she was the person I confided in. The problem with Miranda was that she had made it clear that we were just friends, almost family even, and because I had agreed, it had made the situation carved into stone.

I was starting to wonder if I was actually having feelings for Miranda, and not just because I was already in love with her daughter. I needed to figure it out without ruining our friendship and definitely before she headed back home to Kentucky.

When I went back into the carriage house, Izzy was getting a much needed diaper change. The smell of fresh shit filled the room and I covered my nose. "Eww somebody has a stinky hinny."

"That would be your little cutie over here." Miranda started laughing as she pointed to the wrapped up diaper. I grabbed a plastic bag and held my nose as I walked over toward the stink bomb.

"I will take this outside and bury it," I said as I scooped it into the bag and tied it shut. When I reached the door, I fanned it open and shut. "How can you sit in there and not gag?"

"You get used to it," She laughed.

Izzy ran toward the door. "Bye bye?"

"No. Uncle Ty will be right back," I explained.

I didn't bury the diaper, but I threw it in the dumpster behind the barn. I wanted that smell to be as far away from human contact as possible.

When I got back inside Miranda was cleaning up. "Your cell phone keeps ringing."

I grabbed my phone and noticed I had thirty-seven missed calls. I shook my head and sat down, scrolling through the numbers. Ten calls were from my mother, and the rest were from my friends, including Van and Colt's number. I had seventeen text messages.

Most were asking about Miranda and Izzy, so I answered everyone from Kentucky back that things were fine and I just left my phone somewhere. I had a bunch from Heather, telling me what I had missed out on, and some from my best friend Mike.

Every year the fraternity had a big ABC party. The concept of the party was that you could wear anything but clothes, and let me just say that people my age were very creative. To say that a lot of skin was revealed would be an understatement. The outfit malfunctions themselves left for great entertainment.

Miranda must have noticed me smiling just thinking about it. "What are you smilin' about?"

"There is an ABC party tonight at the frat house. I was just thinking about how much fun it was last year."

"I have always wanted to go to one. I even know what I would wear. I am sure you are goin' to have a good time. Take pictures so I can see them tomorrow."

That wasn't acceptable. "What if I can find a sitter? I mean, we won't go until after nine so Izzy will be asleep anyway."

"We just got here. I don't know anyone to ask. Izzy would freak out."

"My mother will do it. We can find out at dinner."

She shook her head. "I don't know if that is a good idea. We didn't come here so I could go party with college people. I came here to protect myself and daughter."

"I am inviting you to come out for a little while. I won't even drink."

"You really think she will watch her?"

"I think that after spending ten seconds with her earlier, she's filling a craving for her own grandchild, that obviously she isn't going to have anytime soon."

For the next half hour Miranda seemed excited, but still feared my mother would say 'no'. Izzy was running around the couch, itching for me to keep chasing her. Every time I got close, she would scream at the top of her lungs and yell 'no'. I would grab her and tickle her.

I managed to run over and ask my mother if she would babysit, before the girls arrived for dinner. I knew that after seeing Izzy for herself, she wouldn't be able to resist. She agreed without even giving it a second thought.

Dinner worked out great. We brought Izzy's seat over and hooked it right to the table. My mother got herself so excited about watching Izzy, that she had my father run to the church to borrow a porta-crib. While the girls did dishes, we tried to get it set up ourselves. Of course Miranda came walking in and had the damn contraption set up in three seconds flat.

Izzy saw what it was and ran away from it, like it had teeth.

ABC parties required planning, due to the fact that it was an anything but clothes party. I had already set out something for myself to wear, but I had absolutely no idea what Miranda was planning. She grabbed a few things from my mother's pantry and headed over to the carriage house to get ready, while I went in my old bedroom to do the same. My costume consisted of a small orange cone and some caution tape. The cone was to cover my goods, while the tape was wrapped around to cover the rest. Last year I had used the tape and it got ripped off, so this year I secured it better with Duct tape. Because we still had to drive there, I threw on a sweatshirt and some large jogging pants. I tried to avoid my parents as I walked past them, with what looked like a giant hard-on.

My mother gasped and shook her head, probably regretting the idea of babysitting while Miranda and I walked around half-naked.

"It's just a party Mom, and all of the private parts are covered," I assured her.

"I don't want to know," She said as I walked out the door.

I was dying to see what Miranda was wearing, but she already had on a jacket that came down to her knees when I walked in. "Can I get a peek?"

"Nope. You can be surprised just like everyone else." After only being able to see a pair of red high heels, I was more than curious.

I shook my head, feeling like I was going to regret this. This was exactly what Conner did not want happening.

I begged her to show me her outfit the whole ride to the frat house, but she kept refusing. When we finally parked, we noticed lots of people stripping off coats in the parking lot. I pulled off my clothes and turned to see if Miranda was following my lead.

Holy Hell!

My mouth dropped.

Miranda was standing there, in nothing but a tiny strand of saran wrap across her large breasts and some concoction of a very small, very short saran wrapped skirt.

"Holy Shit!"

"Do you like it?" She spun around, probably to tease me more.

"There isn't much there. Maybe you should keep the coat on," I suggested.

"Why? Does it make me look fat or somethin'?"

"Hell no! You look fucking hot! Too hot! My friends are going to bust a load when they see you. Just stay close to me tonight, please. I don't feel like fighting anyone."

She started laughing. "Whatever you say. Lead the way."

I held out my hand for her and thankfully she took it. This was a bad idea. Every guy in this place was going to be mind-fucking her. She gave the word MILF its name.

Just as I suspected, we walked in and people's mouths actually dropped. She may as well have been naked and I immediately felt protective. "Here we go," I said under my breath.

Mike approached us. "Damn boy. Now I know why you didn't call me back. Who is this fine thing?"

I looked over to Miranda. "This......she is my...."

"Hi, I am Miranda. I am visiting from Kentucky," She interrupted.

Mike looked her up and down as he shook her hand. "You are fucking hot!" He blurted out.

I rolled my eyes while he continued to give her his undivided attention. "Follow me if you want a beer."

She looked back at me while he pulled her forward. I

regretted it, but he was my best friend and all he knew was that she and I were together. He wouldn't go against guy code. Mike wasn't like that.

It took seconds for Heather to come up behind me and smack the caution tape over my ass. She let her hand linger. "Why did you bring her?"

"Because I wanted to."

"Is that your baby?" She said as she turned around to face me. She had made a bikini out of beer boxes. The top was light beer and the small bottoms were regular beer.

"That is none of your fucking business." I scoured the room, trying to spot where Mike had taken Miranda.

"Who is she Ty? I have never seen her before and she's clearly staying at your place." She was jealous. I wanted to laugh in her face, but I was too busy trying to find Miranda to give her a second of my time.

"Seriously, Heather, can you just stop throwing yourself at me. I am not interested. Can't you take a fucking hint? What do I have to do to get the point across? I don't want you!"

I never took my eyes off the crowd, and my heart dropped when I saw Mike and Miranda dancing together. She was so fucking gorgeous. Her body was perfect and I clenched my fist when I watched her put her hands in the air and Mike groping her at the waist. The tattoo on her ribs of Bella's name was being displayed for the whole world to see. Then another one of my buddies grabbed her from behind and they were starting to run a damn train.

What the fuck?

Heather continued to talk, but I heard nothing she said. I pushed her out of the way and headed toward Miranda.

Chapter 17

Miranda

I couldn't believe how awesome Ty was being and the fact that he had managed to give me a night out. After almost kissing me earlier, he had gone back to his strict friend demeanor. He kept confusing me. One minute I felt like he wanted me and the next he was making it clear that we were just friends.

The party was in full force and I loved all of the different things people were using to cover their bodies. Ty was nice to have let me hang out with his friend Mike. He was hot, but not as hot as Ty. When he asked me to dance, I glanced over and saw that Ty was with the girl who had been at his place the other night. I didn't want to disturb them, he was probably telling her that I was his family. It hurt a little just thinking about it. I was really starting to wish that we could be more. I had even made an effort to woo him with my choice in attire tonight, but after his initial shocked voice, he stopped looking at me. I was running out of ideas and with having Bella, I wasn't going to throw myself out there anymore.

I had to focus on her, not myself. I couldn't spend time trying to get guys. It just wasn't a priority, besides I really loved Ty's relationship with my daughter and didn't want to do anything to come between them.

After having me take three shots with him, Mike led me to the dance floor. I tried not to look over at Ty. I wish I could tell him how much I wanted him. I had never been friends with a guy like I was with him. I didn't want to lose that. I didn't know if telling Ty the truth would mess things up between us, but part of me was finding it so hard to resist him.

Mike was a good dancer and I loved that he and his other friends were giving me attention. I never went out and didn't have much friends at home. Being a mother will do that. Sometimes a woman just wants to feel desired. I knew I wasn't ugly, but sometimes I needed the reminders.

"So are you and Ty together?" Mike asked.

I wish. "No, it's complicated."

The shots were warming me up and I was starting to let go with my dancing. Mike's hands started lingering like I had given him the go ahead that he needed. He was definitely a good looking guy. His sandy brown hair was cut short and he had pretty light blue eyes. If I had to guess I would say he was a football player or wrestler from the size of his muscles. He had taped a pizza box to the front and back of him to cover his package and the cardboard continued to rub against me as we danced. His rock hard chest was as exposed as almost every guy at the party. Some were not as easy on the eyes, but everyone seemed to be having a good time looking. Mike kept leaning into my neck and brushing his nose into my hair.

"I think I might love you," he joked with a wink.

"Really? I think I have heard that line before. You will have to come up with a better one than that," I teased.

"I will say whatever you want if it gets me a night with you."

I let my head fall back as I laughed. Another guy came up behind me and started dancing with us. I had been too busy laughin' at Mike's comment to pay attention to the other guy. I was having a good time with two hot guys when Ty came up and grabbed me. "Thanks for keeping her safe guys."

They started to moan and groan. "She said you weren't together man. What gives cock block?"

"Fuck off!" Ty pulled my body as close as I could get to him. He had a cone that was about six inches long covering his private parts, so when he did it, it pressed into my stomach.

"Ouch! Why did you stop me from dancin'? I was havin' a good time."

"I don't want them touching you."

We started dancing to blend in with the crowd around us.

"Why?"

"I...um...Colt and Conner would kick my ass, that's why."

Not the reason that I was hoping for. Why can't you want me?

"They ain't here Ty. I am a grown woman. We have been over this before."

A slow song came on and people started getting close and freaky. We looked at each other and Ty leaned into my ear. "I want you to have a good time, but not with these freaks. They want one thing. Trust me I know!"

"Didn't you bring me here to have a good time? I think I can handle myself."

"I want you to do something for me. I want you to pretend we are together tonight. Can you just do that to make me happy? I don't want to worry about any of my pervert friends hitting on you all night."

Ahh, a reason to touch him....I think yes!

I ran my hands over his chest. "How much do you want me to pretend? Is this really for my safety or are we tryin' to make someone jealous?"

He stared at me for a second and started to smile. Before I could argue, he picked me up and I wrapped my legs around his waist. His hands were on my ass and the cone covering his package was no longer an issue in keeping us apart. I reached my arms under his and held onto the top of his shoulders. I felt Ty backing up until we were against a wall. He licked his lips. "I don't need to do anything to make anyone jealous, because just seeing you with me did that."

"So are you makin' someone jealous?" I asked as our lips started to brush.

"Nope. There isn't anyone here I care about."

"What about that girl? The one that was at your house?" I asked.

"Nothing to tell." Our lips brushed again.

To say I was turned on was an understatement. His hands were gripping my ass. Our lips were touching. I nudged my lips over his and started to pull away.

He spun us around and I was now against the wall. The room was crowded with people, and I was hardly worried about anyone seeing us like this. I didn't care at all. It was like they didn't even exist.

Ty pulled away from my face and brought his mouth to my ear. "You are making this so fucking hard."

He looked at me again. I searched his face for answers, but he seemed so confused himself.

"Making what hard?" I was not understanding. "You said to pretend. Who are we pretending for?" God, I was so hot for him. His naked chest pressed against mine. My nipples were hard under the plastic and the more he held me the more they tingled.

He freed one hand and brought it up to touch my face. His fingers stroked my lips as he watched, biting his lip. "I don't want anyone else to touch you. I want them to think you are all mine."

I didn't care what his reason was. I had wanted to kiss him, like really kiss him, for over a year. I had imagined it a million times. He might be faking his feelings, but I sure wasn't.

He didn't have to know that.

"Okay," I whispered.

I licked my lips and watched him getting closer to me. I wrapped my arms around his neck and slowly brought my lips to his. I was so afraid that he was going to pull away that I just froze with our lips pressed, but as his body pressed against me, all I could think of was feeling his tongue. I stroked his bottom lip with my tongue and pulled away, waiting for him to respond.

Ty smiled. He pressed his forehead to mine. "Okay?" He was giving me a second chance to back out.

There was no way I was going to do that with the fire that had ignited between my legs. I had barely any clothes on, but I was so hot. Instead of answering him, I grabbed the back of his head and pulled him into my kiss. If I thought my nipples were overly sensitive from his holding me. Well, when his tongue stroked against mine for the first time, those sensations doubled. I let out a soft whimper as our tongues began to mingle. His lips were so soft and his breathing was becoming heavier. I hadn't come here to seduce him, but if I wanted more of Ty, I knew I had to give it my all.

He was giving me the reigns to continue this little charade, which had been his idea from the get-go. I dug my nails into his back and pulled his body closer to me. I wanted to feel his chest pressing against my sensitive nipples. Just feeling his body that close made them ache. I couldn't remember ever being so turned on from just kissing. I just wanted to feel his hands all over me, touching me in every way that would imply that we were way more than just friends.

I was aware that I was wearing nothing but saran wrap, and that my ass was most likely only covered for the fact that I was pressed into a wall. Our kisses were so deep and I couldn't help but feel like Ty was enjoying them as much as I was. For two people that were 'pretending' we seemed to be more in sync than any other couple at the party.

After several catcalls and some juvenile comments, Ty pulled his lips away from mine. His head burrowed into my neck as he calmed his heavy breaths. "I told you to stop me."

He sat me down and pushed himself away, giving us a good foot between us. I knew he was hard under that cone, he couldn't deny it. His cheeks were flushed and his eyes were fixed on mine. "I wasn't ready to stop. Don't you want to put on a good show?" My heart was beating out of my chest, but I couldn't deny my yearn for his touch. I wanted him.

He looked around the room. "I am pretty sure that everyone here is fully aware of what we just did. I did have a practically naked, hot as shit chick, pressed against a wall with my tongue down her throat. I am certain that neither of us are in any danger of getting hit on."

I tried to act like it was no big deal; like it was just something fun we did as a joke. Still, we both stood there unable to speak, while our eyes were still filled with desire.

I looked down at the orange cone that was fastened to his hips and ass by Duct tape. Under that cone was something I couldn't help but be curious about. The shots had relaxed me and made me feel adventurous. When he still hadn't said another word to me, I grabbed him by that cone and broke the distance between us. His lips were close to mine again. I could feel him breathing. "You seem like you had fun."

Our lips touched again and I felt his tongue slide over my bottom lip. "You have no idea how much."

I got ready to say something, but I heard the word 'whore' being yelled and saw that friend of Ty's walking past us and purposely graze him in the back. At the same time he turned to acknowledge her, I pushed him aside. "What did you just say?"

The bitch didn't back down, but dammit, where I was from, neither did we.

"I called you a whore."

I looked her up and down. "I ain't no whore you stupid bitch!"

She flung herself at me. "Who. Are. You. Calling. A. Bitch?"

I grabbed her by the arm and shoved her ass down on the floor. People started forming a circle around us. I didn't give a shit about my saran wrapped outfit or the fact that it could be pulled apart easily, but Ty must of. He grabbed me and wrapped his arms around my waist, backing me up. "Show is over people," he announced. When he knew I was out of danger, he turned to face Heather. I expected him to help her up, but he leaned down closer to her. "I told you before that we were fucking done. Stay the fuck away from me and from my girl, you stupid bitch!"

He referred to me as 'his girl'. Squeee!

His strong hands wrapped around my waist again as he

pulled me close. "I am so sorry about her. She just doesn't give up. I tried to end things so many times, even before Van found out about us."

I was shocked. "She's who you cheated on Van with?" *I hadn't put two and two together.*

He nodded and looked ashamed. "When I threatened to end things, she threatened to tell Van all about us. At the time, I thought I still had a chance. That night was when I found out. We hooked up after that a couple of times, but only because I was so lonely, and honestly, she was always offering."

"Maybe she's in love with you."

"I don't give a shit how she feels. It was never anything but sex for me. I have never felt anything for her. She puts herself out there with no self respect for herself. That is pathetic."

I looked past Ty and noticed that Heather was being comforted by a few other girls. She had ruined the hot moment between Ty and I, but part of me felt sorry for her. I knew why she wanted him for herself, because I wanted him too.

"Maybe we should just head out of here. I think we have caused enough drama for the night," I suggested.

He grabbed my hand and kissed it. "I'm sorry I suggested playing around. I didn't bring you here to make you almost fight with a girl that can't take a hint."

The animosity in his voice was different than the Ty I was used to. He definitely had no feelings for that girl at all. If there were ever a doubt in my mind about him with the girls from the other night, it was gone. That was her last attempt to get him to succumb to her. She had failed because of me then, and because of me tonight. No wonder she hated my guts.

We held hands to walk out to the car. He didn't bother saying goodnight to his friends, just gave them a quick wave as we exited the frat house. He walked to my side of the car and opened the door for me. It broke my heart to let go of his hand. Our little pretend relationship was officially over, there was nobody left to make jealous.

As he started the car and began our journey home, my swollen lips reminded me of our hot kisses. Unknowingly, I reached up and touched them, closing my eyes and playing out how awesome it had all felt and how hot it made me. Before I was finished reliving it all in my mind, I felt the car pull over. I opened my eyes to Ty staring at me. "I lied."

I turned my body to mimic his position. "About what?"

He took my hands and held them. "Just promise me that this won't change our friendship if I tell you."

I nodded. "Tell me what, Ty?"

"Oh fuck, this is harder than I thought," he shook his head.

Seeing his frustration I gripped his hands harder. "Is this about Heather?"

"Hell no!" He scrunched up his face. "Just tell me one thing. Did you want to kiss me tonight?"

He was calling me out. My lips were aching for his touch, but I was so afraid of admitting my desire for him. "Ty, I......."

He interrupted me and started shaking his head. "I knew it. I knew I fucked up our friendship. GOD DAMMIT!" His fist went into the steering wheel and he jumped out of the car in the pitch black of the night.

I jumped out and followed him toward the back of the car. "Ty please calm down." I grabbed his hand to get him to look at me.

"No, just let me calm down. I am just so pissed I ruined our friendship. I should have never thought I could trick you like that."

Trick me? "What do you mean?"

"Don't act like you don't know what I did Miranda. I wanted you to play that pretend game because I wanted to be the guy who was touching you tonight. You have to know how fucking hot you are. You flaunt that body of yours in front of me and I feel like I need to take a million cold showers to relieve the ache I have for you. I wanted you for so long, even back when I visited

Kentucky. That night at that bar when we were dancing, I was so
pissed when that girl came between us. I could have sworn there
was something between us back then, but everything happened
and you stopped talking to me. I just …… I saw an opportunity and
I took it. Now I ruined our friendship over a couple of damn kisses
and a set of blue balls."

Blue balls….

He thought I was mad at him. He thought he was playing
me.

I thought I was playing him.

Ty wanted me. He wanted me for so long.

"I lied to you too."

He looked up at me with a questionable look. "About
what?"

"I lied when I said we were just friends. I only agreed
because I thought that is all I was to you. I know how much you
love Bella and I just thought you were bein' nice to me."

His mouth dropped open. "Every second I spend with you
makes me want you more." He kissed me softly and then pulled
away. "I have never wanted someone like the way I want you
right now."

A car passed and honked at us before either of us realized
how ridiculous we were dressed, standing out on the dark road.
Our hands were entwined together and his thumbs were stroking
mine. "Take me back to your place and show me how much," I
taunted him.

It was going to be good and we both knew it.

We made a beeline for the car and once we were inside,
Ty pulled back onto the road. His hand reached for my thigh and I
used my hand to slide it further up underneath my plastic skirt. It
didn't take him long to figure out that my plastic outfit didn't
come with panties. He let out a moan as his fingers traced the
smooth skin between my legs, getting a hint of how ready I was
for him. He started to swerve off the road. "Holy shit, you are so

wet." I giggled when I felt the car speedin' up.

"In a hurry Ty?"

"Baby, you have no idea how much I want to pull over and fuck you right in this car," he admitted.

I bit my lip and imagined him taking me in the backseat, or how I could maneuver my body to straddle him while he drove. "Please hurry or I might let you," I said as I leaned over and stroked his leg.

"I can't wait to rip that shit off of your skin." He touched the plastic around my waist.

"Mmmm. I can't either." I slid my tongue over his ear lobe and pulled it with my teeth. "I like it rough Ty."

"Shit! You are killing me right now. I want you so bad. You have no idea how long I have wanted to do this."

I ran my hand up his chest and found his nipple in between my fingers. I pinched it as I ran my tongue up his neck. He liked it dirty and I knew just the things to say. "I am so hot for you Ty."

"My dick is throbbing. If you keep talking like that I am going to come in this fucking cone."

We hit the dirt and gravel driveway and almost swerved into the field he was driving so fast. We pulled up to the carriage house and ran toward the door. Before he even had it open, our lips had met. He flipped on the light and pushed me against the wall. "Stand right here while I find some scissors."

I drug my teeth against my lip watching Ty walk toward the kitchen. I wanted to touch every inch of his body. *This was really happening.*

He brought the scissors over and slid them between my breasts gently, making a point not to scrape me with them. "I have waited so long to see these perfect tits."

I was breathing hard as he slowly cut through the plastic. Even after he cut through it, it still stuck to my skin. He dropped the scissors and cupped my breasts with both of his hands, then slowly pulled the plastic away, revealing my naked mounds to his needy eyes. My nipples were so hard and I wanted nothing more than to watch him kiss and suck them.

I watched Ty's mouth open as he took as much of my breast in his mouth as he could fit. He pulled away and circled my nipple with his tongue, while squeezing the other nipple in between his fingers. I was trying to watch his tongue move around, but the first burst of waves started shooting between my legs causing me to throw my head back against the wall. I had never had an orgasm from just having someone play with my breasts, but as he continued to pinch and lick them, the desire between my legs heated with fire and I felt myself convulsing right in front of him.

He looked up at me, realizing what had just happened. "I swear that has never happened before."

Ty's mouth was on mine again and I felt his tongue breaking the threshold to my mouth, sliding against mine. I loved the way he stroked his tongue over mine. His hand started at my nipple and then worked its way down to my waist. He tugged at the plastic skirt and when nothing happened, he broke our kiss and started ripping it to shreds. I wiggled my way out of the rest of it and then leaned back as he took in my whole naked body. I tried to squeeze my legs together, knowing how wet I was for him, but his hands came down and slid between my folds, separating them while he circled my sensitive spot. "You want me so bad," he said out loud.

"Does that turn you on Ty? Are you ready to fuck me?" I teased.

I could feel him trying to pull the caution tape and cone from his body. "You have no idea how bad I want you. Give me a minute to get this shit off of me. I will meet you in the bedroom." He kissed me one more time before heading toward the bathroom.

Chapter 18
Tyler

The last thing I wanted to do was leave Miranda standing there naked while I ran to disassemble my costume from my aching dick. I fought with that shit ass Duct tape, even taking some of my own skin as I ripped it away from my body. I still couldn't believe this was happening. Once I got everything off of me, I looked down at my throbbing cock and considered beating off so that I could last longer out there for my first time with Miranda. I wanted it to be perfect and just hearing her talk dirty made me want to come.

I couldn't remember ever wanting anyone the way I wanted Miranda. She was so fucking sexy to me and everything about her turned me on. It didn't help that I was crazy about her. I had fought this attraction for too long.

As I made my way into the bedroom, all I saw was Miranda sprawled out across the bed, waiting for me. Her hand came up as her index finger motioned me to approach her. She bit her lip as I got closer and I noticed her staring at my dick. I slid my hands up her legs as I climbed onto the bed. Her bare pussy was so close to my face that I drug my chin against it as I made my way up her body. The funny thing was that I had never liked going down on a woman, but I was so turned on that I stopped moving and pressed my lips against her little clit. I was so tempted to taste what I thought would never have been mine. She cried out as I sucked it into my mouth and stroked her folds with my tongue. I couldn't stop myself. The more I licked and sucked on her sensitive little pussy, the more she cried out.

I wasn't used to making a girl come and definitely not twice, in fact normally I only cared about getting myself off. The more she screamed out in pleasure the more turned on I got myself.

She was so wet and as I brought my face up to her breasts

I was dragging her sexiness all over her stomach. I know she could feel it too, even after I had taken her nipple into my mouth again. I wanted to lick them and suck on them until she cried out my name again. When I finally reached her mouth, she cupped my face and shoved her lips against mine, kissing me even harder than before. I felt her tongue against my lips and I knew she could taste herself.

Her hand slid down and found my hard cock. She moaned against my mouth as she began to stroke my girth. "Do you want it in my mouth?" She asked in between kisses.

"As much as I do, I want to slide inside of you more." I admitted.

I slid over the edge of the bed and reached into my drawer to grab a condom. Miranda backed away and watched as I slid it down my fully erect dick. I was rock hard and ached to be inside of her pussy. I kissed her again while I positioned myself over her. I took my hard shaft and teased her clit with it. "Oh Ty…."

"Say it again." I kept running my cock over her little swollen clit. She was using her legs to pull me closer, but I fought her, just knowing she was so turned on.

She took her fingers and stroked the tips of her nipples. "Please fuck me Ty."

She was so wet that I let go of my cock and slid right inside of her. I had never been with someone that had a child, but you definitely couldn't tell. She was tight and with every stroke I wanted to explode. The friction of driving myself deeper into Miranda was like semen-surged torment. I felt Miranda's fingernails ripping into my back as she bucked her body into mine, matching my thrusts.

Her tongue slid across my lips twice before she let me kiss her. Kissing her was too much and I had to keep taking breaks from moving to keep from going too soon. Miranda used her legs and flipped us around so that she was on top. Her perfect tits started bouncing as she moved her body up and down. She played with her nipples, teasing me while I watched her. The harder she grinded herself into me, the faster I felt my release coming. I grabbed her hips and held her still while I finally exploded.

Miranda collapsed on my chest and kissed my nipples while I tried to catch my breath. "Let me know when you are ready for round two." She whispered before heading into the bathroom.

Holy shit!

After removing the condom, I fell back on the bed and must have fallen asleep, because I woke to Miranda climbing into bed next to me. She smelled of fresh soap and had a wet head. She started to lay on the opposite side of the bed, but I reached over and grabbed her by the waist, pulling her into my chest. "I think I missed you," I whispered.

"I think you were snoring," She joked.

I reached around and cupped her breast into my hand. "I am sleeping like this all night."

She took my hand and pulled it off of her breast, guiding it down between her legs. I let her hand guide my fingers into circular motions over her clit. She moaned as she continued doing it. I rubbed my growing shaft over her ass, showing her that what she was doing was working, of course she already knew it would. I pulled my hand away and turned her around to face me. I took my hand and ran it in between her breasts and down her stomach. "I think you're beautiful."

"Does that mean you're ready for round two?"

Damn.

I smiled and kissed the side of her mouth. "I am considering it, you little nympho." I was more than considering it.

"You of all people shouldn't complain about my love for sex," She said sarcastically as she traced the skin around my nipple.

"You are so aggressive. I think I am scared of what you

might do to me next. I am a fragile specimen you know," I teased.

"Actually, it's funny that you mention it. I want to have a little fun of my own if you can handle it."

Okay, now I was scared!

"What kind of fun are we talking about?"

"Close your eyes and give me your hands." She was very serious.

I must have been crazy, because I closed my eyes and did as I was told. I felt something wrapping around my wrist and opened my eyes to see a very naked Miranda wrapping caution tape around my wrists. "Are you fucking kidding me?"

"Shut up and let me have some fun with you. Stop being a pussy."

She got my hands fastened somehow to the headboard and climbed on top of me. She reached up and covered my eyes with a shirt so I couldn't see what she was doing. I tried to shake it free, but it wouldn't slide off. "Seriously, you are kind of freaking me out," I admitted.

"Shhh, calm down." I felt something cold touch my nipple and move around. After I felt the dripping I realized it was ice. She had planned this.

I cringed at first, but then it started to feel good. "See, it's nice isn't it?"

I nodded my covered head. She pulled the ice away and I could hear her chewing on it. Her hands ran up and down my thighs and I could feel her breath between my legs. I knew she was down there, but she never touched me.

Then I felt something freezing on the tip of my shaft. I retracted my body at the shock of it. "Whoa!"

The coldness traveled all the way down my shaft causing me to get goose bumps all over my body. I felt hands gripping the base as the coldness began to subside revealing soft lips rising and lowering over my cock. Miranda didn't go slow, in fact she didn't take her time at all. Her grasp became loosened and she bobbed her head up and down quickly while stroking me in a varied rhythm. The combination of her mouth and her hands, added to the fact that I couldn't see anything felt so good. Her opposite hand began massaging my balls while she sucked my dick even harder. Just when I thought that it might be possible for me to come again so soon, she lifted off of me, almost appearing as if she left the room. I didn't feel her moving on the bed and I couldn't hear her breathing. When I was about to call out her name, I felt the bed shift.

She removed the shirt from my face and leaned down to kiss me. As she pulled away she shoved one of her tits in my face. "Do you like these the most?"

I tried to catch her nipple with my tongue. "I like the way your nipples feel on my tongue."

She kept coming within inches of my tongue, never letting me make contact. "You want to touch them don't you?"

"Please let me," I begged.

She pressed them both together and pinched them in between her fingers. Then she took her finger and wet it in her mouth, just to be able to run it over her nipples. "This turns me on so much." She continued playing with them within inches of my reach.

I could actually feel my mouth watering as I watched her. She started massaging both of them and then, like heaven opened up and let me have a peek, she pushed one up and licked her own fucking nipple. "Oh fuck yeah! Do it again." I bit down on my lip as I watched her wiggle her tongue over her erect nipples one at a time.

She started grinding herself into my stomach and I could feel her getting wet again. The idea that she was still so turned on, even after a shower, made me hornier than before. I wanted to free my hands and touch every inch of her body. She was making me crazy.

"What do you want me to do now Ty?"

"Baby, I don't care what you do to me, but I have got to be able to touch your fine ass. Please let me have my hands, I promise that I will let you have free reign."

Miranda laughed. Her lips found mine and as our tongues began to mingle, I felt her releasing my restraints. I immediately reached around to her flawless ass and squeezed her cheeks in my hands.

"Turn around. I want to watch your ass while I am fucking you," I ordered.

Miranda seemed to get off on the dirty talk, which in turn, got me off. She was down on her hands and knees and if I thought she was fucking perfect from the front, well it was the same case in the back. I ran my hand all over her ass cheeks and started to dive right in. Realizing I hadn't applied protection, I reached over for the nightstand.

"I get the shot Ty. I can't get pregnant for two more years. I haven't been with anyone for over a year now, if you are worried about that."

I always used protection before and I don't know why I didn't just grab a condom, but I drove myself right into that pretty pussy. She let out a loud moan every time I thrust in and out. I used her hips to pull her deeper.

"Please don't stop Ty. Ohh, it feels so good..."

I leaned over and grabbed both of her tits, squeezing her nipples while I fucked her. I let one of her tits free and grabbed the headboard, using it to thrust myself even faster into Miranda. I could feel the walls of her pussy tightening around my dick. I knew she was coming. She was crying out my name and I just lost it.

I collapsed on top of her back and caught my breath. I kissed her back before slowly sliding down next to her. "That felt so good."

She was laying on her stomach facing me, while I was on my back. Her finger traced the skin on my chest. "It did."

I grabbed her hand and kissed it. "I could have had that months ago?"

She shrugged and smiled. "Yeah, but we are even better friends now and neither of us is on the rebound. It's just us."

"I haven't asked anyone to be my girlfriend since I was fourteen years old, but after the way I felt tonight at the party and now this, I don't think I can handle it if we were still just friends."

She scooted her body over and put her head on my chest. "I don't think we have ever just been friends. I've wanted you to kiss me for so long. I just thought I was just a friend."

"Have you ever looked in the mirror at yourself? Do you have any idea how gorgeous you are? Do you have any idea how hard it was for me to tell your family that I didn't want anything from you besides your friendship, when all I could think about was touching you?"

She ran her tongue over my nipple and then kissed it. "So was I worth the wait?"

I let out a cackle. "And then some. I've have never been with anyone like you before. You are fucking amazing."

"So are you."

I leaned down toward her face. "Can I get one more kiss before I close my eyes?"

I was exhausted and with her in my arms, I felt like I could fall right to sleep, but I had to just feel her lips one more time before I did.

It wasn't a soft peck. Instead, Miranda kissed me with her mouth open and let me skim my tongue across hers before pulling away. "Goodnight Ty."

I wrapped both of my arms around her back and held her close. "Promise me that when I wake up, you will be right here. I am still thinking this was all the best dream I ever had."

"I promise."

After hearing her words, I let my eyes close and fell asleep with the most amazing girl sprawled across my chest. I couldn't remember feeling so satisfied and happy all at the same time.

Chapter 19
Miranda

When I woke up, Ty's arms were still wrapped around me. I still couldn't believe that all of this had happened. The truth was that I had wanted it for so long. I had to admit that I never thought it was going to happen. All of the signals were there, but neither of us had the nerve to act on them. If it hadn't been for Ty's plan he had concocted at the party, it still wouldn't have happened.

I didn't know what to think about us hooking up. I had fantasized about it for so long, but hadn't thought about what would happen after we did. I had a child to think about, so having random hook-ups was just not an option for me. I had to put her before everything else.

But this was Ty.

He had been a part of her life since the day she was born. He loved her.

He was also one of my best friends and now I was so afraid that somehow we had damaged that friendship. Maybe not today or tomorrow, but at some point I would have to go home and Ty would stay here. How could I imagine a future for us when it just wasn't possible?

I felt Ty's arms tightening around me and looked up to see him smiling back at me. "Hey."

"Hi."

He smiled and started rubbing my back. "I was afraid to open my eyes, on account of last night just being the best dream ever."

I giggled. "It wasn't a dream. Trust me. I was there."

"Yeah, I remember." Ty reached down and kissed my head. "You were…..my god you were so hot last night. I couldn't get enough of you."

I let my hands slide down under the sheets and felt his

morning girth. "I am right here if you want some more."

Normally I would have worried about my hair or breath, but Ty was so different. He pulled my body up and planted his lips right on mine. Before he could do anything further, we heard a knock at the door.

"Oh shit! It's probably your mom telling us that Bella is giving her a hard time," I suggested.

Ty jumped up and started putting his boxers on. "Damn, I promised her if she watched Izzy that we would go to church with her and my dad."

"Why didn't you tell me?"

I jumped up and watched as he started putting on a pair of khakis he found in his closet.

"I will stall them, just get dressed as fast as you can," he stated as he pulled a shirt over his head, kissed me and walked out of the room.

I heard him opening the door and talking to his mom while I ripped clothes out of my bag, looking for something appropriate to wear. I hadn't actually had time to plan about places I might have to go or people that I needed to impress. Everything was all so sudden. Thank God I found a skirt and a sweater that at least looked presentable. I went over to the dresser and grabbed a brush. My hair was a mess from getting out of the shower and jumping right into bed. It didn't help that I was rolling around on pillows half the night. I finally gave up and threw it in a messy bun. After brushing my teeth, I made it outside in less than ten minutes. Ty winked at me like we had a big secret and I couldn't help but smile.

He already had Bella and was taking her back inside to get changed. I followed behind him. "Wait! I will get her dressed."

"Okay, I was just trying to help."

"Sorry," I shook my head. "You know I hate mornings."

I continued to get Bella changed while Ty grabbed a couple things to add to her diaper bag. Luckily his parents weren't ready to leave, they were just giving us time to get the baby ready. I was able to primp a little more and add some makeup to my tired eyes.

We decided to follow his parents instead of switching car seats and also having to stay after church was over. Ty explained his mother would stay for hours at coffee hour, gabbing with her friends. I still wasn't awake, but he was kind enough to run in the house and fill a whole travel mug full of coffee. It was the little things like cups of coffee and helping with Bella that made me so crazy about him.

"I am so sorry about this morning. After everything that happened last night, it must have slipped my mind." He grabbed my thigh and gave it a squeeze.

I gave him a smile and grabbed his hand into mine. "You look really happy."

"You're the reason."

I felt my cheeks flush, but I didn't know what to say.

I realize that thinking about sex in a church was probably a horrible sin, but as the reverend discussed his lesson on unanswered prayers, lasts nights actions kept running through my mind. The lesson discussed praying for something to happen for so long and being so upset when God didn't answer them. He explained about a man who was involved with a woman all throughout high school. That woman went off to college and left him behind. He prayed and prayed to have her return so that they could have a life and a future together. After years of hoping he ended up meeting someone and falling in love. They were married and had three great children. After being married for twenty years, the woman from his past came back into town and tried to rekindle their relationship, even though the man was married. Despite her attempts the man realized that because of his unanswered prayers he was already with his real true love.

I thought about all of the times I prayed for Tucker to change and want us to be a family and how those prayers were never going to be answered. Then I looked over to Ty, with Bella on his lap, and my hand in his. My heart felt so full of love. Last night wasn't a one night stand and Ty wasn't using me for sex while I was here. This was much more than that to him. Him protecting me and feeling jealous when other people looked at me, he obviously wanted me to be just his.

Bella was exceptionally well behaved during service and even more so when a bunch of nosey people noticed that Ty and I were there together and I had a child. I had no clue what they were thinking or saying about me, but Ty never let go of Bella, or my hand, even after we got outside of the church.

"So we have exactly five hours before dinner will be ready," Ty said as we headed out of the church parking lot.

"What are we havin' for dinner?"

"Mom always makes something big on Sunday's. It's a family tradition."

"I don't want to keep imposin' Ty."

He pulled the car over slowly and put it in park. After taking my hand and kissing it, he looked me right in the eyes. "You know we should have been a couple for months now. If it wasn't for your cock block brother, it would have happened sooner. Now, I can't change the past Miranda, and maybe waiting all these months gave us the time to get our heads on right, but now that the cat is out of the bag, I'm not holding back. I am crazy about you and I want you to be a part of my life. I don't want this to be temporary. I am sorry if you think I am rushing, but dammit, I have never felt so happy before and I'm not about to let it go."

I honestly didn't know whether to laugh or cry. I just sat there, staring at him.

"Please say something, baby, you're making me nervous."

I looked down at our intertwined hands and started to tear up. I was far from sad, but after everything that I thought I wanted for so long, I realized it was finally happening. "This is usually the time where I tell you that I have a baby and if you can't handle that, then we probably shouldn't see each other anymore, but since you love my child almost as much as I do, I think we can skip that conversation," I joked. It was the best I could do. I think I was still in shock.

"Does this mean I don't have to sleep at my parents anymore?" He teased.

"I guess it does."

He leaned over and kissed me full on the lips. "Then don't fight me about family dinners."

"I wasn't fightin' you. I just don't want to be needy."

He started pulling back on the road. "You can need me all you want. I'm not kidding Miranda, I am tired of being alone. Spending the past few days with my two favorite girls has made me the happiest I have been in over a year. Waking up next to you this morning was fantastic, even with your wild hair."

I rolled my eyes. "Should I cut it?"

"Hell no! Sometimes I need to be able to grab it."

We both started laughing.

Sunday dinner turned into late night cards. Ty and his parents entertained me with stories of Ty when he was younger and things that Bella had done while they were babysitting. Before we got ready to head back over to the carriage house, I headed into the kitchen to help his mother with getting everything cleaned up.

She smiled when she saw me coming in the room. "My son is smitten over you."

I smiled and grabbed the dish towel to start drying. "If I can be honest, I am pretty crazy about him too."

She turned the water off and looked directly at me. I actually felt scared. "Ty has been through Hell this past year and one thing that has always put a smile on his face is when he talks about you and that little girl. I know that you are only supposed to be here for a short time, but I have to ask that you will consider his feelings in all of this. I'd hate to see him heartbroken again."

"Mrs. Mitchell..."

"It's June or Mom, not Mrs. Mitchell when it's family dear."

"Sorry, June, I ...well Ty and I just started whatever this is between us, but I can promise you that I have no plans of hurtin' him. I really care about him. I have for a long time."

She shook her head. "I can tell. I just know my son and I have never seen him look at anyone like he does you, not even Van." She reached over and touched my chin. "Do you hear what I am saying?"

No! Say what you mean in English.....

"Yes, Ma'am."

"When you first came here I thought he was getting in over his head, but after I saw him with the two of you, I realized he was already starting to fall in love. You are good for him Miranda, you and Bella."

Love? He couldn't love me....

I had been here for three days and already been accepted by his parents. Ty made it clear that we were a couple. I felt his arms wrapping around me before I could answer his mother. "You ready to head over. I need to go to bed so I can get up for work tomorrow."

Ty let go of my waist to grab Bella and after he had walked away, I reached over and hugged his mother. "I won't break his heart, I promise," I whispered.

She gave me a smile and grabbed my hands. "Do you want to go into town tomorrow? I have to grab some groceries and a few other things."

"That would be great. I will see what we need over there and make my own list."

We said our goodbyes and finally headed back to the carriage house.

Surprisingly, Bella stayed asleep while we carried her and laid her down in the porta crib. Since Ty would clearly be sleeping in his bed with me, she needed to be comfortable herself. I wasn't really sure if I should take off my clothes or sleep in underwear, or put on a big shirt, so I sat on the edge of the bed and waited to see what Ty was wearing. He stripped out of everything except his boxers and climbed into bed. "What's wrong?"

"I guess I am not used to sleepin' next to someone who just wants to sleep."

Maybe that sounded weird.

"I really hate that you have never been appreciated by a boyfriend before. Get into something comfortable and climb in here next to me. " He patted the bed beside him.

I stripped down to my underwear, while he watched and smiled, and climbed in beside him. He pulled me in closer and kissed the top of my head. "A real man makes his woman feel wanted and always keeps her safe. Close your eyes, baby."

I closed my eyes but I couldn't go to sleep right away. I kept thinking how at some point I would be expected to go home. I had basically committed myself to a relationship with Ty, one that I wanted more than anything, but I had no idea how it was ever going to work. At some point my brother was going to find out and he was going to kill him.

Then I started thinking about Ty's mother and how she thought he was already falling for me. Ty had never acted like this before with Van, I knew that for a fact. I just couldn't get why he wanted me, when nobody else ever had.

His gentle snores reminded me that I was in his arms, and for the time being, he was mine. I didn't know how long I could keep him, but I would do anything to stay this happy. I didn't care what anyone else thought of him, he was perfect to me.

Chapter 20
Tyler

I hated when my alarm went off indicating that I had to get up and get ready for work, especially since I had the most beautiful girl in the world sleeping in my arms. It was a good thing that she was such a heavy sleeper. I managed to get up and put on my entire uniform without waking her or Izzy. After using the bathroom to do everything else, I snuck over to my parents for a cup of coffee. The coffee at the auto shop was worse than my mothers and I never felt like stopping anywhere else.

The morning drug on forever and all I kept thinking about was my amazing weekend with Miranda. Looking back, I know that the timing had never been right for us before, but it still made me sad that we had wasted so much time already. Izzy was getting so big and I wished that I had been there more.

I caught myself daydreaming more than once and my boss was really getting on me to finish up an air conditioning job before the day was out. The customer had already waited an extra three days for the part to come in. I kept myself occupied on the task at hand until it was time for everyone to break for lunch. As I was walking out to the parking lot, I saw three familiar faces heading in my direction.

My mother, Miranda and Izzy smiled as I met them halfway in the parking lot. "What are you guys doing here?"

"I had to run into town and offered to bring Miranda with me," she explained.

Miranda held out a brown bag. "Your mom said that you really like this place so I got you lunch while we were there."

"Ty up!" Izzy held out her arms for me. I hated grabbing her in my dirty uniform, even though Miranda said it was okay. After giving her a fry, my mother finagled her out of my arms and walked her around.

I leaned over and kissed Miranda. "Thank you for lunch."

She nudged me in the arm. "Thank you for wanting me."

"Just to be clear, I think I have always wanted you, sexually of course. Curious at least," I added.

"You know I don't mean like that."

"I know and please don't thank me. This," I pointed from her to me, "is what I wanted. This is right."

"It feels so natural, almost like we have been together for a long time already," She agreed.

"I think all those late night phone calls helped us. We don't have to go through that getting to know each other phase." I took my sub out and started eating it. Miranda wrapped her arms into mine and put her head on my shoulder.

"That is true. I even knew what buttons to push when we got freaky. That was a plus."

She leaned in to kiss me. "Definitely a plus."

"Your mom really loves you." She changed the subject.

"Yeah, she obviously really loves you too. She never liked Van. You should have seen when everything went to shit. She kept telling me how she had told me all along Van was the wrong girl. The fact that she likes you amazes me." I didn't want to tell her that at first my dear mother had told me to stay clear of Miranda. That only lasted until they met Izzy.

"She helped me shop for you today. I am going to start making dinner during the week for us at the carriage house. She told me everything you like and don't like so that shouldn't be a problem."

She had no idea how depressing my life was before she walked back into it. I felt like I had died and gone to heaven.

"I hope you can cook good," I teased.

"I hope you like everything well done." She seemed pleased with her comeback.

I looked over and saw my mother putting Izzy in her car seat. Miranda must have noticed too because we both stood up. "I guess I will see you tonight?"

"Dinner will be ready for you."

"I feel like an old man."

"Am I an old lady?"

"I've seen you naked and you have no wrinkles....like none anywhere," I joked. "You going to give me a kiss so all these dick heads I work with can stop staring at my girl?"

Miranda wrapped her arms around me and slapped me with a very long, very tongue involved kiss that left nothing for the imagination. I heard whistling as our kiss broke and waited until they pulled away before walking back into the shop.

"Where'd you find that?" My boss asked.

"None of your damn business."

"Touchy! This one must be good in the sack," he implied. *You have no idea.....*

"Her name is Miranda. She's my girlfriend and I would appreciate it if you kept your thoughts to yourself."

"Hey guys, it looks like Ty here has finally found himself a keeper," he called out.

"It's about time. Is he pussy whipped already?" Someone yelled from the back.

I rolled my eyes and went back to my station, ignoring them for the rest of the day.

When I got off work it was starting to get dark. Pulling up to the farm and seeing the lights on at the carriage house really made me feel content. Walking in the door was even better. Izzy came running up to me grabbing on my legs while Miranda was busy getting the table set for the dinner she had ready. I still felt like I was in some kind of dream. A week ago I was coming home to an empty house. I didn't have a girlfriend and honestly I didn't know if I even wanted one, but from the moment Miranda walked in my door everything changed.

"Ty up." Izzy dangled between my legs. I pulled her up and gave her a big kiss on the cheek.

"Hey cutie. What did you and Mommy make for dinner. It

smells so good."

"We made you peach and thyme glazed pork chops with rice and broccoli." Miranda smiled like she had accomplished something tremendous.

I walked over and grabbed her for a hug. "I would have been fine with hot dogs and beans."

She kissed me slowly. "We can have that tomorrow."

"Or next week, cause you will still be here," I kissed her again. "or the week after..."

That is exactly what happened too. After three weeks had passed, we were happier than ever. During the week I would work and come home to the girls. We spent the weekends going places or just hanging out with my parents. Miranda fit in like she belonged with us and the longer we were together, the more sure I became. In a few short weeks everything about my life had changed and I never wanted it to go back to the way it was.

Van had called to talk to both of us several times, but we decided to keep our relationship a secret, to avoid the time bomb that would go off when our Kentucky family found out about us. She knew we were friends and that we hung out and that is where we left every conversation. Miranda's mother had been keeping tabs on Tucker's release. It hadn't happened as early as they first assumed, but he had been out for a couple weeks before they heard anything from him. The phone calls to Miranda's old phone started up and with those calls came the threats. The voice was muffled and the number was always blocked, but it was clear who was doing it. As much as her family hated it they knew she was safe staying at the farm.

Miranda and I had been trying to figure out how to keep her there for a longer period of time. At some point the verbal threats weren't going to be enough to keep her with me, so she had to either tell them we were together or find a different reason that she needed to stay. With the help of my mother, she found a salon in town that was looking for someone to fill in while their regular shampoo girl/receptionist was on maternity leave. It was just temporary but would give us two months without the family breathing down our necks. I had to give it to my mother. Not only did she keep our secret, but she welcomed Miranda and Izzy into our family, sometimes too much.

Even my father stepped in and suggested that we clean out the back of the carriage house, which was for storage and still had wooden garage doors on it, and finish it off to give Izzy her own room. His argument was that it increased the value of the property, but their desperate attempts to secure my happiness made me appreciate them. Who better than them to know how pathetic my life had become before the girls came into it.

Miranda's mother didn't take the news of her daughter wanting to stay here, but with her ex being such a threat, it worked to our benefit. They still video chatted and talked at least a few times a week.

My mother was all too happy to be able to watch Izzy three days a week while Miranda worked. The salon was on the same block as my shop so not only did we ride to work together, but I got to have lunch with the hottest girl in the world every single day she worked. The guys at the shop finally stopped giving her a hard time. Once they got used to seeing her all the time, they knew how serious we were.

Because things had become so serious, I had decided that I was going to give Miranda a romantic night out. Even with a little one running around, we got to spend time together, but it wasn't like we could run around naked having wild sex all night. Most of our alone time consisted of hot showers while Izzy napped or waiting until she fell asleep so we could quietly have sex.

It was a Friday and our official one month anniversary. My parents were taking Izzy for the night and Miranda and I had reservations at a little restaurant an hour away. She wore a red dress similar to the one she had worn months ago on the night that should have been ours. Of course she looked gorgeous and I couldn't take my eyes off of her. She had curled every strand of her long blonde hair in fancy ringlets. Her makeup was perfect and she smelled like heaven. I even wore a pair of dress pants and a black v-neck shirt. While Miranda was getting into the car, I ran back into the house and set up her surprise for when we returned. My father was going to set the rest of the things up once we were gone.

I had everything planned out. Our dinner was going to be perfect and when she got home she would be showered with attention. I had never felt this way about anyone and she needed to know that I was pretty damn sure that this was it for me.

Miranda seemed nervous on the ride to dinner. "You okay, baby?"

"I've never been to any place fancy before. Are you sure I look alright?"

We were already holding hands, in fact I never drove without her hand in mine. I pulled it up to my lips. "You are the most beautiful woman on this planet. You deserve to be taken to fancy places."

She leaned over and kissed me. "I can't believe that it's been a month already Ty. If I would have known that we would be this happy, I never would have held back my feelin's."

"All that matters is that we are together now."

Dinner was perfect. We had a candlelight corner table and Miranda looked so excited. Instead of sitting across from me, she scooted her chair closer to mine and I rubbed her leg under the table. She had no idea that her night had just begun and I wanted it that way. I had so much more planned.

On the way home from dinner, she cuddle up next to me as I drove. "Our dinner date was wonderful. Thank you Ty."

I kissed her head. "You're welcome, baby."

Her hand started sliding up my leg and stopped at the zipper to my pants. "I've never been so happy in my life," she whispered in my ear and then licked the lobe.

I felt her hands unzipping my pants and then one of her hands sliding inside. "Ahh." I was trying to focus on the road as she pulled out my cock and started stroking it with her hand.

She said nothing before unfastening her seat belt and dipping her head between my legs. I felt her take my erection into her mouth. "Jesus Miranda...."

I held the steering wheel with one hand and put my other hand on her head. It was extremely hard to keep my eyes on the road when Miranda was working her magic. No one had ever got me off the way she could. I finally had to pull over to the side of the road until she finished. I needed to close my eyes and enjoy it. We had a baby at home and blowjobs just weren't something that happened that often. Her mouth lingered over my erection even after I had finished. She slowly pulled away with a big smile on her face, like she had made some huge accomplishment. "Thanks again for our date Ty."

"You.Are.The.Girl.Of.My.Dreams."

She giggled as I pulled back on the dark road. I had sent my father a text telling him that we were on our way home before we had left the restaurant. He knew to wait a little while before he went over and got everything set up for me.

We pulled up and I jumped out of the car before Miranda and headed to open her door for her. "Let me get that for you."

"Thank you. We are home now. You don't have to impress me anymore," she said.

"I have a surprise for you." I covered her eyes and slowly walked her into the house and straight to the bedroom. Candles were lit around the room and my father had done a great job putting the rose petals all over the bed. A bottle of wine was chilling and chocolate covered strawberries were on the nightstand. I slowly removed my hands from her eyes.

Miranda put her hand over her mouth and her eyes filled with tears as she took everything in. "How did you do this?"

"I had some help."

She walked over to the bed and touched the real rose petals. "This is amazing."

"Sit down, baby." She followed my lead and sat down on the bed. I grabbed a strawberry and fed it to her. "Do you have any idea how happy you make me?"

She kissed me with her strawberry lips. "I have an idea."

"I get lost in you every single day. I love you so much." It wasn't how I planned on saying it, but there it was just flying out of my mouth like it couldn't stay unsaid any longer.

Her tear filled eyes looked directly into mine. I started to feel like I was going to pass out. "You love me?"

"I do. I have never loved anyone like I love you."

She lost it. She buried her head into my chest and started bawling. I held her tight, afraid that she didn't return the feelings and perhaps my sudden confession has just caused me to lose both her and Izzy. I couldn't speak. I just sat there holding her.

Finally when I was about to cry myself, she looked up at me. "Nobody has ever really loved me, not like this, not for real."

"This is real Miranda. I don't know why anyone couldn't love you, but it's their loss and my gain."

Even after I kissed her on the lips she still cried.

"Do you love me?" I needed to know. My heart was beating out of my chest and I felt like I couldn't breathe.

"Ty, yes I love you. I have wanted to say it so many times, but I didn't want to scare you away."

I ran my fingers over her cheek. "I'm not going anywhere, baby. Now stop crying and celebrate with me. I got you wine and chocolate and not to mention I planned on giving you one hell of a massage later."

She laughed and nestled her head into my neck. "I'm just so happy."

"Good. You deserve to be."

She looked up at me. "So do you."

"You really love me?"

She stood up and grabbed my hand, pulling me to stand with her. Miranda ran her fingers over my lips then pressed her mouth to mine. "I do." She brought her lips to my ear. "Make love to me Ty. I don't want to go fast tonight. I want to kiss every inch of your skin and look into your eyes when our bodies come together."

Chapter 21

Miranda

My body was trembling after Ty's confession. I had never been so overemotional, but as his fingers slid the straps to my dress off of my shoulders, I started shaking. Tears streamed down my eyes and it wasn't because I was sad or in any pain. I had never felt anything like this. I had Ty's heart, the one that he had never really given anyone, including Van. I couldn't react to his shocking confession. In the back of my mind I had always been comparing myself to her. I don't know how it happened. He came crashing into my life and never backed down. He'd never disappointed me and he adored my daughter. To everyone at home I had always been trash, but Ty never looked at me that way. Not once.

Passion filled kisses started at my neck and slowly made their way to the back of my shoulder, sending heated flames between my legs. I felt the zipper slide down my back and his hands free the dress from my body. As it fell to the floor I heard him gasp at the matching bra and thong I had picked out to surprise him. My surprise had nothing on his. "You are so beautiful," he whispered in my ear as his fingers traced over either of my ass cheeks.

"I know how much you love red," I said as I turned around to face him.

He licked his lips and ran his two pointer fingers over my breasts, until he hit the lace of my bra. "I do love red, especially when you're wearing it."

He kissed my neck and I tipped my head back. "Maybe I should wear it every day."

He slid both of my bra straps down my shoulders, making sure to kiss each one before sliding it down off of my breasts. I watched him taking in my naked breast, licking his lips before meeting my gaze. He stared into my eyes as he reached behind me and released the hook, allowing the bra to drop to our feet. His lips pressed between my breasts and kissed the skin. I felt his tongue sliding down to my stomach until he reached the base of my panties. Ty kissed my underwear directly where I was ready for him underneath. His hands seized either side of the elastic as he pulled them down and off my legs. He stayed there on his knees running his hands up my thighs and then back to my ass. I was hot for him as I watched him taking in every inch of me.

He stood up and backed me up onto the bed before removing his shirt and dropping his pants to the floor. I was wondering why he kept his boxers on until he grabbed a bottle of lotion laying on the bed. Ty turned me around to lay on my stomach and I felt the cold lotion being dispersed over my back. At first it was cold, but then I felt his hands rubbing it around. He started at my shoulders, slowly kissing all over each part of skin that he finished. He worked magic on my upper back and let his fingers slide over the sides of my breasts.

When Ty got to my lower back I could feel him rubbing his erection over my ass, as if to remind me that this was not just for me to relax. Once he got to my ass it was obvious that it was his favorite part of the massage. He gripped both cheeks and lathered up the lotion to provide to a slippery service. He circled his hands around my butt and down my thighs, letting his fingers gently touch the heat between my legs. When he got to my feet, he turned me around. I watched as he sat on his knees and placed one leg at a time on his shoulders, massaging each foot separately.

He paid attention to what he was doing, but I caught his eyes lingering around my naked body. I continued to tremble in ecstasy. While his hands moved slowly up my legs, my breathing got heavier knowing he was inches away from my sex. He sensed my anticipation and teased me at my thighs before placing soft kisses where I was burning for him. I felt his tongue on me and started to shudder as the heat intensified. I was so hot from his touching me that when his tongue hit that most sensitive spot I cried out in pleasure. "Ohhh! Please. Don't. Stop."

Ty grabbed my ass and continued licking as my body finally began to quake. He let his lips linger over my sex, giving me shivers. Finally, he moved his lips up to my stomach and then each breast. He kissed each nipple before our mouths made a happy reunion. I could taste my orgasm as I kissed his lips and it got me even hotter.

I wanted him to spin me around and drive himself right inside, but Ty took his time. We were making love, which was something I wasn't very good at doing. I had never been with someone that took their time. I guess I had never been with someone that really loved me.

I felt Ty's hands sliding between my legs and I opened them to make it easier. "You are so wet, baby." His fingers slid right in and the friction was causing me to push my hips into him. "Tell me you want me."

It was hard to speak when Ty had two fingers inside of me and his other hand was pinching my nipple. "I...I want you Ty."

"Oh, I can tell you do. It's so hot."

Just hearing him talk about it made me want to scream. Thank goodness he finally positioned himself over me and slid his whole girth deep inside of me. Ty rocked in and out of me with a slow precision that I also wasn't used to. The slower he went the more I screamed out in pleasure. His movements made everything more intense. I watched as the sweat trickled down his chest and he never took his eyes off of mine. I wanted to close my eyes and bite down on my lip, but he kept kissing me, driving his tongue over mine then pulling away to see my expression. He moved the hair out of my face and buried his head into my neck as I felt him tightening, then eventually collapsing his hot body over mine.

As if that wasn't just the best thing I had ever experienced, he rolled over, pulling me with him. He looked directly into my eyes. "I love you Miranda."

"And I love you Tyler."

Most of the small tea lights had already burned out, but Ty got up and blew them all out before coming back to bed. He grabbed the wine and worked to get it open, while I reached over for the tray of strawberries. He had his feet hanging off the bed so I climbed up behind him on my knees. I held one up to his mouth and watched his perfect teeth bite down on it. He looked so sexy doing it that I was already wanting to have him touching me again.

When he finally got the darn cork out, he took a big drink from the bottle. "Now that is classy," I teased.

I reached my arms around his back and hugged him. "You keep pressing the twins against my back and I will have to show you what my version of classy looks like."

"That sounds like a promise."

He turned to face me. "Let's get a bath."

"That tub is not big enough for both of us."

He reached his arms out as he stood up. "We will make it work. Bring the wine."

In order for the bubble bath to work, Ty had to get in first while the water ran. In fear of it overflowing, I scooted myself between his legs with my back against his chest. The bubbles filled the tub as Ty reached around and ran the soap all over my wet body. We took turns hitting the bottle of wine until the thing was empty.

This was another first for me. Having someone sit in the tub, washing my body with such gentleness. When he was finished, he wrapped his arms around my chest and held me until the water started to get cold. I had started to drift off when he stood up and grabbed me a towel, wrapping me up before getting one for himself.

"You ready for a sundae?" He asked as we walked out of the bathroom.

"I'm not really hungry."

"Will you at least watch me eat some?" There was something loaded in his question.

"I guess."

He let his towel drop to the floor and pulled mine off, before pulling my naked body into the kitchen. Before I could react, he lifted me up onto the counter and turned to the refrigerator. He handed me chocolate syrup, cherries and cool whip and then turned around to face me. "You forgot the ice cream."

Ty put one hand on either side of my legs. He kissed my neck and then my chin. "No I didn't."

"Yes you did." I pointed to the items on the counter. He grabbed the chocolate and poured some on his finger. I gasped when the freezing cold chocolate hit my nipple. He laughed as he started doing the same thing to the other side. "You are crazy."

He leaned down and sampled the chocolate on one of my nipples. "Only for you, baby."

"Holy hell! It's freezing."

"That is a contradiction my beautiful girlfriend. Now lay back so I can hook this shit up."

"What do you mean?"

He gently pushed me to lay down on the whole counter. I felt like an idiot just laying there naked, well, that was until he started making it very enticing.

Ty filled my belly button with maraschino cherries. He used half a can of cool whip between my legs and I could feel the chocolate syrup drizzle down there, as I started laughing in hysterics. He covered both of my breasts with cool whip and added one cherry to each side, then stood back like he had created a masterpiece.

"Why did we even take a bath?"

"It was on my to do list," he said confidently.

"Are you just going to look?"

His eyes roamed from my breasts to my crotch. "I don't know what I want first." He leaned down and filled his mouth with one of my breasts. When he pulled away his face was covered in whipped topping. "This is the best sundae I ever had."

No sooner had Ty dove into his food concoction between my legs, did a knock come from the door. He stood up covered in chocolate and whipped topping and in walked Van.

"Miranda, are you in ....OH MY GOD!" She turned her eyes away from us. "Jesus, what did I just walk in to? Holy shit!"

"Just let us get dressed and we can explain," I begged as I tried to stand up without dessert toppings running all over the floor. Ty just stood there in front of me. In the midst of being caught by his ex, a potential snitch to our secret romance, he leaned over and kissed me, then took my hand and led me into the bedroom.

I tried to towel off the stickiness, but I knew I would have to shower. Ty got dressed and waited for me without saying a single word. A part of me worried that maybe he would regret our relationship now that she knew about us. I was so afraid to face her, especially since Ty and I had been lying to her for a month.

He took my hand and walked into the living room. She stood over us and paced back and forth. "How long has this been going on?"

"Does it really matter?" Ty said rudely.

"How could you two get involved knowing what it would do to the family? Do you have any idea how pissed they are going to be? This is exactly what Conner was afraid of. You two can't have casual sex and think it will be okay."

"There is nothing casual about this." Ty was confidant and he never let go of my hand. Van stopped pacing and looked at both of us.

"What are you saying? You are in some kind of relationship? Now isn't that a joke." She started laughing.

Ty squeezed my hand and I knew he was getting pissed. "It

ain't a joke. Miranda and I are together, like for real together and I am in love with her."

Van's eyes got really big and she looked from Ty then back to me. I was still speechless. Her and I were friends, but she was also his ex.

"That is impossible. I know you Ty. You can't be in a relationship."

"Well things change Van. The past year has been Hell for me. I lost everything. Do you have any idea how many nights I sat alone wishing I could just end my life? The only thing that put a smile on my face was Isabella. Miranda and I had become good friends and after the last visit, when you all sent me away, I knew there was something between us. When she showed up at my door and we were forced to be alone I couldn't fight my feelings for her anymore. Once I knew she felt the same way, we never looked back. We have been living together for the past month. "

Van finally sat down. I don't know if she could see it in my eyes, or the fact that it all made sense, but she just sat there. She turned back to Ty. "How do you know you love her? You told me the same thing for years. I think you are confusing sex for love."

He gave me a smile before answering Van. "Look Van, I am not trying to hurt you, but what you and I had was just a puppy kind of love. I cared about you and I wanted to believe that you would be the one for me, but be honest, you and I both know it wasn't real love." He looked over to me and winked. "When Miranda walks into the room, my heart skips a beat. She's beautiful and confident and knows how to make me laugh. She's the best mother and always puts her daughter before anything. I love her smile and to be there for her when she needs to cry. When we are apart, I feel lost, like a part of me is missing. I've never felt this way in my life and there is no doubt in my mind that it's real."

Van started to tear up. She wiped her eyes and looked over at me. "Congratulations you tamed Ty. Now tell me how the hell you two are going to handle this when everyone else finds out? I won't have this ruin my wedding."

"Van, Ty and I are adults. Frankly it's none of their business. I don't understand why I am not allowed to be happy. Why is it so bad that I found someone that loves me and my daughter?"

"Because it's Ty." She started rubbing her temples.

"This is why we didn't tell you," I explained.

"Well I would have rather found out on the phone then walking in on Ty with his face between your legs."

"We are celebrating our one month anniversary actually. If you don't believe me you can check out the bedroom," Ty said sarcastically.

"No thank you! Jesus, this is not at all how I saw tonight going."

"Why are you here? Did they send you here for her, because she isn't leaving."

"No dumbass. I am trying to plan a wedding and since my mother, Brina, and now Miranda are all here, I flew in to go dress shopping. I left a message for Miranda this morning explaining everything. Obviously someone didn't check their messages."

I don't think Ty liked her attitude. He stood up and walked over to Van. "You really are being a bitch about this. It pisses me off that you get to be happy but we can't; like we aren't good enough to have happiness."

"Screw you Ty. I just think Miranda should know how you promised to love me forever while you had your dick in other girls."

I put my hands on my face and tried to block the two of them out.

"I fucked other girls because I was never satisfied with you. Get off your high horse and take some responsibility. You're the one who screwed my cousin in my fucking bed while I lay in the hospital."

"You were in the hospital because you got caught screwing Heather and stole a car when you were drunk. It was your fault."

I stood up and screamed. "STOP IT!" Ty and Van looked over at me. "We all know what happened. It isn't necessary to rehash things. Van is marrying Colt because she loves him and she deserves to be happy. We aren't going to let anyone know about us until after the wedding. You don't have to worry about it. And as far as Ty's cheating goes, well, I have to believe that he loves me enough to not do it. If it happens then he knows he loses me and Bella. I trust him, more than I trust anyone. He has never given me any reason not to. I've actually met Heather and I am pretty sure that little bitch knows he's taken."

Ty started laughing. "She thought Bella was my kid and it was part of the reason you left me."

Van put her hands over her face and shook her head. "This is so fucked up."

"Just spend time with us. I promise you will change your mind," Ty suggested.

Van stood up and grabbed her purse. "Brina dropped me off so I could get my car. She wanted me to invite you out tonight, but obviously I interrupted you. Just give me my keys and I will come back tomorrow when I know you will be dressed."

I walked her toward the door and handed her the car keys. "I have to grab the car seat."

We got outside and she finally turned around to face me. "Ty lies Miranda. I just want you to know that before you get your heart ripped apart. You are one of my best friends and soon to be cousin. I would hate to see you hurt."

She handed me Bella's seat and got into her car. "Are you going to tell on us?"

"Honestly, I wish I didn't know. I won't say anything."

"See you tomorrow." I watched her pull away, but her words haunted me. It took me forever to walk back into the house. I didn't want to doubt Ty, but maybe I was being a fool for thinking I could have a perfect life.

Chapter 22
Tyler

Of all the people in the whole fucking world, Van had to be the one to ruin my perfectly planned night with Miranda. To make matters worse, Miranda came back into the house like she had been slapped in the face.

"What happened?"

She shook her head and started cleaning up the mess in the kitchen. "It's nothin'."

I grabbed her and pulled her to face me. "What did she say to you, baby?"

She wouldn't look at me.

"Please talk to me," I begged.

"Let's just say that she warned me about you. She doesn't think I should believe everything you tell me." When she finally looked up I could tell she was crying.

"I don't lie to you Miranda. I swear that I love you and I have never thought about being with anyone else. You are all that I want. I will spend the rest of my life proving it to you if I have to."

She studied my face. "The rest of your life?"

I put my head against hers. "I don't fucking care what anyone else thinks about me. I am madly in love with you. I only want you. Our relationship is nothing like mine and Vans, you know that."

She finally wrapped her arms around me and I let out a sigh. "I love you too. I don't want to doubt you. She has her reasons for not believing you have changed."

"You changed me. You and Izzy. Do you really think I would risk losing this?"

She shrugged. She fucking shrugged. I let my arms drop and walked into the bedroom. After finding my phone in the pocket of my pants I handed it to her. "Just to start my lifetime of proving that you are all that I need, here is my phone. Take it. Keep it for as long as you want. Go through it. I deleted every girl's number the first night after we had sex. I haven't been on Facebook for months, but I will give you that password and you can delete anyone you want. I don't care if you delete the account. I have nothing to hide from you. The only secret that I ever had was that I wanted you and fell in love with you. I swear."

"Do you still have feelings for Van?" As much as I didn't want her to ask that, I knew it was coming. I deserved to be asked, after all, she was the one who had listened to me cry over her months ago.

I pulled her onto my lap on the couch. "I love three women. My mother, Izzy and you. Van is marrying my cousin and we grew up together. She was my first and I will always care about her, although right now I am pretty pissed off at her."

Miranda ran her hand over my face. "I have never felt this way and it scares me. It would kill me if I lost you. It would kill Bella."

"Baby, you aren't going to lose me. I swear to God that you are all that I ever want. Can't you just see how much I need you?" I held her so tight. She really was my everything. There had to be a way to convince her how serious I was. A way to prove to everyone that this wasn't temporary.

I knew exactly what I needed to do, but I would need my mother's help again. Miranda finally calmed down and we watched a movie before heading to bed. Our night had been so perfect. What was it with people just walking in my door? All of this could have been avoided.

I was so happy once I got the bed cleaned off and Miranda climbed into my arms. I needed to feel her there, especially now that she was having doubts about me. If I could take anything back about my past it would be that I cheated. Then again, if I hadn't I would have never been able to be with Miranda now. It all happened to get me exactly where I needed to be.

With Van being a ticking bomb, it was only a matter of time before Colt and Conner came beating down my door forcing her to go home. I wasn't about to let that happen. I needed to make sure there was no way they could keep us apart.

Miranda woke up in a much better mood. She showered me with kisses and talked me into getting a very long shower with her. There was no way I could resist a naked Miranda. I washed her hair and then every single inch of her body. As I lathered up her breasts she began stroking my dick with her hand. She teased me with her tongue, not letting me kiss her lips. It turned me on and she knew it. She pushed me back against the shower wall, before turning around and sticking her ass against my erection. To have a girl that offered doggy-style was like getting a diamond in a Cracker Jack box. As I thrust myself inside of her, she put her hands up on the opposite shower wall and pushed against me. The friction from the water combined with how wet she already was enabled me to hit it faster than usual. I grabbed her wet hair and heard her moaning and lost it. The visual of me behind her was burned into my head for the rest of the day and I think she knew it would be.

My mother had gotten up and made breakfast, so Van picked Miranda up for dress shopping while we were all still over there. Van and my mother spoke for only a few seconds. I did notice that my mother purposely hugged and kissed Miranda in front of Van. It was spiteful, but maybe in some way my mother knew that Van would spend the day filling Miranda with doubt. I walked outside with them and kissed Miranda like we were back in the shower. When she pulled away she patted the crotch of my pants. She knew it was good, hell she knew she was that good.

Once I watched them pull away, I sat back down with my mother. She knew things were about to get serious and gave me all of her attention. My dad took Izzy and headed outside to collect eggs. She loved chasing those chickens around.

"What's the matter?" She asked.

"Van walked in on us last night. It didn't go over very well."

"Well you don't want her back do you?"

I scrunched up my face. "Hell no, Mom. She got Miranda all upset, telling her that I couldn't be trusted and that I would eventually cheat."

"If she spent half a second with you two, she would know how crazy you are about each other."

I grabbed my mother's hands. "Mom, I need your help and your blessing."

She shook her head but still smiled. "I was wondering when you were going to have this talk."

"I need to have Grandma's ring changed. I know Van wore it for only a day, but I want Miranda to have something brand new. I know you have always wanted me to use that ring, so I was wondering if we could have some things added to it."

"I supposed that it can be done. You sure this is what you want? You won't just be committing to Miranda you know."

"I have never been more sure about anything in my entire life. I know it's fast and maybe if the circumstances were different I would wait years, but I can't lose them, Mom. It would kill me to be that far away from them."

If I would have known that Van was going to bust into my romantic night, I could have asked sooner. There was still a chance that Miranda would think this was all way too soon and quite frankly say 'no'.

I had to at least try.

"Well, you know that we love her already. Bella is the cutest little girl. I'd love for her to call me Mimi, like you used to call your grandma." She looked at me like her heart was full of love. My mother had never liked Van, so for her to be happy about Miranda and Izzy, she must have been excited.

"I have an idea of how I want to do it. Do you think we could call Mr. Harper at the jewelry store. I need to get this taken care of as soon as possible. Is he even open on weekends?"

While my mother got out the old phone book, I headed back to the house to grab my grandmother's ring. It was just plain white gold band with a solitaire diamond set high in the center. It was a half carat in size, but had a kind of antique look to it. I knew what I wanted done to it, but I didn't know how long it would take.

Someone in heaven must have been looking out for my sorry ass, because the jewelry store was open. I hated sneaking around behind Miranda's back, but I felt like us getting engaged would be the only way to make this more permanent, aside of marriage of course.

I'd been so caught up in our relationship to actually look at the big picture. There was one thing that I knew for certain. One thing that I would give anything to have. I needed Izzy to be my daughter. She needed to have my last name. Tucker had given up his claim to her and I would be damned if anyone took that little girl away from me now. Aside from living so far away, I had done everything to be a part of her life since the day she was born. I had no intentions of ever letting her down. If something happened to me and Miranda, I would still want to be her daddy.

I knew that nobody would understand the way I felt about her, even from the beginning I heard their comments. They looked at me like I had some fetish for small children. Sick Bastards!

I loved that little girl more than anything in the whole world. I had to believe that I was meant to be there when she was born. Everything that happened from that day on had led me right back to her. I may not have supplied the sperm, but it didn't matter to me. She was my everything.

The jeweler was waiting for us to arrive and when we did, he sat me down and listened to my idea. He said that what I wanted would be easy to do and would take about two weeks. I handed him my bank card and watched as he removed two thousand bucks from my account. I honestly didn't care how much it cost. I needed it to be perfect.

With the ring being taken care of, all I needed to do was keep my cool until the jewelry store called to tell me it was ready to be picked up. I had time to plan.

Izzy spotted my dad as we pulled back into the farm. My mother really got a kick out of how smart she was. In the past month she had gone out and got herself a car seat for her own car and had my father get some of my old shit out of the barn attic.

"Hey Dad. You got a minute?"

My father put the rake he was using down and walked over toward me. Izzy ran toward him and pointed toward the chicken house. "Chicks."

"Wait a second and I will take you to see the chicken again."

"I need your advice." My father was a quiet man. He stayed out of people's business and he liked it that way.

"What's bothering you Son?"

"Would you be disappointed in me if I asked Miranda to marry me?"

He shook his head and removed his hat. Colt did the same thing when he didn't know what to say. "I can tell you really love the girl and this little one here too. I reckon after everything you been through that your just coming to a point in your life where you are ready to settle down. You already know that your mom and I approve. Hell, I plan on starting that addition in the next couple of weeks. I appreciate you asking me though."

"Do you think I am rushing things?"

"Do you think you are?"

I shrugged my shoulders. "Sometimes I guess. I mean, I love them so much and I know that they are it for me. I know it's fast, but I want Izzy to have a daddy. We need to be a family."

"You already are a family in my book. You take care of each other and you love that little one. I am pretty certain that you are already a daddy in her little eyes."

I looked at Izzy. She was playing with my dad's old sweaty hat. She looked so much like Miranda and sometimes I just wanted to hug her and never let go. "Her mother and brother don't want us together. They will do whatever they can to break us up once they find out we are together. I have to secure their life here."

"As long as Miranda and you are on the same page, you do whatever has to be done. I don't want any drama here like with your cousin. You know I don't like that stuff." He let Izzy down and started walking away from us. "We will meet back at the house. This little one wants to see the chickens."

"Don't be too long. She needs her diaper changed." I walked back to the house and just sat on the couch. My stomach was in knots and started wondering how much more bullshit Van was filling Miranda's head with. I went to grab my phone and send her a message, but when I did I realized that Miranda had my phone.

After I got Izzy a fresh diaper we played outside for a little while until she started falling all over the place, crying for no reason. We went inside and laid on the couch together. Within ten minutes she was fast asleep on my chest. I played with her hair and watched her sleeping. There was no way that I could ever be without them.

It would just kill me.

Chapter 23

Miranda

Dress shopping with three people that had major issues with my boyfriend was not my idea of a fun time. From the moment that Van picked me up, she began to give me the third degree about Ty. Apparently, she had been up all night so upset that I let myself get involved with such a 'man whore'.

There were a couple times where I felt like slapping her out of her current conversation. As if that wasn't bad enough, her friend Brina, who was a total bitch, talked trash about Ty the rest of the day. At one point I ducked into a bathroom and started crying.

They could say everything they wanted about Ty, but I didn't know the guy they were talking about. My Ty wasn't selfish. He never put himself before Bella and I. He wasn't rude. He never looked at other girls. He didn't keep secrets. He never lied about where he was.

They didn't want to hear that he changed, or that maybe he just never found the right person to make him happy. All they wanted to do was convince me that I was making a horrible mistake.

I loved Ty. They weren't going to change my mind. There had been something brewing between us for over a year and in that period of time we had become friends. We couldn't hold back what we wanted any longer and I was so glad that we hadn't. He treated my child like he was her father. He loved her, bought her things and took care of her. There was nothing that he wouldn't do for that child.

To see them together, just reassured me how serious he was about being with us. All along he had known I had a child. He wasn't trying to get into my pants. I had been with a lot of guys. My track record was worse than his. If anyone should be running, it should be him.

After spending the entire day listening to them and trying on a million dresses, she finally drove me home. I was so happy to walk in that door and see the two of them sleeping. Van came in behind me and just froze when she saw them. I felt like turning around and giving her the finger after the earful that I had gotten all day. She was a great friend, but Ty talk should have been off limits.

To be nice I had invited her to dinner. It was unlikely that she would actually stay, but I needed to make sure that my mother and especially my brother didn't find out about my relationship. I was an adult, but they would make my life miserable anyway. My biggest fear would be them threatening to take Bella away from me, on account of me being an unfit parent. My family was close, but they would do anything to prevent me from being with Ty.

When I walked over to grab Bella out of Ty's arms, he woke startled and squeezed her tighter until he saw me. He smiled and finally let go. I was glad she stayed asleep long enough for me to lay her down and return to the living room before they killed each other.

"How long have you been asleep?" I asked.

"What time is it?"

"Six."

"Shit! Over an hour. I guess we were comfortable," he admitted.

"Do you want me to order a pizza?" I asked.

He stood up and stretched, before leaning over and kissing me on the lips. "No, baby. I will make something."

I caught Van rolling her eyes. "Do you want any help?"

Ty shrugged and kept walking toward the kitchen. I sat down on the chair next to her as Ty pulled out some bacon and started cooking it. "BLT's good? I had a lot to eat last night and I am still feeling really full."

It took everything I had not to laugh at his comment. I

know what he meant and it wasn't the food he was talking about. The comment was for me, but Van got it too.

"You're sick!" She blurted out.

"You're a prude," he retorted.

She turned to face me. "How can you be in love with this guy?"

"He's is perfect to me. How can I not?"

"Well you must give really good head to have him be so faithful and honest. That is all I can think of." Van looked from me to Ty waiting for a response.

Ty leaned over the counter and looked directly at Van. "She gives the best head that I have ever had. In fact, last night on our way home from dinner, she gave me the best blow job in the history of blow jobs. You know what else she's good at?"

He was taunting her now. I just sat there, speechless.

"I am afraid to ask," she noted.

"Everything. Just close your eyes and think of the kinkiest shit possible and she's good at it. She can also put her legs behind her head. It's fucking awesome."

I was laughing so hard that I was crying and Ty loved that he had finally shut her up. He winked at me again before attending to his food preparation.

A messy haired Bella came walking out into the living room looking around. "Ty?"

"I'm over here sweetie."

My heart melted every time she would look for him. With one arm he scooped her up and accepted her booger faced kisses. She started to point toward Van when she got over her Ty obsession.

"Hey little girl. Can Aunt Van get a hug and kiss?"

Bella shook her head and hid in Ty's chest. "No!"

Of course Ty had to rub it in. "Can Ty get a kiss?"

Without hesitation she puckered her lips and kissed Ty.

"You brainwashed her, dickhead," Van said while laughing.

"I didn't have to brainwash either of them. They love me all by themselves. And I love them too."

Van looked around the place. I knew she had been here a million times. Even though I knew that they weren't ever getting back together, it still made me jealous. I hated the reminder of who he had been with.

Ty finally finished making our plates and we all sat down and watched movies. I caught Van a few times just watching the three of us interacting with each other. She seemed especially interested in the attention that Ty gave to me and Bella. He was constantly stroking my arm or kissing my hand and head. Bella jumped all around on our laps and he welcomed her in as well.

When the movie finally ended Van said she had to go. We both stood up and walked her out to her car. Bella leaned down and finally gave her a kiss, making her smile a little more.

"I don't know what to say about you guys. I mean, it's clear that this isn't about sex, but I just don't get how the two of you have changed so much for each other."

It didn't matter what she thought. I wasn't trying to be rude about it, but this was clearly between Ty and I.

"Are you going to tell Colt?" I asked.

"No. I told you before that I don't want to get involved. If they ask I will tell them that you and Bella were here alone. You two can be the bearer of bad news. After my wedding of course."

As Van climbed into her car, Ty slapped me on the ass. "Now let's get inside and have hot sex all night long."

She rolled her eyes and rolled up her window. I think she actually floored it when she pulled away from us.

"Way to scare off our company," I joked.

"She was being a prude. How much bullshit did she give you today?" He asked.

I shrugged. He really didn't need to know, it would only hurt his feelings. "You know how they talk. I didn't listen to them."

"I think I need a lot of kisses for reassurance. No actually, I think I need some naked time."

Bella started jumping in between us. We separated and started chasing her around the room. "The naked time will have to wait until after someone goes to sleep."

"Promise?"

"Promise."

Well we can chalk that promise up and stick it in the jar of IOU's. Ty was nice enough to give Bella a bath while I cleaned up the rest of the house. It wasn't really that messy so I finished in less than ten minutes. I laid on the couch just listening to the two of them playing in the bathroom. He better have put towels down because with the amount of splashing that was going on, we might have a flood. I must have fallen asleep, because the next thing I knew, I was being carried to the bed.

Just like every Sunday, we woke up and started getting ready for church. Ty was in a really good mood, considering he didn't get his naked time. He woke me up with kisses and coffee before getting Bella dressed in a new outfit he insisted on buying her. She was wearing a little sailor dress and little matching shoes with anchors on the toes. He got her two matching bows for either side of her hair and made his best attempts to style it himself.

"Hey, baby, what do you think? Did I do good?"

"Aww, she looks so cute." She did too.

"I was thinking we should all get sailor suits and wear them next Sunday," he said sarcastically.

I was standing in front of the bathroom mirror, trying to apply eye liner and busted into a laughing fit. The eye liner smudged all over my eye lid. "There is no way I am doing that."

"Oh come on, it will be fun."

"It sounds like a terrible eighties picture." I was now removing my makeup to start over again. He didn't understand that I wanted to look my best for him all the time. I never wanted to give him a reason to look anywhere else.

"Why are you putting that stuff on your face? You look beautiful without it." Ty came up behind me and wrapped his arms around my waist.

"You're just tryin' to get me to hurry up." Although, his statement gave me butterflies.

"I fed Izzy and we are ready when you are."

"Okay. Be out in a second."

When I walked into the living room, Ty and Bella were sitting in front of the T.V. They were watching some little baby show where giant animals were dancing around. Bella was dancing all around to the music, while Ty recorded her on one of our phones.

A little girl came on the screen next with a man that was reading to her. It was clearly her dad and he was tucking her in for bed. The little girl snuggled up to her daddy telling him that she loved him. Bella just stood there staring at the television. I kept watching her realizing how close she was getting to turning two. We still had a few months, but time was flying by. She was paying more attention to things, like she was to this particular show.

She freaked out when Ty came up and turned the show off. "No Ty!"

"I'm sorry Iz, we have to go to bye bye."

She looked at him curiously. "Bye bye?"

"Yep, your mommy is finally done her primping." I stuck my nose up at him.

We finally got packed in the car and were on our way to church. Things got super quiet in the car for some reason or another and out of the back seat I heard my daughter saying something that made my stomach drop. "Daddy. Daddy. Daddy."

Three times right in a row.

I thought Ty was going to roll us into a ditch. He looked from me to the rear view mirror. "Did she just?"

I held my hand over my mouth. "Yeah."

"Do you think she knows what it means?"

I looked back at Bella who still kept repeating it. "Daddy. Daddy." This time she was pointing. Right at Ty.

I knew he saw her in that mirror. I was speechless as I watched his shocked face. We were pulling up at church but just sat in the car instead of jumping right out. Ty turned around and looked at Bella, sitting in her car seat, pointing at him. "Daddy."

I had no idea how she could pick that up from watching a show, but she knew exactly what it meant and she thought Ty was her daddy. There was no denying it. Ty reached back and touched Bella's foot. Tears rolled down his eyes. I didn't know how to react. I was still in shock from hearing it myself. If I ever wondered if he was serious about being with both of us, his actions were giving me the answer.

"Are you okay?" I asked.

He laid his head against the seat to the car and wiped his eyes. "She called me Daddy."

"Daddy." Of course she said it again.

"She thinks you are." I rubbed his arm while he just kept looking at her.

"I love her so much."

"She loves you too Ty. You know she does. Even as a tiny baby she loved you. Remember how you would sing to her through video chats?"

He laughed. "You weren't supposed to be listening."

I smirked. "She was an infant. I couldn't leave her alone. It was sweet."

"I want to be her daddy." My heart dropped out of my stomach. Now I was the one crying. I had applied my make-up twice and it was now running down my face.

"Really?"

"Isn't it obvious Miranda? I want it more than anything. I want her to always be able to count on me, no matter what happens." He ran his fingers over my tears and wiped them from my cheeks.

I opened my mouth to say something, but someone started knocking on the window. It was Van and her mother. "You guys going to get out of the car? I want to sit with you."

I looked to Ty. "What if Bella says it in front of her?"

"She already hates me, so I really don't give a shit. It's between us, not her." He climbed out of the car and immediately reached for Bella, while I straightened my face, again.

Bella was in rare form in church and even Ty's parents couldn't occupy her. They were sitting in the pew in front of us and she kept wanting to climb back and forth, disrupting everyone around us. Thank goodness we were in church so people were more forgiving. Van and her mother sat next to us and Ty made it a point to never let go of my hand during service. Even as we stood to sing, he would wrap one arm around my waist. I could feel their eyes on us. As we got seated in between songs, the room got quiet. Bella was in front of us climbing on the pew. Then she held out her arms to Ty and said it, in front of the whole congregation. "Daddy."

Her little fingers were moving for him to grab her and that is exactly what he did. I couldn't look over at Van and her mother, in fact I couldn't even look at Ty's parents, who had turned around with the happiest look on their faces. I knew Ty was ecstatic. Bella had chose him. It was as if she knew all along he would be her daddy.

It was beautiful.

Chapter 24

Tyler

There are moments in life where you just know you will never forget. That day when Izzy called me 'Daddy' in front of the entire church congregation was one of those moments. She chose me on her own. I didn't even have to ask her mother first. Izzy knew that I was her daddy and that I loved her more than anything.

Van and her mother let out a simultaneous gasp when they heard it. It's funny how things happen at the precise moment when you don't want them to. I myself didn't care that they heard it, but Miranda looked mortified that it happened in front of so many people. She had been judged her whole life and tried to stay out of the spot light. She had no idea that her beauty made that impossible.

So I had this plan where I was going to ask Miranda to marry me with Izzy holding a sign asking if I could be her daddy, but since she was already calling me it, my plan went to shit. I ended up having more time to get a new plan, because the ring wasn't ready in two weeks. It actually took five.

Van went home that weekend and kept her promise about telling the family that Miranda and I were involved. For the first week Miranda freaked out whenever someone from home called. As the time passed, she realized that we were in the clear. Colt and Van's wedding was only five weeks away. Miranda and I had been living together for over two months and every day got better than the one before it. I had to sneak out on my lunch break one day to pick up her ring. I took it out of my pocket a million times to stare at it. I had the jeweler add a circle of diamonds around the single solitaire stone. It changed the look of the ring completely and I was pleased with how it turned out.

I remember the night I asked her, like it was just yesterday. Miranda had to work that day, so we rode in together. The ride home I was so quiet and she sensed that something was up, but I wasn't about to blow my surprise. She kept at it though, driving me completely insane. She knew me so well and I hated that I had a secret, but was super excited about it too.

When we finally got home we walked over to get Izzy from my mother's. Of course she came running out to me. "Daddy."

"There's my girl." I gave her big kisses before giving her to Miranda. Sometimes she didn't even want to give Mommy kisses. I felt kind of bad about that.

I hadn't told my parents that the ring was ready, so they had no way of knowing that I was planning on popping the question. They kept inviting us to eat dinner with them. I gave them weird looks and tried to signal that it was a special night, but they kept insisting.

While my mother and Miranda worked on getting dinner ready, I found a piece of paper and wrote down the exact words I had thought of using. I was so nervous and the sweat was rolling down my face, even though it wasn't hot in the room at all. Izzy was being so ornery and I hoped that she would help me with my plan, in fact she was the biggest part of it.

I could hardly eat dinner, due to the fact that my stomach was in knots. I had never considered that she might say 'no'. My family kept watching me at the dinner table asking what the hell was wrong, but I insisted I was fine.

I waited for the ladies to get dinner cleaned up. The waiting was so hard. Izzy was getting tired and my parents had a show they watched so I needed to get the show on the road. Miranda walked in and sat down across from me. I took a deep breath as my mother sat next to her. I had no idea what they were talking about, because I think my heart was beating so hard that it was preventing me from hearing.

"Izzy, come here to Daddy." Saying that was never going to get old. I reached my hands out for her. I gave her the folded piece of paper. "Give this to Mommy."

She walked the paper over to Miranda perfectly and I giggled when she came running right back to me, as if she knew my next move. Miranda opened the paper and looked confused.

The piece of paper read : *Daddy wants to know if we can change our names to Mitchell?*

I put the ring on Izzy's thumb and told her to take it to her Mommy. She looked down at it and walked it over to her.

"Here." Izzy said like a little angel.

I got down on one knee in front of Miranda. "I know this is sudden, but please be my wife. I want this to be forever. I want us to be a family."

Miranda was shaking and crying. My mother rubbed her back. I just sat there waiting for her to answer. The suspense was killing me. She finally nodded her head. "Yes, I will marry you."

I slid that ring on her finger and kissed it. "Then I guess we are getting married."

"I guess this is why you were acting so weird earlier?" She asked.

"I was sweating bullets."

My dad walked up and hugged Miranda. "Welcome to the family, darling, even though you were already a part of it."

She gave my mother a big hug and I noticed that even my mother had tears in her eyes. I couldn't believe that they loved Miranda so much. Bella was clapping even though she had no idea what had just happened.

For the next two weeks Miranda walked around glowing, but the closer it got to us having to go to Kentucky, she started to get tense. One night she was really in rare form. Everything I did and said couldn't relax her.

"Baby, what's wrong?" I grabbed her into my arms.

"I don't want to be away from you Ty. I am so scared to face them. They are going to try everything to break us up. They aren't going to care about this ring or what it stands for."

I hated that she was so sad. I looked over to my sleeping

little girl, yes *my* little girl, and thought about being away from them. I closed my eyes and tried to remain calm. "Let's just get married. We can apply for a license tomorrow and get it taken care of before we go to Kentucky. If we are married they can't tear us apart."

"Are you sure? I don't want to force you into it."

"Baby, I love you and our little girl. The sooner you have my last name, the better."

She wrapped her arms around me. "I love you so much Ty."

"Since we are talking about it, I want to know your take on my adopting Izzy. She needs to have my name Miranda. I want to be her only daddy. How do we get him to sign off on that without your family finding out?"

She pulled away from me and smiled. "Actually, that won't be a problem. You see I kind of lied to Tucker when Bella was born. He wasn't really there for my pregnancy and my mother was freaking out about how much of a loser he was. She insisted that I not add him to the birth certificate. At the time I hated the idea, but after he left the hospital that night and didn't even act happy about being a father, I got pissed. I left the birth certificate without a father listed. Tucker doesn't know. He thinks I just gave Bella my last name because we weren't married. He used to threaten me about taking her, but he has no legal right to do it. Changing it might cost some money, but I think she deserves to have your name."

I was so excited. "Seriously? I can have both of my girls all to myself, forever?"

"If you want us," she teased.

"Want to catch a flight to Vegas and get married right now?"

"I think we can wait two days." She kissed me slowly and as her tongue stroked my lip, I knew she wanted to celebrate in a different way.

I looked over to Izzy, who was sound asleep in the porta crib. My father and I needed to get our asses in gear with adding those rooms. My little girl needed her own room.

"Maybe we should wait until we are married," I joked.

She sat back and studied my face. "Seriously?"

"Hell no! Give me that ass."

I grabbed her legs and pulled her down where I wanted her. She kissed me slowly, stroking my cheek with her finger tips. "You really know how to be romantic," she teased.

I took both of her hands and lifted them above her head, tangling my fingers into hers. "I can be romantic, but right now I just want to be inside of you."

Miranda sat up and grabbed the bottom of my shirt. She pulled it over my head without saying a word. After pushing me down on the bed, she climbed on top, straddling me. I tugged at her shirt and she obliged by removing it promptly. I tugged at her pants and she rolled her eyes and she lifted up to remove them. "You going to ride me, baby?"

She ran her hands over my chest, making sure to pinch each nipple. "Is that what you want?"

Miranda was wearing my favorite hook in the front bra. It made her tits protrude out of the top. With one hand I reached up and unhooked it. She used her forearms to keep the bra over her breasts. I licked my lips knowing what was under that lace. "Stop teasing me."

She pulled the bra down just enough to where I could start to see her pink nipples. "Is this what you want to see?" Her hips moved ever so slightly against my sudden erection.

I went to grab the bra, but she slapped my hand away. As she began to grind herself more against me, I watched her biting her lip, waiting for my next reaction. I took both of my hands and ran them up her thighs. When I reached the soft skin to her ass, I guided her movements. Now, I was still wearing pants, so knowing that she was naked and ready to go was tormenting the hell out of me.

I slid my fingers over her pussy just to satisfy what I already knew. She was so ready for me. She rocked her body against my fingers, tempting me to slid them right inside. Miranda let out a little cry when my fingers entered her. I moved my hand slowly as I used my thumb to circle her soft clit. She threw her head back, closing her eyes tightly. "Tell me you want me."

She covered her mouth and she let out soft cries, trying not to wake Izzy. Her eyes met mine and she looked like she was tipsy. "You know I do."

Miranda was unbuckling my belt and managing my zipper without me even asking. She shuttered when I removed my hand so that she could take off my pants. As much as I loved touching her, there was something else that I wanted inside of her. As she climbed back over me, she bent over and drug her tongue over my lips. "Touch me please."

I hadn't even noticed that her bra had finally dropped and her beautiful breasts were right within reach. I slid my hands up her perfect waist and cupped both of her breasts into my hands. Without much force, I pulled her down closer in order to take one into my mouth. I sucked on her nipple, making it hard against my lips. As I circled it with my tongue, I lifted it just enough that she could lick it with me.

Holy fucking shit that is the hottest thing ever!

Miranda didn't even know what was happening. In a matter of one second I had gripped her ass and position her to slide myself right inside. She leaned back and accepted my whole girth. When Miranda was riding me I never could last very long. She teased her nipples with her fingertips, knowing that every time it set me crazy.

While my hot ass girlfriend was riding the hell out of me, I had to start closing my eyes. She dug her fingernails into my chest, making me open them.

"Please kiss me." She leaned down, shifting my cock just

enough to remind me that I was about to come any second. Her lips hit mine and I felt her warm tongue sliding inside of my mouth. My body tensed and I grabbed her ass, forcing her to stop moving. At the height of my explosion, she swayed her hips just enough to tickle every inch of my skin.

I grabbed her hands and pulled her down over my chest. Miranda kissed me gently while I started to trace her back with my finger tips. "I love you Ty."

"I appreciate that considering I am such a horrible person in everyone else's eyes." I don't know why I said it, but it pissed me off that what Miranda and I had was real and people just couldn't believe it, Van mainly.

Miranda looked up at me. "You know that isn't true. We both have shitty pasts Ty. None of that matters to me. You have proved time and time again how dedicated you are to Bella and I. Don't you ever doubt that I don't notice."

"Do you believe that everything happens for a reason?"

She shrugged. "I don't know. Why do you ask?"

"I've been thinking a lot about everything that happened. If I hadn't been such a bastard boyfriend to Van, she wouldn't have gotten with Colt. I would have never followed her to Kentucky and been there when Izzy was born. Not to mention the crap with Tucker being a total ass-hat and doing all of the stupid shit he did to you. We wouldn't have become such good friends. I never would have known how fucking hot you were, or how much I wanted to see you naked. I wouldn't be here right now, happier than I have ever been in my life. I feel like I was supposed to be in that car that day. This was all supposed to happen exactly like it has."

She pressed soft kisses over my lips repeatedly. "When you put it like that it does sound perfect."

"Are you sure you want to marry me? You can still back out."

I ran my fingers in between hers and pulled her hand up to

kiss the ring on her finger. "I am sure."

Yeah, so my friends would be calling me a sappy ass pussy bitch, but if that's what I had to be to have this life, then that is what I was. My ass-backwards life plan wasn't for everyone to understand, it was hard enough trying to explain it in my own head. Nothing mattered to me except those two girls. They were my reason for breathing.

Chapter 25
Miranda

I guess most girls would imagine having a huge wedding with fancy dresses and a room full of people that celebrate the coming together of two people that love each other. My wedding was nothing like that at all. We applied for the license and two days later we were walking into the court house. I don't know where he found the time, but Ty had gone out and got us two matching white gold bands. His parents and Bella went with us. Ty held her the whole time, even though the Justice of the Peace guy thought she was a distraction. He probably thought we were crazy, or maybe I was pregnant again.

Ty carried me out of the court house. We went out to dinner and went home just like every normal day. Except for the piece of paper, nothing felt different between us. I was ecstatic that I was Ty's wife, but he already had my heart regardless. Ty's mother, my new mother in law, helped me make the necessary calls about having Bella's name changed to Mitchell. I had to fill out a bunch of forms and then contact social security administration to get a new card for her. Because there was no father listed on the birth certificate, it was easy to have it done. I lied and said he was the father on every piece of paper. I wasn't worried about Tucker ever coming around. He never wanted her in the first place.

Ty and I decided that if he ever came around we would deal with it then. In my heart I knew that he was Bella's daddy in every way that counted. They didn't need blood to have that father daughter bond. She was his before he was ever on my radar.

Sometimes I had to laugh at how it all had happened. Perhaps Ty had been right when he said we were always meant to be together. I had never believed that before, but I started to think back to our first time in church. The unanswered prayers had worked to our advantage and now we had each other.

As we both started to prepare for Colt and Savanna's wedding and our official coming out, things became stressful. It didn't put a strain on our relationship, but it was obvious that we were both worried. There was no way of getting out of the visit. We were both in the wedding party. Ty had asked Colt to have Conner be his best man. He had a few reasons behind his decision. I think the first one was that he hated Brina, who was Van's maid of honor. The second reason was that he insisted on being paired up with me in the bridal party. I liked that part of his reasoning the most. The third being that if the family overreacted and we had to leave, they could go on without us and have to change nothing.

I was trying to be optimistic, but my brother was a dick and there was no getting around the fact that he told Ty to stay away from me and he promised that he would. When it came to my brother accepting us, I knew it wasn't going to happen. He was still sending Ty random text messages about it, like he was reminding him.

The day we packed up the jeep was beyond nerve-strickening. Since we were in the wedding party we had to go a week earlier than Ty's parents on account of wedding festivities. We decided that at first we weren't going to say anything. There was no need to cause drama before the big day. We would keep our distance and act like friends. The problem was that I couldn't be in the same room with Ty and not look at him like he was my whole life. Not to mention that Bella called him Daddy all of the time. In fact since he had been promoting it. She had completely forgotten that he had any other name.

Ty tried to keep my spirits up on the way there. He tickled my leg and reached over to kiss me at stop lights, but my nerves were shot. I wanted to vomit. I was supposed to be living at the farm as a temporary situation. Not only was I sleeping with whom they thought was the devil, but I had up and married him, and

185

filled out the paperwork to change Bella's name.

Our web of secrets was going to give me an early heart attack.

"Baby, you need to calm down. No matter what happens, we are going to be together. If they don't accept it right away, we can deal with it. They will come around once we prove that this is real. I promise."

"Maybe you should just pretend that you are still upset about the wedding and go home."

"Are you seriously telling me to drop you off and drive all the way home without you?"

When he put it that way it sounded pretty stupid. "You know Bella will spill the beans."

"So what if she does. I have nothing to hide. They can't do anything to us now."

Ty was starting to talk with his hands. He only did that when he was frustrated. I tried to ignore it, but it was making me more nervous. "Oh yeah? Who says?"

"The state of North Carolina for starters."

"I am sure that our family will be glad that the state of North Carolina is on our side," I said sarcastically.

Aside from worrying about all of this, I was also worried about the Tucker situation. Things had been quiet, but I knew the whole town knew about Colt's upcoming wedding. Word travels and Tucker would know I would be there. Ty knew it was on my mind, and reassured me a thousand times that I was safe. It was just hard not to worry.

"I think you need one of Van's pills."

I rolled my eyes. "I'm glad you find this so entertaining."

"Its…." Ty was interrupted by Bella screaming his name.

Apparently her daddy thought it was cool to teach her that when she saw the golden arches she could have fries. Her little finger pointed toward a McDonald's billboard with a picture of fries. "Daddy. Daddy fri fri."

Of course Ty forgot about what he was saying mid sentence. "Daddy will get you fri fri's, baby."

She started clapping in the backseat. "Yay!"

I shook my head. "You know if you give her everything she wants she will expect it."

"So what. I can't help it. She has me wrapped around her finger," he teased.

"Obviously."

Once Bella got her fries, she concentrated on shoving them in her mouth. To prevent her from choking in the back of the car, I only gave her three at a time.

By the time we got to the ranch, she was sound asleep. I was relieved that I could at least get hugs and kisses before she woke up and called Ty 'Daddy'. Before getting out of the car, Ty grabbed my hand. "We should probably take off our rings."

As much as I hated hearing him say that, I knew it had to be done. "I hate this."

"I bet they are going to make me stay at Colt's. How fucked up would that be?" Ty whispered.

He was trying not to use bad language around our daughter.

I saw Lucy and my aunt coming out of the house toward the Jeep.

"Shit! I don't even get a kiss."

"I love you Ty." I gave his hand one last squeeze.

"I love you too."

The door swung open and the hugging had begun. Ty ran over and grabbed his aunt, spinning her around. "Aunt J. Your favorite nephew is here," he teased, knowing my brother was also her nephew. In fact she and Colt were our only connection.

Lucy and OUR aunt looked in the back at Bella. "Oh my goodness she's so big."

They hadn't seen her in almost two and a half months. I couldn't tell how much she had changed, but I wasn't surprised they thought she had.

"How was the drive?" She asked Ty.

"It was fine."

Bella started to stir in the backseat and I saw Ty turn as white as a sheet. "Why don't you guys go inside. I can get the car unloaded," he suggested.

He tried not to look at me and I tried not to look at him. This was impossible.

I grabbed Bella out of the car while Ty stood where she couldn't see. "So where is my mother?"

"She's down at the house. You should go surprise her on the golf cart. She has missed you so much. Speaking of that. When will that job be over? It was nice of you to offer to help out, but we want you to come home."

Oh no, not this already...

"I miss you all too. I think surprising my mom is a great idea. Just have Ty put my stuff in my room for now. We will be back soon." I almost ran away from them. When I said Ty's name Bella's started looking around for him.

I hopped on the golf cart and started driving toward my mother's house. Ty was going to have to go to Colt's. He was going to be pissed at me. "Shit...Shit...Shit!"

"Shit!" Bella repeated.

"Oh God! Honey that is a bad word. No, no!"

"Shit."

I am doomed!

My mother came outside and met us. She scooped up Bella and showered her with kisses. "Hi pretty girl. How is my baby?"

She grabbed me for a hug while still holding Bella. "Hey, Mom. How has everyone been?"

She gave me a funny once over. "You look fantastic, honey. I think being away from guy drama has done wonders for you."

If she only knew. Shoot me now...please.
"Thank you."
"Shit."
My mother looked down at my now potty mouthed daughter. "Has she been spending time with Tyler?"
Thank God she said Tyler. Bella didn't recognize him being called that. "No, she learned that from her mother. I just dropped something and for the past ten minutes she hasn't stopped sayin' it."
"Well they pick up on everything at this age. Their minds are like sponges."
We walked in the house and saw my brother standing there. "What's up sis?" Standing behind him was Courtney aka Miss Kentucky. Her hands were tucked into his back pockets.
She saw me and rolled her eyes.
"Are you kiddin' me right now?"
"Something I need to know about?" My mother asked.
Conner gave me a warning look like he would hurt me if I told my mother about his bitch ass girlfriend. "No it's nothin'."
"So did the dickhead keep his hands off you on the ride here?" He asked.
"Watch your mouth around my daughter."
"Sorry." He came up and nudged my side. "Did he?"
Bella went running toward my mother and she took her into the other room. I looked him right in the eyes. "No, we pulled over and fucked for over an hour at least three times. Bella cried the whole time, but we didn't care at all that she was watchin' us." I shoved my brother clear across the room. "Nothin' changes with you. What the hell is that bitch doing in our house?"
He turned around and looked at Courtney. She was standing there with her hands on her hips. All I could think about was her swooning over Ty. I hated her even more now than before. "We are kind of seein' each other. Be nice to her."
"Screw you."

189

"Have you talked to Van today?" He changed the subject.

"No. Why?"

"Her and Colt decided to have a coed bachelor party. You know how Colt is. Anyway, we are all going out tonight together. I can't wait till Ty see's who my date is."

"Why would he care?" I probably should have just been quiet, but it pissed me off that Courtney not only was here with my brother, but he was implying that Ty would want to hook up with her.

"Why are you takin' up for him? Somethin' I need to know about?"

"No!" I looked right at Courtney and just couldn't help myself. "Last time he was here he told me that she was an annoyin' drama queen and there was no way in hell he would hit that."

Courtney looked pissed. I got happy. Point for me.

"Why would he tell you that?"

"Because we are friends. Friends talk about things. Obviously, you must only have acquaintances."

Conner grabbed my arm and stared at me. After a few seconds, I pulled out of his arms. "Mom, do you care if I run over to Van's real quick? I need to talk to her about tonight."

"Sure honey. Bella can stay here. Just leave me her diaper bag."

I shot my brother a dirty look and ran out of the house.

Chapter 26

Tyler

I no sooner pulled up to Colt's when I saw Miranda pulling up on the golf cart. She was crying her eyes out. Without any regard for the chance Colt was around, I instinctively ran toward her. She flung into my arms. "What happened, baby?"

"I can't do this, Ty. I just want to go home."

I grabbed her face and forced her to look at me. "It's going to be okay. I promise."

"No, I can't do this. My brother is an asshole."

"What happened?" I clenched my jaw trying not to lose my cool.

"Well I walked into my mother's and that bitch Courtney had her hand down his pants for starters."

I rolled my eyes just thinking about how annoying that chick was. "Wow he has nerve talking about me."

"Exactly. Then he started on me about you, warnin' me that he was going to let you know Courtney was off limits."

I hugged my wife in my arms and smelled her sweet shampoo while I thought about what I could say to make her feel better. "Baby, I don't want Courtney. I never did. As far as your brother goes, just ignore him. He has always been a punk."

"I know. I just don't want her looking at you. I kind of said that you thought she was annoying and that there was no way in hell you would ever touch her. I couldn't help myself."

She was cute when she was jealous and I liked her taking up for me. "I can't stop women from looking at me, but just know that no matter where I am, all I am thinking about is being with you. I have no interest in anyone, especially Courtney."

"We have to go out tonight. Coed bachelor party."

"Listen to me Miranda. Whatever happens with our family this week doesn't change anything. We are a family. We made sure of it. I would rather go out with you than see any strippers anyway, cause, darling they ain't got shit on you."

She finally nodded and gave me a half smile. "Yeah right."

I kissed her so softly, almost savoring her lips. "It's the truth. I swear to God that you are the most beautiful woman in the world, to me. Besides, I've seen you dance and there ain't a stripper out there with those moves."

She smiled again and bit down on her lip. "Keep talkin' like that and we are goin' to have to find someplace private."

"Don't you dare tempt me. We just got here."

"I love you so much."

"You know how much I love you Miranda. You have no idea how much it would crush me if you ever left me for someone else. Please don't ever leave me, baby."

She looked up into my eyes. "Never Ty. I will never do that to you."

I believed her, because if she even felt half of what I felt for her, than I knew she was telling the truth. I didn't even notice girls anymore. I had no interest, because I knew that the most beautiful and perfect woman was already mine.

"Where is my Izzy?"

"At my mom's house. I am afraid to have her near you. Once they see you two they will know everything."

From the porch a familiar voice started talking. "You two really don't know how to lay low do you?"

I ran up on the porch and spun Van around in a hug. "Van, I am so happy to see you."

"Why are you being so nice Ty?" She looked from me to Miranda who was laughing at me.

"No reason. Just super happy about my life."

"Seriously something is different. You better spill."

I wanted to tell her for a few reasons. Van and I were friends, but ever since she found out about me and Miranda she had been distant. Miranda wanted to keep our marriage a secret for the time being and I had to respect that. "It's nothing. Where is Colt?"

"You are lucky he isn't here because he would be beating the shit out of you if he just saw you two."

Miranda walked up and hugged Van. "I hear we are going out tonight."

"Yup, but you two need to stay away from each other, like dance with strangers or something."

"Not happening!" It just flew out of my mouth.

"You can't be together, you know that." Van put her hands on her hips like she meant business.

"Whatever! What room am I staying in? I need to put all my shit in it."

Van shook her head. "Same one as last time."

"Oh good, I figured you would have it painted in baby colors for your slew of babies you will start popping out."

Miranda started laughing at my joke, which in turn caused Van to start fuming. "How can you love him?"

I didn't look back. I didn't have to. Miranda loved me and there wasn't shit anyone could do to change it.

It took me a while to get Miranda calmed down enough to go back to her mother's. I promised her that somehow I would figure out a way for us to spend time together.

Colt finally came home and we hung out for a while shooting the shit. I wanted to tell him about my life and how happy I was, but there were no words to sugar coat things. He was going to be pissed.

Van was being her new normal self and once Brina's bitch ass showed up I wanted to shoot myself in the head. I got ready to go out and stayed up in the bedroom sending text messages to my hot wife.

What are you wearing? -Ty
I am totally naked.- M
Me too! –Ty
Liar! –M

U 2-Ty

I miss your lips-Ty

I hate this-M

And your ass – Ty

I love you. Your daughter misses her daddy.- M

I miss her too. This fucking sucks. Why did I marry my cousin :)-Ty

You are so dumb. We are not related.- M

I bet you smell fantastic –Ty

I do –M

I want you so bad right now. – Ty

Cut it out. –M

Don't look too hot. Dress like an old lady. I don't want to have to kick the shit out of anyone for looking at my wife. –Ty

I am wearing a corset and my tits are hanging out –M

Be there soon. Love u.- Ty

If she was wearing a corset, I was going to freak out.

Thank god she wasn't, but what she did have on wasn't any better. Just like every time, our outfits kind of matched. I had on dark jeans and a gray shirt. Miranda was wearing a gray dress that barely covered her fine ass. It came down almost to her abdomen and tied around her neck. She tried not to smile, but she knew that the dress was going to drive me crazy. I needed to raid her closet and throw all that shit away.

While everyone was causing a commotion I snuck next to her. "The only way you are wearing that is if that wedding ring is planted on your finger."

I reached in my pocket and jingled the rings.

"Behave. I am acting the part."

I smacked her on the ass right before everyone came in the room. Conner immediately gave me a once over. I held out my hand and gave him a half hug. He was family after all, well kind of, well literally now.

I wanted to see my daughter before we left, so I snuck

back inside, telling everyone I forgot something. Bella was walking around near the foyer. I scooped her up and kissed her. "Daddy loves you."

"Daddy."

I saw Lucy heading our way, so I ran out the door leaving my daughter, who had started to cry. Miranda was going to kick my ass.

Colt had arranged a limo to pick us up at the ranch, so we all piled in and set out for a night on the town. Conner was all over that bitch Courtney. Van and Colt were up each other's asses and Brina was busy on her phone. I slid my fingers over Miranda's while her purse covered our hands. I needed to check out her cleavage, but I wanted to survive the ride to the bar.

We were almost there when Conner got a hair up his ass. "Was it necessary for you to dress like that?"

Would she even be mad at me if I beat his ass?

"I look hot?" She turned to look at me of all people. "Ty do I look hot?"

I held my hands up in the air. "Don't bring me into this."

"You are such a jerk. I hate how you act all protective. I am going to start calling you Conner Jr." At first I was confused, but then I finally got it.

Conner took the bait. "You are lucky guys like us care about what happens to you."

"Yeah, I feel so lucky."

We climbed out of limo and Conner pulled me to the side. "I know you and my sister are friends. I don't feel like havin' any drama tonight like the kind that happened the last time we all went out. If you could hang out with her and keep her out of trouble it would be cool." He also wanted to make sure I didn't want his bitch ass girlfriend.

After shaking his hand, Conner walked away. Miranda stayed back with me and squeezed my hand before we walked in. She had just manipulated her brother into thinking us hanging out was a good idea. "Have I told you lately how much I love you?" I whispered.

"It doesn't get old." She said through her teeth.

For a while we all just hung out around the bar. Brina and Courtney became fast friends and I use the term *fast* lightly. Conner was stuck up the beauty queen's ass, which was where I wanted him to stay. Van and Colt were obsessed with each other. I was jealous, but not of them being together. I was jealous that I couldn't put my hands on my own wife.

Miranda had straightened her hair and it hung perfectly down her back. From working at the salon she had been tanning and had her nails manicured all fancy. Her green eyes sparkled and when she smiled it sent chills to my cock. She knew it made me crazy when she looked so hot and I caught her several times giving me 'the look'.

Once everyone had a few drinks, they really stopped paying attention to Miranda and I. Even Brina was hanging all over some guy she had just met. The bar got crowded and Miranda and I blended in on the dance floor. I tried so hard not to touch her too much as we danced, but you can't mix alcohol with a horny man and sexy as shit wife without something happening. Her smooth dress felt so good under my fingers. Her back was facing me as she grinded that perfect ass into my dick. The girl knew what she was doing. We were bumping and grinding all over each other, until Van came walking up. "Seriously you two. You may as well be screwing."

Part of me wondered if she was jealous. I didn't care, but she sure did get in my shit a lot.

I took a big drink of my beer and looked at Miranda. She had a huge smile on her face, the kind she got when she was ready to get all freaky. "Sorry. I just can't help myself." She bit her lip and pulled me back out on the dance floor. I held up my hands like I was helpless and followed her lead.

We probably would have gotten away with things if

Miranda didn't start moving my hands all over her body. I did good for a while stopping her, but the more she drank the friskier she got. "Calm down, baby."

She whined. "I can't help it. I want you so bad Ty."

Fuck!

I never would have thought I would be asking Van for favors, but I knew if I wanted to keep the peace, I needed her help. "I promise you that I will do whatever your pretty heart wants when we get home, but you have to calm down."

"But I want you right now."

"I want you too, but we have to wai...." Her lips were on mine. I wanted to pull away, damn I wanted to protect her, but her magic tongue found mine and I couldn't stop. It was like we were back at home and rediscovering every inch of each other again. Miranda's hands went up my shirt and I felt her nails against my skin. I grabbed her ass and pulled her against me.

I felt an arm dragging me away from my wife. When I looked back I noticed that Van was standing with Miranda. I turned around to see Colt and he was pissed. He shoved me against the wall in the men's room. "Do you want to live to see tomorrow?"

"What the fuck is that supposed to mean?"

He shook his head. "Did you think she wouldn't tell me?"

I got a half smile across my face. I should have assumed. "I love her."

"You think you do, but what are you goin' to do when she moves home?"

"She ain't coming back."

He raised an eyebrow. "The hell she ain't."

"You don't understand Colt." I leaned up against the counter and tried to think of what to say to my cousin. "Damn, this is bullshit. Why is it so hard to believe that I love her?"

"Her mother will never let you be together." His hand was on my chest, keeping me from moving.

"It's not her decision. Miranda is a grown woman." I flung his arm away from me. "Nobody can ever take her from me."

He started laughing, like my words were a joke. "And why is that?"

I held my hands up in the air. "Because she's my wife."

Colt's smile disappeared. "What did you just say?"

"You heard me."

He ran his hands through his hair and started pacing around. I wasn't sure whether he was going to beat my ass, or drag me outside and let Conner do it. Or both.

He shook his head and huffed and puffed. "When did this happen?"

"A couple weeks ago."

"Married?"

"Married."

He slammed his fist into the wooden stall. "What the fuck were you thinkin'?"

"I was thinking that I loved her and I wanted to spend the rest of my life with her."

He shook his head and put his hand on my shoulder. "You are my family, actually, you are both my family, so this is how things are goin' to happen. You and Miranda are goin' to go home tonight and keep up the charade that nothin' is goin' on. I won't let you ruin this for Van. I can't believe you did this shit."

"That's it?"

"Well, I would like to hit you, but then I would have to explain why I did it."

I held out my hand and shook Colt's. "I swear to you that this isn't some kind of game. I can't live without her man."

"Time will tell, cuz. I am promising you though, if you hurt her, you have to answer to me."

Colt left me standing in the men's room. Miranda and I couldn't have anymore close calls. I wondered how long it would take Colt to tell Van about my being married. She was going to flip her lid.

I headed back out to try and locate Miranda. My petite little wife couldn't handle her alcohol. Neither of us really drank a lot anymore. We were so happy that we didn't ever need to. When I approached her, Van gave her a little push. "How much did she drink?"

I laughed. "Maybe two beers and one or two shots."

"For the past ten minutes she hasn't shut up about how amazing you are at...never mind, I can't even say it out loud."

I busted out laughing. I knew one thing she thought I was amazing at and it was something I barely ever did to Van. She rolled her eyes and walked away.

"Am I in trouble?" She asked.

"You were bragging about my skills, why would I be mad about that?" I teased. "Come dance off the alcohol, baby."

Miranda wasn't physically acting like she was drunk. She walked fine and even danced normal, it was just the way she was talking. If I could keep her mouth shut, everything would be okay.

For the rest of the night, she behaved herself. We danced like we were friends and I even got a nod from Conner at one point. After about an hour, Miranda finally was calm enough to get back to just pretending I was her annoying babysitter. Colt and Van relaxed and we all had a good time.

The limo ride on the way home was hard. With the exception of Brina, who somehow was finding another way back to the ranch, the two other couples in the car were steady making out. I played with Miranda's fingers again, just imagining how I was going to rip the dress off of her later.

Conner caught me whispering in her ear, but I told him I was talking shit about Brina and he laughed it off.

Instead of going home, Colt and Van invited everyone back to their place. The limo dropped us all off and we went inside. We were all having a good time, but it was so hard pretending that she meant nothing to me. Love was in the air and I wanted her in

my arms.

Chapter 27

Miranda

I thought Ty would have been the one to get us caught, but no, it was all me. I couldn't help it. I couldn't be that close to him, touching his skin. Thank goodness Colt and Van stepped in when they did. I was pretty sure that Ty wouldn't have been able to stop me himself.

The after party at Colt's was nice, but I kept catching Ty's gazes and I knew he wanted to be alone. Ty went to the bathroom and I waited a few minutes before heading in that direction. Everyone pees, so they couldn't think it was a secret meeting plan.

I walked into the bathroom and felt his lips on mine. His hand slid right into my dress and caressed one of my breasts. He pressed me up against the wall and I threw my head back as he buried his face into my neck.

"This is so hard," he whispered.

"Don't stop Ty."

He didn't need my permission. Ty lifted me up and pushed the dress around my waist. In two short moves he had opened up his pants and pushed my panties aside. He carried me over to the sink and sat me over it. I felt the cold porcelain against my ass as he thrust inside of me right away. His mouth never left mine and his rough kisses sent chills throughout my whole body.

I knew they were all right down the hall. We shouldn't have been doing this, but I couldn't stop.

It started to feel so good that little cries were coming out of my mouth with each thrust. Ty covered my mouth with his hand and he pushed into me harder. I dug my nails into his ass, holding him as tight as I could. I leaned my head back against the mirror and pulled my dress away from each of my breasts. Ty got one look and closed his eyes as his body tensed up. It was like my breasts had magical powers.

As soon as he started to relax against my body, we heard my brother talking and the sound was moving toward the bathroom. He pulled away and buttoned up his pants while he pointed towards the toilet. Ty crouched down behind me, just as the door swung open.

"What's goin' on?" Conner asked.

"I don't know man. I was taking a piss and she came running in here, throwing up. I have already flushed the toilet twice. She can't have much left in her." I started gagging like I was puking. Ty held my hair out of the way.

I made a few more spit sounds and reached for the toilet paper. When I turned around, my brother looked concerned. "Jesus your face is blood red. She needs to go home and lay down."

I was shaking so bad. It couldn't have looked anymore genuine.

He put his arm around me and led me out of the bathroom. I couldn't look at Ty on account of my possible busting into laughter. My husband was brilliant.

Instead of trying to argue about staying, I let my brother lead me out of the house and get me seated on the golf cart. "Hold on."

He didn't say a word as he drove me to the main house. I climbed off and started walking toward the door.

"You okay?" He hopped off and started to approach me.

"I'm fine Conner. Not that you really care. In fact, all you care about is giving me a hard time. Why is it so important for you to know my business? Why do you have to threaten every guy I am friends with?"

"You're drunk. Just go to bed."

"No! Screw you Conner. I'm not drunk. I'm pissed." I should have let it go, but he needed to cut his shit out.

"What's this about Miranda? Is this about Ty? Did you fucking sleep with him In North Carolina? I will kill him."

Not only did it happen in North Carolina, but also about ten minutes ago...

"This is what I mean. I never even mentioned Ty."

It has everything to do with him.

"Tell me the truth Miranda. Has he ever hit on you? I need to know. I never wanted you going out there to stay. I can't believe mom sent you to live with that man whore."

"Stop it. He has never been anything but nice to me and Bella. This is exactly what I'm talking about. I am a grown woman. If I decided to pick some guy up at a bar, it's my choice, not yours. Why do I have to have a damn babysitter? Do you think Ty wanted to hang out with me all night when he could have been having a good time himself? Do you ever think about anyone else?"

I had to pat myself on the back for the Ty part. I am pretty sure he was exactly where he wanted to be.

"It's my job to protect you."

"Just leave me alone. If that is your idea of protectin' me then I would rather be in danger. If it was your choice I would be alone forever."

"You don't need to be puttin' yourself out there. Do you think about your daughter?"

I smacked my brother right in the face. He turned his face back to me and looked pissed. I didn't care.

"Screw you! Why don't you go fuck your little slut beauty queen and stay the hell out of my life."

"Miranda, wait!"

I kept walking. There was nothing else I wanted to say to him. I loved my brother, but I hated him just as much.

When I got into the house, I straightened up my clothes and ran up to my old room. I grabbed my phone and sure enough I already had a message.

Close call, baby. –Ty

Sorry. – M

Make sure the kitchen door is unlocked. I will come over when everyone goes to bed.- Ty

Okay. –M

We are doing a horrible job staying away from each other. – Ty

It makes me want you more. I can't help it. – M

Love you c u soon – Ty

After changing into a t-shirt and shorts, I ran downstairs and unlocked the door for Ty to be able to get inside the house. My aunt and Lucy were already in bed and with people coming and going, nobody would make a big deal out of Ty being in the house. He was family.

I felt like it took forever, but as I started falling asleep, my mattress moved and his strong arms wrapped around me. "Is Izzy at your mom's?"

"Yeah."

He kissed my neck. "I checked her room and she wasn't in there."

"Sorry."

I turned around to face Ty. I ran my fingers over his cheek. "What's wrong?"

He shrugged and looked sad. "This is the first night since you guys moved in that I didn't get to tell her goodnight. Even when she stays at my parents I get to see her."

"You saw her earlier babe. She knows you love her."

"I know." He pressed soft kisses over my lips. "I love it when you call me babe and when you wear my rings." He slipped my wedding rings back on my finger.

I wrapped my arms around him and cuddled my body into his. "You're such a good husband and daddy."

"Goodnight, baby."

Since I hadn't been living at the house in a long time, I didn't have any alarms set. Ty and I both woke up to voices in the house, and they were getting closer. The sun was shining through my bedroom window. It was obvious that we had overslept. "Is the door locked?" I was panicking.

"Of course it is. Can you calm down and tell me good morning before you start freaking out."

I leaned in to kiss Ty and heard someone at my bedroom door.

"Tell Mommy to wake up." My mother voice sent my heart racing.

"Mommy." Bella was beating on the door.

Ty and I looked at each other. He jumped up and ran into my closet. I wanted to laugh, but I was too upset about it all. "Mommy is coming."

I opened the door and saw Bella and my mother. "Hey, baby."

I had immediately started to worry when I realized that my closet had sliding doors and there was no way Ty could close them without making a sliding noise. I had to keep my mother from walking all the way into my room.

My daughter grabbed my legs and tried to climb up them. "Mommy." Bella then went walking in my bedroom. She was looking around. I knew exactly who she was looking for.

Before I could turn around and stop her, or say something to distract her. I heard her little voice get all excited. "Daddy! Daddy! Daddy!"

Shit shit shit!

From the shocked look on my face, my mother knew that I was hiding something, or someone. She pushed right past me and found Ty standing there in my closet, holding Bella, in his boxers.

"Hey Aunt Karen."

"Oh Jesus Mary and Joseph." She covered her mouth with her hands and collapsed on the bed, looking from me to Ty.

"Mom, we can explain." I stood in front of her trying to block her direct view of Ty.

"You better start."

Bella climbed down and walked over to my mother. As if things couldn't get any harder, she turned and pointed to Ty. "My Daddy."

Of course Ty burst into laughter. The fact that he couldn't hide his excitement of Bella's love for him didn't make it easier for my mother to take. "All night she kept asking for her daddy. Can one of you please explain why she thinks that Tyler is her father."

"Mom, it's kind of complicated."

"You better start *un*complicating it; RIGHT NOW!"

I sat down next to my mom and looked over at Bella holding her arms out for her daddy again. She showered him with kisses like we weren't even in the room. "Ty and I are together."

"What's that supposed to mean? You are practically family. I changed his diapers." I have no idea why my mother threw that last bit in, and I chose to just ignore it.

"Aunt Karen, we have been living together since she came to stay with my parents. We are in love."

She shook her head and wiped away her tears. "This is not happening."

"Mom, please don't be mad at me. I wanted to tell you, but Conner threatened Ty before about me. I knew if you found out you would make me come home."

"You're damn right I would. This charade is over right now. You are moving home as soon as this wedding is over. This is not going to continue!" She threatened.

I saw Ty clenching his jaw. He was only going to take so much more. "We aren't moving back Mom."

She stood up and put her hands on her hips, as if it made her more powerful. "There is no discussing this. You are coming home."

"I'm so sorry, but you can't make me do that."

"There is no way I am going to let someone like Ty influence my daughter and grandchild."

I walked over to Ty to almost shield him of my mother. "Ty

loves us. He wants to be Bella's daddy. You can't tell me you haven't ever noticed how close they are."

"You two shacked up together is no environment for a little baby. Don't make me file for custody of that child Miranda."

I started crying immediately, even though I knew it would resort to this. "Don't you dare threaten her with that shit!" I felt the vibration of Ty's voice against my back.

"Get out of my daughter's room. I will do what's best for her."

"What's best for Miranda is for her to be with her husband." And there it was. The time bomb had exploded.

We should have kept our rings hidden in the car, but after our emotional reunion last night, we wore our rings to bed. My mother looked down at my hand and gasped in horror.

"You didn't?"

"It's one hundred percent legal too. We have the judge's signature and everything," Ty said sarcastically. I elbowed him in the stomach for that one.

"There is no way I will let my granddaughter be raised by my own nephew."

"Jesus Mom, we aren't even related. Besides, you don't have a choice in the matter."

She put her hand on her face and started to cry. "How could you both do this?"

"Can you please think about my happiness for one second? Don't you want your only daughter to be happy? Why can't you just try to be happy for me? I love him Mom and he loves us. He has taken complete responsibility for Bella and loves her like she's his own flesh and blood. I couldn't ask for a better father for her."

"He's not her father. What are you going to do when her real father comes into the picture?"

I walked over and put my arm around my mother. "He isn't going to. He has no claim to her anyway. I never added his name to the birth certificate like everyone thought. There is no father listed. That's why it was so easy for Ty and I to petition to have her name changed." *Oops. I probably shouldn't have said that.*

"You didn't? This isn't happening."

Ty got down on his knees and looked at my mom. "I've done everything right. I have a good job and we have a our own house. My dad and I are putting an addition on it right now to give Bella her own bedroom and playroom. Miranda and Bella are on my health insurance plan and I make plenty to support us. I would do anything for them. They are my whole world. I swear to you that I am telling you the truth."

My mother just stopped arguing. I don't know why and I didn't care. "Looks like you have covered all of your bases. You have to understand if I need time to be able to accept this. I didn't send my daughter away for her safety thinking she would run off and get married. It's a bit too much, that's all."

"Am I safe enough to put my pants on now?" Ty asked with a smile.

My mother nodded.

We watched Ty carry his clothes and go into the bathroom. Of course Bella followed behind him and he turned around and picked her up. My mother just watched them. She said nothing for at least five minutes. We could hear Ty talking to Bella in the bathroom. He was teaching her how to brush her teeth and they were singing some dumb song they heard on one of her shows she loved.

"He's all she talked about last night. I honestly thought it was just a phase she was going through. She really seems to love him doesn't she?"

I let out a little cackle. "Sometimes I think she loves him more than she loves me. She really is his world Mom. It was impossible to *not* fall in love with him. Just spend an hour with them and you will see what I see."

"It's just so sudden."

"We have been getting to know each other for almost two years and even before that we knew each other as family. If you think of it that way it isn't really too fast. I've known Ty my whole life practically. Isn't it better that he isn't some stranger?"

"Are you saying that you were involved before you moved?" She looked concerned about that.

"No. Ty and I never even kissed until I moved. He has never done anything but be a gentleman around me. He makes me feel safe. He always has."

She put her hand on my leg just as Ty and Bella walked out of the bathroom. Bella came running over toward us. "Mommy, Daddy bwush."

She was trying to tell us that she brushed her teeth, not that daddy was a bush.

When my mother finally stood up and held her arms out for both of us, neither me or Ty hesitated. She had both of our faces close to hers, let out a sigh and smiled. "If I didn't love you both I would ring your necks right now. Tyler Mitchell, you know better than to wed my daughter without asking. Her daddy would have hunted you down for that."

"I know. Sorry, I just couldn't take the chance of losing them," he admitted.

While I ran into the bathroom to change, I heard my mother continue to talk to Ty.

"I can't promise you that everyone is going to be as calm as I am Ty."

"I know."

"My son is not going to be happy for the two of you. He talked about coming to get Miranda the moment she pulled out of the driveway. When he finds out that he was right about the two of you, I won't be able to control him."

"Aunt Karen it's fine. I can handle it. I wouldn't expect anything less from him."

"You have to stop calling me Aunt Karen. It's very

209

inappropriate."

"Okay Mom."

"I can feel the gray hairs filling my scalp."

After brushing my teeth I ran back out to my room. My mother was right, my brother was not going to be thrilled. Colt needed to get his ass to this house pronto.

"Is Colt here yet?" I gave Ty a warm smile, reminding him that I loved him.

"Everyone is downstairs but the two of you. Of course I had no idea that you were in here together."

"Maybe Ty should just wait to come down. If they don't know we were together then they don't have to find out yet. I don't want anyone to have black eyes for the wedding photos. Van would kill us."

Ty laughed and shook his head. "Go ahead down. I will wait ten minutes and join you."

In front of my mother, he smacked my ass as I was walking out of the door. I turned around and gave him a laugh before following behind her.

She was right. Everyone was in the kitchen. Lucy had made a huge breakfast and food was all over the island. Everyone said hello and then got back to their previous conversations, not even paying a bit of attention to me. I shrugged and happily made myself a plate. Bella was walking around with a piece of sausage in her hand. She liked to run around the kitchen island because it never ended. So, with her sausage held up high, she was running around screaming at the top of her lungs. Everyone stopped talking because they couldn't hear each other through her screaming. That is when Ty decided to walk in the room. Bella's screams stopped but only for her to go running toward Ty. "Daddy! Daddy!"

He picked up Bella and turned beet red. My brother dropped his fork and stood up straight. Ty held Bella with one arm and held his hand up for Conner to stop coming at him. Of course on his hand was his damn wedding band. To make things ten times worse, I jumped in between them waving my hands in the air at my brother. He reached over and grabbed my arm, staring at what was on my own finger. The room got silent. There were a few gasps, most likely from my aunt and Lucy, but everyone mainly just stared at me, Ty and Bella.

"No fucking way!" Conner said under his breath.

"Just calm down Conner," I begged.

"Don't tell me to calm down. I am going to fucking kill him," he threatened.

Finally Colt stood up and came to stand next to Ty, while Van threw herself in front of Conner. "I don't care what you all do after the wedding, but until then, nobody is fighting. I will not pay someone to Photoshop black eyes off of my groomsmen."

My mother stood in the corner shaking her head. I felt so bad for her. She was really astonished that we had done something like this.

Conner finally backed away, knowing that if he took a step forward Colt was liable to kick his ass. He took his plate and threw it in the sink. "This is bullshit!"

Bella heard the word shit again, so on top of the animosity in the room, she started yelling 'shit' over and over.

The rest of my family just stood there, waiting for us to come up with a good explanation as to why Ty and I were married in the first place.

Chapter 28
Ty

Even if I tried to picture the worst scenario of how it could have all played out in my head, it still didn't compare to what Miranda and I had woke up to this morning. It was important to me that everyone knew how serious we were about each other. This wasn't some stunt.

Once Conner left the room and walked out back, everyone just stood there waiting for me or Miranda to say something. Obviously Colt hadn't told Van about the marriage part. She looked like she was about to throw up. Her eyes were full of tears and she kept looking at Miranda's hand.

It didn't take her long to break through the crowd of people in the room and grab Miranda's hand. She studied it then finally looked up at me, not Miranda. She dropped Miranda's hand and went running out of the room. I really felt bad for Colt. He must of really been taken back by the way she was acting. I didn't know what her problem was, but she was acting like she was jealous.

He went running after her anyway.

Miranda's mother finally broke the silence in the room. "Everyone who isn't related to me needs to leave this room right now."

Brina and Courtney, who had been standing around enjoying the entertainment, walked out annoyed. Even Lucy left the room.

My aunt was waiting for my new mother in law to tell her what was going on. I reached over and grabbed Izzy another piece of sausage. She hopped down and started running around the kitchen island. With one motion of her hand my aunt pointed to the small kitchen table. Miranda and I sat down at the round table. "I think I have pretty much figured it out, but we need to decide what's going to happen next. My son is to be married in one week and clearly this is a problem."

Colt's mother resembled Miranda's but was older by a few years. She had a little more gray hair, but after losing her husband almost two years ago, she had a more aged look. Ever since I was a little kid I had called her Aunt J, or sometimes Aunt K, just to be silly. She was the sweetest lady I had ever met. I could tell she wasn't happy with me.

Miranda had her hands folded on the table. I reached over and ran my fingers across them, sliding my hand into one of hers. I gave her a short squeeze before I cleared my throat to start explaining.

"There is nothing to discuss. Miranda and I are married. This should have nothing to do with Colt and Savanna. It's none of their business."

"Tyler Mitchell, don't you dare say that. If it's causing problems between he and Savanna then it's a quandary."

Miranda, who had been super quiet, must have gotten frustrated. "I'm sorry but it isn't our fault if Van is acting this way. Ty and I are happy. Can't anyone be happy for us? Has anyone realized how much they are hurting me? Don't you think I would like to be congratulated. Don't we deserve our families support at all? I mean, I know we did this behind your backs, but look at how everyone is acting. None of you would have supported our decision. That's what this was too, it was our decision. Ty and I are adults and we want to spend our lives together, raising our daughter, then we will."

Her grip on my hand was deadly, but I didn't dare pull away.

"How can you expect anyone to act happy Miranda. You married someone who has been your family your whole life. You lied to all of us for months. Did you just call her your daughter?" Aunt J announced.

My poor aunt Karen, I mean Mom, sat with her hand in her face, shaking her head.

"Would either of you have supported us? It's obvious that I already know the answer. I'm sorry we hurt your feelings, but this wasn't your decision to make. As far as us being family, well we all know that Miranda and I are not related. We share the same cousin. It doesn't even matter. We can sit here until we are blue in the face, but it isn't going to change my mind. Miranda and I are married. We are a family. If this is going to continue to be such a problem for everyone, then I will pack up the car and take my wife and daughter and go home."

Conner was standing at the breakfast room door. He was outside, but the windows were open. He had heard my every word, yet he just stood there with his head down.

My aunt reached her hand over to her sister. "I am very confused about the daughter part. Is there something I need to know?"

She almost snorted. "No. Ty adopted Bella. They had her name changed to Mitchell."

"I'm the only father she has or will ever have. Is that going to be a problem too?"

The room was silent and I could hear footsteps approaching us. I knew it wasn't Conner coming to kick my ass, because he was still standing at the door fuming.

"There isn't goin' to be a problem." Colt's voice filled the room and when we turned around I saw him holding Van's hand. That was a good sign, at least I hoped it was.

"Is everything okay between the two of you?" My aunt asked her son.

Colt and Savanna pulled up two chairs and we scooted over to make room for them. Izzy was getting bored and came running over toward me. "Daddy up."

I picked her up and just out of pure habit I filled her face with kisses. Everyone at the table stared at us.

While still watching me and Izzy, Colt answered his mom. "Everything is fine. Van just got upset for a minute. I think it would be better if she explained it though."

Van gave a half smile but still looked sad. She played with the napkin on the table and wouldn't look up. "You two being together was a shock at first. I just never expected the two of you to fall in love. I'm so close to both of you and never had any idea about it. When I came to visit and saw you together, it was hard at first, but I got used to it. This might sound terrible, but I never expected Ty to ever change. At first I was scared for Miranda, afraid he would just hurt her like he hurt me. When I saw him with Bella I was shocked. The way he loves her is just beautiful."

I gave Van a smile. I couldn't believe I got a compliment out of her.

She smiled back and continued talking. "It hurt me that he was so happy, not because I wanted to be with him, but because it made me feel like I was the reason he was always unfaithful. I saw him and Miranda and the fact that they were just as in love as Colt and I and it hurt me. Then I saw the ring. For years I thought that ring would be mine and to see that he had not only given it to her, but had it changed just for her....I don't know. I just snapped."

I felt bad for Van. She was right, but it wasn't to spite her. "I didn't do any of this to upset you Van. I changed the ring because she deserved to have something new that came from my heart, not something that an old girlfriend wore for a day. Her wearing that old ring seemed wrong to me and it wouldn't be fair to you either. I would have got her a whole new ring if it weren't my grandmother's."

"No, you did the right thing." She reached over and grabbed Miranda's hand. "You know I love you. I am so sorry that I doubted your relationship. I was being ridiculous. I can tell it's real between you. Ty looks at you like Colt looks at me. I didn't want to admit it before, but it's the truth."

Colt looked across the table and put his arm around Van. "Ty, we don't want you to leave. Our wedding won't be the same without you both in it. You are our family, my blood, nothing is going to change that."

"Thanks, Colt, but I think we need everyone to be okay with it." I explained.

Conner came rushing through the door, pointed his finger toward me. "There is no way in hell I will ever be okay with the two of them."

I gently handed Izzy over to her mother before standing up to face Conner.

"Boys you need to calm down and talk this out." I wasn't sure if my aunt said it or Miranda's mom.

I held my hands up in the air, letting him know I had no interest in fighting him.

"What is your real problem with me Conner? Ever since Izzy has been born you have been nothing but a dick to me. What did I ever do to you?"

She must have heard me saying her name and climbed down from the table. Izzy was at my ankles, grabbing my legs. "Daddy up."

Conner watched me pick her up and shook his head. "That is my problem. You think I didn't notice how you were with that kid. Everyone else might have been busy with other things, but I noticed. Every time you came to visit, you spent more time with her than anyone else."

"I watched her being born Conner. You are pissed at me for loving a child?"

"It wasn't normal."

"So your beef with me is because I love Izzy?"

"Bella." I heard everyone saying at the same time.

"She is my Izzy." I shook my head.

"No, you just aren't gettin' it. I knew all along that if you loved Bella than my sister would want you. Even I know nothin' is more attractive to a mother than to see a man carin' for her child. You came around lovin' all over her, lettin' her sleep on your chest. It got even worse after you saved her from Tucker at that bar. She never would admit it, but I knew there was somethin' goin' on between you."

"There wasn't Conner. I swear," Miranda said from behind me.

Conner put his hand up. "Save it. You might not have acted on it, but it has always been there. The way you were always lookin' at each other. Are you really goin' to deny it now?"

I didn't have to look back at my wife. I put my head against Izzy's and at the same time as Miranda we said 'no'.

I heard her mother gasp. "This explains why you didn't fight me about going to North Carolina."

"Mom, I didn't know and neither did Ty. We never talked about our feelin's. We were just friends."

"But you had hopes?"

I was afraid to turn around to look at Miranda on account of Conner standing in front of me.

"Yes." I could hear that she was getting choked up.

Conner shook his head, letting out some air as he let out a cackle. "How long did it take once she got there? How long did it take the two of you before you just couldn't take it anymore?"

"That is none of your business." I reacted too fast and if my child wasn't in my arms, I was sure he was going to pounce on me. I swung her around just in case.

"Actually, I want to know. I sent my daughter to Ty. I think we should all hear the story."

Oh mother fucking hell! I am dead!

"So Ty, how long did it take you to get into my sister's pants?"

I considered telling them a total lie. It would have been easier.

I looked from Conner to Izzy. "Uncle Conner wants some hugs." Conner gave me a dirty look but reached his arms out for Izzy. She gave him a quick hug.

217

"This is goin' to be good if he had to hand me the kid."

I looked around the room at my family. With the exception of Van I had known everyone my whole life. "I didn't even know Miranda was coming. I'd been working late every night and left my phone in my Jeep. Things hadn't been going good for me. Aside from work, I spent most of my time alone."

Everyone in the room was looking at me.

"Daddy." Izzy reached her arms out for me.

I grabbed her before continuing. "Miranda showed up at my door and after helping her get settled I slept over at my parents. Since I knew she was upset, I offered to take her and Izzy to a petting zoo. Anyway, after spending the day together, I was invited to a party and I asked her if she wanted to tag along. My mother really took to Izzy, and the party didn't start until after her bedtime, so it wasn't like I was asking her to be a bad parent."

"Obviously. Because goin' out to parties is what every mother should be doin'."

"Conner please. Your sister is a good mother. Don't act like she isn't allowed to have a life. The child was asleep and with family." My new mother in law took up for me. Conner wasn't happy.

"I wanted to go to the party. It was an ABC party. You know, the kind where you have to wear somethin' other than clothes. I always wanted to see what they were like."

Jesus Christ Miranda! There are some details they didn't need to know.

"I had no idea what her outfit was going to be. I got dressed at my parents and when I picked her up she was wearing a coat. I should have known that it wouldn't be good, but I just wasn't thinking. Miranda decided that saran wrap was a great idea for a costume. I'm not talking like she wrapped her whole body. Very little was covered. Trust me when I say that I mentioned both Conner and Colt's name when I saw what she had on. Once we got into the party, everyone had their eyes on her. I freaking panicked."

Miranda started laughing. I was glad to have her take over for the next part. "Yeah, he wasn't too happy with my clothing choice. I started dancing with these two guys and Ty got all protective. He forced me to pretend that I was his girlfriend so that I wouldn't be approached by anyone else. But....there was one little problem with that. The more we were pretendin' the more real it got. Ty pulled away from me and distanced us. I swear he did."

I shook my head just thinking back on that night. "She's right. I pushed her away. I pulled her out of that party and headed home. The thing was, I felt so bad about kissing her that I pulled over to talk about it. That's when we both realized there were real feelings involved. The rest is history."

There was no way in hell I was going to tell them about that first night. Miranda and I had experienced many hot nights since then, but that topped them all. The anticipation alone was insane.

"In other words, you screwed her twenty four hours after she got there."

"Come on Conner can you be respectful please." Colt was starting to get as annoyed as I was at him.

"It's the damn truth," he added.

"Well, since you know, what do want to do about it? She's my wife Conner. I did right by her and Izzy. There isn't another man on this planet that could love them like I do. That child is mine in every way that it counts. If you hate me for that, then I am not going to apologize. In fact, I'm not apologizing for any of it. I've never been more happy. They are my whole world. I'm just sorry that you can't understand it."

Finally what I said seemed to hit a nerve. Conner went flying back out of the door and this time he didn't stay close.

I took a deep breath. "That went better than expected."

"Boy, if you were a stranger you would be in deeper shit

than you already are." My aunt chimed in.

"Shit!" Izzy said her new favorite word.

My aunt put her hand over her mouth. "Sorry."

"Mom, I kind of need to know what you are thinkin' over there. Now that the cat is out of the bag, I need to know that you will support us."

She put both of her hands flat on the table and looked from Miranda to me. I could tell she was really trying to think about what she said. "I'm really hurt, but I understand why you felt the need to do things the way you did. I just always pictured my daughter having a real wedding. Aside from the shock, I want you to be happy. I know Ty has made mistakes, but I can't deny that it's obvious you love each other."

"I think I have an idea to make this all easier on all of us to take. If I can arrange it, would you be willing to renew your vows tomorrow night?" My aunt asked.

"They can get re-married in the barn. It's already half way decorated." Van added.

Colt turned to look at her. "You sure that is okay, darlin'?"

She nodded. "I think it will be fun. Besides, after how I have been treating them, I kind of owe them."

"So how about it you two? You up for letting that hard headed brother of yours walk you down the aisle, so he can have some kind of redemption?"

Miranda started laughing. "I don't know if he will want to do it, but of course I am up for it. I would marry Ty a million times."

I loved that she looked right at me when she said it. It was like watching someone throwing a kiss and the other person catches it and puts the invisible kiss on their chest. Well, it was something like that.

"Then it's settled. We are now in double wedding mode. Everyone help clean up breakfast. Us girls have to go out shopping for a dress and the guys need to finish getting that barn decorated." My aunt stood up and everyone followed suit.

Miranda and I just looked at each other. "I guess we are getting married again."

"I really hope we don't have to sleep in separate rooms tonight," I joked.

"I heard that Ty. I think pretending you aren't married yet would be a fantastic idea," Miranda's mother noted.

I shook my head and decided I needed a laugh. "That's just mean Aunt Karen. Cousins should be allowed to sleep together before they are married. Everyone does it."

She threw a dish towel at me. "Tyler!"

"Shit! Shit!"

"Thanks Aunt J for teaching my daughter cuss words!" I announced.

"Miranda you really have your hands full with this one," she said as she came up behind me and kissed me. "My hard headed nephew."

Chapter 29
Miranda

One minute I felt like I was being disowned and the next I was being pampered. After our family meeting, my aunt and mother drug me out to find a last minute dress. Ty insisted on keeping Bella so that I could relax and enjoy my day. I think he wanted her around so that my brother would be reluctant to start trouble.

He and Colt were put on decoration duty. As an added surprise, I called Ty's parents and begged them to come. It wasn't just my idea, in fact my aunt sprung for them to fly. She called the airline and bought two round trip tickets like it was nothing.

She had more money than she knew what to do with and she never spent it unless she had a reason. I suppose my wedding was a good enough reason for her. We had lived on the ranch since my father died when I was ten. I was the closest thing to a daughter that she would ever have. She and my mother weren't just sisters, they were best friends. The two of them made me try on so many dresses.

I didn't want anything big and formal. They seemed upset that I didn't want a real wedding dress, so we settled for a dress that was white and long. It was strapless and had a light purple beaded design over the top and around the waist. It was very straight and came down to my feet. After trying it on, I knew it was perfect.

They also insisted on buying Bella a different dress than she was wearing In Colt's wedding. We found her a little white dress that had purple beads just like mine. It was so cute and I knew she would get a kick out of us matching.

Just to set my mind at ease, Ty agreed to send me random text messages letting me know that he was alive. Of course I should have known that every single one would be totally inappropriate.

Make sure you buy crotchless underwear. −Ty
I don't plan on wearing any. − M
Even better.-Ty
Everything okay? − M
Izzy and I decided to go cow tipping- Ty
I love when you teach your daughter about nature −M
I love when you are naked. − Ty

Leave it to Ty to request crotchless underwear. I wasn't really sure if my aunt would be buying those anytime soon.

Our late lunch was relaxing. I had been spoiled all day. It was nice to no longer feel like a disappointment. "Thank you both for everything."

"Honey, it's our pleasure. We just want you to do this the right way. I don't want you regretting not having had a real wedding," my mother replied.

"I am really sorry for lying to everyone. I just didn't think anyone would ever understand," I admitted.

"Miranda we may be old but we aren't blind. If you weren't attracted to Ty we would think there was something wrong with you. That boy is very easy on the eyes. I appreciate how much he has always looked out for you. I really had no idea," my mother looked to her sister and smiled.

"I agree, my nephew has the handsome gene, but let's not forget how gorgeous Miranda is. You two remind me of Ken and Barbie. Seeing you both interact with Bella is just something else. She sure does love her daddy."

I started to tear up thinking about it. "We never told her to call him daddy. They watch this show together and one day she heard it on there. The dad was reading to his child. I will never forget the day she did it. We were in the car on our way to church and she pointed to Ty and kept sayin' it. He just started cryin'. It was the sweetest thing I had ever seen."

"Isn't that funny that he was there for her birth? Almost like he was meant to be her daddy all along," my aunt suggested.

"He says that too. She's the luckiest little girl. He reminds me of daddy the way he holds her. When he walks into the room she lights up. She hates being without him. You should see when we pull up at his work now. She recognizes the building and starts yellin' for him. If she wants somethin' she asks daddy, because she knows he will give it to her."

"This morning I heard him singing with her," my mother added.

"It sounds like she's a very lucky little girl," my aunt replied.

"Are you mad at me for changing her name?" I asked.

My aunt winked. "Mitchell is a good strong name."

"The more I hear about him, the more I realize that I may have been completely wrong about my nephew….uh…son in law. Sorry, it's still hard to change that. Sweetie this morning was a shocker, but now that I have had time to process things *and* I have gotten the picture of Tyler in his underwear out of my head, I have come to accept things. You are an adult. As far as Tyler being Bella's father, well if he isn't the perfect daddy than I don't know what is. Besides, Bella chose him herself. I think you really didn't have a choice."

We all started laughing. "You are probably right about that."

My mother reached across the table and took my hand. "I love you and I know that things haven't been easy for you. Losing your daddy was the hardest thing for a child to ever deal with. I honestly still don't know how we made it through. What broke my heart the most was seeing you look at other kids with their fathers" My mother started to cry. "Your daddy loved you so much, you and your brother. If I could bring him back I would. I still miss him so much." She wiped her face before continuing. "When I think back to when you got pregnant, I remember how much family meant to you. I wanted Tucker to want to be a father to Bella, because I knew it was all you had ever wanted. When he did the exact opposite I saw how much it hurt you. No mother wants their child to be called a mistake. You know I never remarried because no man was ever as good as your father. It's so hard finding someone to take full responsibility for a child that isn't theirs. For Tyler to be that devoted to that child is a God given miracle. From the way you describe him I have to wonder if your daddy is out there somewhere looking out for you. Whatever put him in that car that day changed both of your lives."

The people around our table must have thought the three of us were nuts. We were all three crying and smiling at the same time. I held up my glass. "Here's to flat tires."

Just to appease my mother, Ty spent the night in my room, while I stayed at my mother's house. He did however spend the whole evening with us. Conner had made himself scarce. He didn't come home for dinner and wouldn't answer my mother's calls. I couldn't help the way my mother smiled when she watched Bella with Ty. She was even more impressed at how he refused to leave until he had told her goodnight.

"So I guess I will see you tomorrow Mrs. Mitchell."

I laughed and kissed him. "Yes you will Mr. Mitchell."

"You sure you don't want to have a quickie?"

I wrapped my arms around him and didn't answer.

"You okay, baby? You know you can't back out of this, on account of us already being married."

"I'm not backing out. I just wish my brother would stop being such a dick. I am so afraid he's going to ruin tomorrow. This is really important to my mother."

"Stop thinking about him. I better go before I decide to stay."

He pulled my hand as he started walking away from me. "Love you."

"Love you too!"

Sleeping was totally out of the question. I was a little overwhelmed with feelings and suddenly understood why the

225

courthouse was so appealing to me. I tossed and turned until finally I just sat up.

I decided to see if Ty was having the same problem.

R u awake? – M

No-Ty

I can't sleep –M

We should have had the quickie – Ty

I am serious –M

SO AM I – Ty

I miss you – M

Keep that in mind if you ever want to leave me – Ty

Whining wasn't working. It was time to break out the guns.

I am so horny tonight I can't stop touching myself. – M

Play fair – Ty

My nipples are so hard. – M

I know for a fact that Izzy is asleep next to you. –Ty

Please, babe –M

Come open the door. I am outside. – Ty

Ty being outside meant that he had already left before I sent the sexy messages. He wasn't playing fair at all.

Once we got into my room, we climbed into bed with Bella between us. "Are you mad at me?"

"No. Go to sleep. I can't have my wife looking all tired tomorrow."

When I woke up I saw Ty curled up with Bella. She had turned to face him in the middle of the night. They would both be sweating but never separate from each other.

I met my mother in the kitchen and started pulling a cup of coffee.

"Are Ty and Bella still asleep?"

I turned around with the guiltiest smile on my face. "Guess you heard him come in?"

She ignored me. "Are you hungry?"

"No. I feel sick. Did you ever hear from Conner?"

I felt arms wrap around me and almost spilled my hot coffee. "Morning."

Little footsteps followed behind Ty and a very grumpy little girl emerged. She got one look at Ty hugging me and smacked him in the leg. "No Daddy."

My mother put her hand over her mouth and started to giggle. "Somebody is jealous."

Of course Ty had to make it worse. He started kissing me all over my face. "I love mommy. Oh, mommy gives good kisses. I love her so much."

My daughter literally sat down on the kitchen floor and started crying her eyes out. After we all got a good laugh at her, Ty reached down and grabbed her. "Daddy was just teasing you. Mommy is a terrible kisser."

I smacked him on his butt and started laughing. "Don't tell her that."

"Give daddy kisses Iz, I have to go get ready."

"Izzy bye bye." She held her hands up.

He crouched down in front of her. "Today you and mommy are going to be princesses. Do you want to be a princess for Daddy?"

Her face got all pouty. "No!"

He let out a laugh. "Please be a good girl. Get dressed and you can come see Daddy."

It took Bella twenty minutes before she stopped screaming for her father. I was half tempted to send her dress with him and let him get the child ready. She finally calmed down when she saw her dress. It was fancy which meant it was a real princess dress.

My aunt had agreed to go pick up Ty's parents since he still didn't know they were coming. Van showed up and started taking a million pictures of me and Bella. At first Bella liked it, but it got old really fast.

We hadn't invited anyone else but Ty's parents, so there

were no guest coming. The minister told my aunt that he could only come at lunch time. At quarter of we all started to head to the barn.

When I climbed off of that golf cart and saw my brother standing there in a tux, I started to ball.

"Stop cryin'. You'll mess up your face and I will never hear the end of it."

Van led Bella in front of me and music started from somewhere inside of the barn.

"What are you doin' here?" I said as I put my arm under my brothers.

"Ask your husband."

I didn't know what Ty had said to my brother, but here he was, walking me down the aisle. Bella was in front of me the whole time. All she had to do was see her father and she went running. I tried not to cry, but I just couldn't help it. My brother was a hard head, but I loved him and he was the only person in my life to understand what we went through when we lost our father.

Thank goodness for waterproof makeup and tan skin. I didn't wear foundation and the mascara I put on didn't even come off during my showers, so I knew that was intact. When I got up to that makeshift altar and saw Ty standing there, more handsome than I had ever seen, with tears in his eyes, I freaking lost it.

Chapter 30

Tyler

I knew that this little service was all for show, but it felt so real. Especially when I walked into the barn and saw my parents there. I had no idea they even knew this was happening. Colt had called the tuxedo place and arranged for us to get our wedding attire early, so all of us guys were all decked out. It was weird seeing Van walk up that isle first. Her eyes were fixed on Colt's and I couldn't have been more happy for them.

They had spent the entire afternoon helping me decorate enough for our small group of family. Flowers covered either side of the aisle and there were balloons everywhere. I have no idea how my aunt did it, but there was even a two tier cake sitting on a table. It was all so surreal.

I know Miranda would have liked Izzy to walk slow and drop pretty little petals with every step, but she saw me and came running. Her little head full of blonde curls was bobbing up and down causing me to laugh as she ran. She looked so pretty in her little dress, especially when she jumped right into my arms. "There is my princess"

She pointed to the barn doors. "Mommy."

Nothing could have prepared me for when I first saw her walking in. A huge lump formed in my throat as I watched her taking each step toward me. I had never in my life seen anything more beautiful than Miranda in her wedding dress, with a bouquet of flowers and her arm wrapped around Conner's. I never cared about weddings or dresses, but damn she could have been on the cover of Bridal Magazine. Her head was completely full of curls and her makeup looked beautiful, even with all the tears she had in her eyes. I don't know what kind of shit she had on her lips, but they were super shiny and it was hard not to just reach over and start kissing her.

Conner gave me a friendly nod as he kissed his sister and

walked to his seat. Finding him last night was hard enough, but then in the middle of our talk, Miranda started texting. She thought I was in bed, but I was actually sitting out back of her house, begging her brother to get over himself and let us be happy. After spending the better part of the day pouting, he was in a calmer mood. I was still a little apprehensive until I saw him walking in the barn with Miranda. He had finally come to terms with everything, well the best that Conner could do at least.

I would have liked to take both of her hands into mine, but with Izzy in my arms, I was only able to hold one. I tried to look up into her eyes, but I felt the burning in my eyes and knew the tears were coming. I stroked Miranda's fingers and took deep breaths. For some reason I felt like we weren't married yet, like this was the real thing.

"Mommy no cwy." Izzy reached over and tried to wipe her mother's face. We both started laughing.

I clenched my jaw and looked at Miranda. Her smile was so perfect. I mouthed the words 'I love you' while the reverend was speaking. I honestly have no idea what he was saying. I was too captivated by my wife. Never in my life had I wanted to fall to the ground and cry, but the more I stood there in front of everyone that we loved, the more in awe I became.

Our ceremony wasn't like a normal wedding. Since we were already married we only had to repeat our promises. We already had our rings on our fingers. I don't know what came over me, but right before he was about to declare us, I interrupted him by turning to face our family. "I just need to say something real quick."

I whispered to Izzy. "Can you stand up for a second? Daddy will buy you fries."

Yes, I had to bribe her...It was necessary.

"I know everyone is here to see me and Miranda promise ourselves to each other again, but I think there is someone else who is just as important." I let Izzy down, got on my knees and grabbed both of her hands into mine. She was swinging her body back and forth, giving me a huge smile. Tears were rolling down my eyes so fast that I couldn't even see. I could hear Miranda sniffling and knew she was a wreck. I closed my eyes and took some deep breaths again. "Isabella Mitchell, I promise to love you and cherish you. I will protect you and never ever leave you. I promise to be the best Daddy that any little girl has ever had." I could barely speak. "Daddy loves you so much Izzy. Can I have a kiss?"

She leaned in and kissed me. I hugged her close to my body until I felt like I could stand up and face Miranda. I held on to one of Izzy's hands and grabbed Miranda's as I came to face her. She was crying so hard that I had to pull her against my chest. The poor reverend was just standing back behind us. Finally, when it was obvious she couldn't calm down he took over.

"I now *re*pronounce you Mr. and Mrs. and little Miss Mitchell. Whenever they are ready, they can kiss."

I started laughing and looked out at our family. I don't think there was a dry eye in the room. Including Brina, which I didn't invite, but Miranda insisted on being nice.

I turned to Miranda who was still a big ole mess. "Can I please have my kiss now?"

Her lips met mine immediately. Every time we pulled away we just kept coming back for one more kiss. "I love you so much, baby."

"I love you too."

Colt put his hand on my shoulder and then pulled me into a hug. Surprisingly, Izzy got down and started running around. Everyone came up to us at once and there was just a huge crowd of our family standing around us.

My aunt had some restaurant drop off a shit load of food for all of us, so we just all stood around hanging out. It was actually pretty cool that we were all sort of already family. There were no introductions needed. Colt got us some music going and everyone seemed so happy.

Izzy clung to my leg and I was walking while dragging her around. She didn't understand that daddy had metal in his leg. It was nothing that some Tylenol and a few beers couldn't fix.

I was so happy to see my parents there. Miranda pulled us over toward them and when Izzy saw my mom, she went running. "I can't believe you guys are here."

"Miranda wanted to surprise you," my father answered.

I turned to look at my wife who had a big smile across her face. "Surprise!"

She kissed me and never stopped smiling. I know because I could feel her teeth touching my lips. "You are fucking perfect," I whispered in her ear.

"So are you."

It was funny. I think we gave everyone hugs and kisses while still holding each other's hands. I couldn't let go of her.

Van came running toward us. "Picture time! We need pictures."

For the next thirty minutes Van had Brina taking every possible wedding pose known in the history of wedding poses. I could tell that she had studied the magazines until they fell apart in her hands.

Soon after the pictures, I started to realize that mine and Miranda's night was turning into a dress rehearsal for Van. She was running around, ordering us to cut cakes and open cards and finally dance.

When the music started and I had Miranda in my arms, I stopped letting Van and her little bossy self bother me. I was captivated by the most spectacular sight in the entire world. I stroked her cheek. "You are the most beautiful thing that I have ever seen in my life."

She giggled. "I bet you tell that to all of your wives."

"I hate to break this to you but you are the only one." I reached down and kissed Miranda softly on the lips and talked while I continued to kiss her. "There. Will. Never. Be. Anyone.But.You."

"What you said to Bella was the single most beautiful thing I have ever heard in my entire life. I don't know how you got through it. It was so perfect Ty. I don't know where I would be if you weren't in the car that day. I have wondered that every single day since she was born."

I ran my hands up and down her back, finally leaving them on each of her ass cheeks. I pulled her closer into my embraced as we swayed around to the music. Other people were dancing, but Miranda and I were in our own little bubble. "I can't even imagine my life without you both. Fate has to be real Miranda. I wasn't even supposed to be in Kentucky. I will never forget being in the back of that car, holding you on my lap and watching Izzy taking her first breath. From the moment I saw her, I fell in love. I remember chasing after the ambulance. I felt like I had to be there with you."

"Aren't you glad you were?"

"It was one of the happiest days of my life. I think about it every time I look at her. When she lays with me I look at her skin and her little fingers and how fragile she was when she first came home from the hospital. I remember the first time she smiled at me. It was so awesome."

Miranda started laughing. "I think I know when your most favorite memory was."

I chuckled. "Yeah. The day she called me daddy. My heart just melted hearing that. It still does. Miranda, I don't care how many children we have, she will always be blood to me. Nothing will ever change that. She's mine in every single way. If you find some rich man and end up leaving me, I will still never stop being her father. I would rather die than live without either of you, but I couldn't bear to not be her daddy."

"How could I ever find anyone else that makes me fall in love with them every single day like you do?"

I looked around at everyone having a good time. It was basically just a party with everyone dressed up. "Did you ever in a million years think this would be happening to us?"

"No." She laughed.

"Do you regret rushing into it all? I think that is what everyone is so mad about. They think that people like you and I can't be tamed."

"I don't regret anything Ty. I feel like we were always supposed to be together. My daddy would have been proud of the man I love. As far as everyone else, well, screw what they think."

Her smile did things to me. I couldn't help but slowly press my lips to hers again. Her tongue brushed against my lips and as I pulled away I saw that look in her eyes. I pulled her back into another kiss and this time I found her tongue and stroked it against mine. I closed my eyes and imagined we were back at home and alone.

"As much as I love our family, I can't wait to get home and get that addition done so we can sleep naked every night."

"You know your daughter is still going to climb into our bed every night. I hardly believe you would tell her no."

I laughed against her mouth. "Your right, well she can't come in every night. We need to make more babies. I want Colt to have to explain how he's related to our kids over and over again."

Miranda wrapped her arms around my neck and busted out laughing. "You are so sick."

"Seriously though, I do want more kids. Not right away but in a couple of years. We shouldn't wait too long because I don't want Izzy to be that much older than her little brothers or sisters."

We were distracted by Conner dancing around with Izzy. He had her in his arms. The more he swung her around the faster she laughed. It was nice he finally calmed down. It wasn't like I hadn't proved myself time and time again to him. All along I had been protective of her.

"So how many kids are we having, because this body won't look the same for long?"

"We could be like that family on television that has twenty kids. That would be awesome. They could do a background story on us and how we are related."

She buried her head into my chest and started snorting she was laughing so hard. "I don't think my vagina can handle that, babe."

"Fine we can start with one, but I have seen you pregnant and your sexy as shit. I might need to see you like that more than once." I spun her around and pulled her back into me. "You called me babe and said vagina in the same sentence. I am so turned on right now."

"Daddy! Mommy! Up!" Obviously Izzy was done her dance with her uncle.

There was only one thing that could stop me from kissing my wife and it was Izzy. We pulled her up into our arms and danced with her between us.

"Guess we will have to continue that later tonight." I acted disappointed, but I really wasn't. I was used to Izzy coming before our sex life. Miranda always made up for it by being the little seductress she was. I think having to wait sometimes made it even better.

"Don't make me wait too long. These crotchless panties aren't that comfortable."

Oh Shit!

I buried my head into her neck. "You are killing me here."

"I only did what you said. Do I need to show you the message?"

"No. I clearly remember it."

She giggled. "There is like nothing there. Even I got turned on looking at them." Her eyes intently sent me a message I was very familiar with.

"Don't give me that look. You know I can't resist it. You

look so damn beautiful right now, it's killing me. Did you have to buy the one dress that would result in me staring at your tits all day?" I licked my lips just thinking about how hot she looked under that dress.

Miranda started laughing. "The first thing I thought about was how much you would love this dress because of how my tits looked. And just so you know, I bought red ones."

She backed away just enough that I could take her in. I knew she was talking about her damn panties. "Can I get a peek?" I pulled her back into my one handed dance.

"Nope. You have to wait to remove them. Be a good boy and try not to think about it," she teased.

"You will be the death of me."

If there were a picture that represented the word perfect, it was our life. There was no telling what we had in store for us, but whatever it was, we were going to do it together. I had my girls and that was all I needed to be happy at the end of the day. It was amazing how one little miracle had changed every aspect of my life, but it was true. That little girl was a gift from God. Miranda likes to think it was her father sending her happiness from heaven. If it was him, I would like to thank him because I couldn't imagine spending one single day without them.

Of course it didn't hurt that I had the sexiest, freakiest, most beautiful woman on the entire planet. Some people might say that I did all of this because of the child. If they spent five minutes with me and Miranda they would change their minds. She was my obsession; the one person in the world that could satisfy me completely. Sometimes you have to go through Hell before you can find Heaven.

I had no idea what kind of life was in store for us, but I was willing to work my ass off to make sure it was the best it could be.

End of Book Two

If you enjoyed this book, please share a comment or review.
Let me know what you think of this book by contacting me at the following:

www.jenniferfoor.com

http://www.facebook.com/JenniferFoorAuthor
www.jennfoor@gmail.com
http://twitter.com/jennyfoor

www.jennyfoor.wordpress.com
http://www.goodreads.com/jennyfoor

Jennifer Foor lives on the Eastern Shore of Maryland with her husband and two children. She enjoys shooting pool, camping and catching up on cliché movies that were made in the eighties.

CPSIA information can be obtained
at www.ICGtesting.com
Printed in the USA
LVOW04s1947201016
509597LV00012B/911/P